THE
RISING
OF
BELLA
CASEY

MARY MORRISSY

BRANDON

First published 2013 by Brandon, an imprint of The O'Brien Press Ltd,
12 Terenure Road East, Rathgar, Dublin 6, Ireland.
Tel: +353 1 4923333; Fax: +353 1 4922777
E-mail: books@obrien.ie
Website: www.obrien.ie

ISBN: 978-1-84717-576-2

1 2 3 4 5 6 7 8 9 10
13 14 15 16 17

Layout and design: The O'Brien Press Ltd.
Cover photograph: copyright © Mark Douet
Printed and bound by CPI Group (UK) Ltd, Croydon, CR0 4YY
The paper in this book is produced using pulp from
managed forests.

The quotations from Seán O'Casey's work that appear in the text are reproduced by kind
permission of the O'Casey estate.

The O'Brien Press receives assistance from

For Ruth Morrissy as promised a long time ago

Acknowledgments:

I would like to thank the New York Public Library where much of the research for this book was undertaken on a fellowship at the Cullman Centre for Scholars and Writers. The centre's director Jean Strouse, her deputy, Pamela Leo, the librarians at the Berg collection, as well as my fourteen fellow 'Fellows', all contributed, either directly or subliminally, to the making of this novel.

A final draft of the novel was completed during a residency at the Centre Culturel Irlandais in Paris, under the directorship of Sheila Pratschke, to whom I also extend thanks.

Mary Foley, librarian at University College Cork, came to my rescue with invaluable material, and the Rev Patrick Comerford steered me towards Church of Ireland research sources.

I would like to acknowledge my first intrepid readers – Rosemary Boran, Joanne Carroll, Valerie Coogan, Colbert Kearney, Douglas Kinch, Margaret Mulvihill and Orla Murphy – and, in particular, Molly Giles, whose clear-eyed vision allowed me to consider the novel afresh.

The spark that ignited my interest in Bella Casey came from Colbert Kearney's study of the oral tradition in O'Casey's Dublin trilogy, *The Glamour of Grammar*. I drew on Seán O'Casey's six volumes of autobiographies for inspiration in creating Bella's world. I read a great deal of background material while writing the novel, too voluminous to mention here. Three books deserve special mention, however – *Kildare Place: the History of the Church of Ireland Training College and College of Education, 1811–2012*, by Susan M Parkes, *London's Women Teachers: Gender, Class and Feminism 1870–1930*, by Dina Copelman, and *Dublin Tenement Life, An Oral History*, by Kevin C Kearns. There is a wealth of biographical scholarship on Seán O'Casey, but Christopher Murray's *Seán O'Casey: Writer at Work* provided a broad overview of his life and work, while Martin B Marguiles's *The Early Life of Seán O'Casey* offered an intimate and witty examination of the playwright's youth.

EASTER MONDAY, 1916

'A skirmish,' Bella Beaver declared with more certitude than she felt. 'That's all it is.'

'*They* said it was a rising,' her daughter, Babsie, shot back. 'Isn't that what they called it, Starry?'

Babsie had been stepping out with Starry Murphy for a couple of months. His given name was Patrick but a doting aunt had likened him to a celestial gift, being the only boy in a clutch of girls, and the name had stuck. He was one of *them*, a Catholic, an RC, but though she disapproved, Mrs Beaver had held her tongue.

'That's exactly so,' Starry said.

A dapper boy, he reminded Mrs Beaver of her dead husband. Something about his dark tossed hair, his jaunty manner. Her

Nick as a young man, that is. Before he'd been tainted, before she'd been destroyed . . . but no, she would not dwell on sorry history for it was a wound to her.

Starry had been on duty at Jacobs for the holiday weekend to keep the ovens ticking over and Babsie had gone to meet him when he came off shift. 'He was on the fitter's floor,' Babsie began for she was in the habit of speaking for Starry even when he was present, 'when he and the other lads heard this ragged bunch galloping up the stairs, taking them two at a time, all business. They marched right into the "King's Own" room without a how do you do, full of bluff and declaration and, I swear to God, waving guns they were. Isn't that so, Starry?'

Starry nodded.

When Mr Bonar, the overseer, approached the belligerent band to sort the matter out, he was pushed roughly aside.

In the name of the Irish Republic . . . one of them announced unscrolling a parchment and reading from it.

'The Irish Republic, whatever that is when it's at home,' Babsie said. 'Starry thought it all some kind of a caper or a crowd of travelling players putting on a free theatrical. Then the tricked-up soldiers rounded everyone up, bar Mr Bonar and the watchman, and herded them out on to the street saying there'd be no more baking biscuits in Jacobs this fine day.'

A crowd had gathered. Women mostly, howling like Revolution furies at the pretend soldiers.

'Youse boyos should go off to France and fight, instead of

turning guns on your own,' one of them hollered waving her fist as a couple of them appeared on the roof of Jacobs and ran up a strange flag of green, white and gold. And then a shot rang out.

'And that decided us,' Babsie said, speaking again for Starry.

On their way home they passed the General Post Office. All shuttered up and sandbags built up at the entrance, and the self-same declaration pasted on the doors with stamps.

'The Post Office no longer belongs to us,' Babsie reported. 'It's the headquarters of the New Ireland.'

'The New Ireland,' Mrs Beaver repeated wonderingly. Then she retreated to her original position. 'It's a skirmish, that's all.'

They lived through the rest of the day and the day following by report alone – or the hiss of rumour, though it was a principle of Mrs Beaver's to discourage idle gossip. The Germans were coming, Mrs Clarke said, whole battalions of them to prop up the rebels. The length and breadth of Sackville Street was destroyed. And further afield, too, according to Sadie Kinch, second next door. Chancellor's, the opticians, gone, she said, Court Photographers a pile of smoking rubble and Pickford's all but demolished, its windows all blown in.

'And the looting!' said Sadie. 'My husband saw it for himself. Doxies parading about in fur coats from Marnane's and ropes of pearls filched from Hopkins and Hopkins.'

'Sure that's nothing,' Mrs Clarke piped up, 'I heard there was a crowd of scavengers in Manfield's windows, brawling in full sight. And sure everyone knows they only display the left shoes.'

'And hats,' Sadie Kinch countered, 'there were blackguards going round with three and four piled up on their heads, as trophies for their wives.'

As she listened to her neighbours, Mrs Beaver wondered how they were so knowledgeable about such lawless behaviour. She would keep a sharp eye out in case said Sadie Kinch might sport some new and unexpected millinery in the near future.

When she awoke on Wednesday morning, the rumours flying up and down the lane had been replaced by a solemn Sabbath calm. Mrs Beaver wondered if the tall tales were something she'd dreamt up, a feverish kind of fantasy like one of those moving pictures at the Royal. After two days behind closed doors, there wasn't a morsel left in the house and they were reduced to tea grounds used twice over and drunk black. She would have to venture out. Valentine offered to escort her.

'You'd never know, Mam, it might be dangerous out there.'

She took her son up on the offer although she did not credit the talk of cannon roar and devastation and fully expected to find everything as it had been. She would go as far as the Pioneer Stores for a loaf of bread and a twist of tea. But when she and Valentine arrived at the shop, they found the shutters padlocked and the double-doors bolted giving the place a bereaved air as if someone had died within.

Having made it this far with not a hint of trouble, she suggested to Valentine that they might light out towards town in the
hope of finding some other establishment open. They could do
with kindling and paraffin for the lamp, else they'd be sunk in
darkness for the rest of the week. They saw nothing untoward, bar
every other huckster's shop showing closed doors, until they got
as far as Amiens Street. Deserted, not a single omnibus running
and the train station silent as the grave. They halted at the mouth
of Talbot Street. There was a strange smell in the air, singed and
sulphurous, as if a fire had been guttered out. As they stood there,
a man accosted them, putting his hand up like a constable.

'Take your mother home direct, Sonny,' he said to Valentine,
'for youse are in mortal danger here.'

He was a portly fellow with pot belly and ruddy cheeks.

'But we're in search of bread,' Mrs Beaver told him.

'Bread, is it? There's no bread getting gave around here, Missus.
The place is in a state of chassis and youse should not be out.'

But the eerie quiet gave a lie to his pronouncements. And he
was out, was he not, if only to be a prophet of doom?

'There's a gunboat pounding the bejasus out of the Custom
House, not to speak of snipers on every rooftop.' He pointed in
the general direction of heaven. 'Better to be home with your
belly growling than be shot down on the street like a dog.'

Men like him, Mrs Beaver thought, can get all puffed up
with calamity. He knew no more than they did, going only
on the overheated gossip of the last ignorant person he had

come across. And he was enjoying himself too much, issuing his florid warnings.

'I'm not for turning,' Mrs Beaver told him sharpish.

'Please yourself, Missus,' he said. 'But I advise youse not to be walking out so brazenly. Youse should creep along and hug the walls for there are gunmen everywhere.'

Valentine drew her aside.

'Maybe yer man's right, Mam,' he said, 'maybe we should go home.'

'We'll go as far as Gardiner Street,' she said, reckless with authority.

By right, it should have been her son itching to see some action and she, his mother, staying his hand. Instead, Mrs Beaver sounded, even to her own ears, like a bargaining child, come too late to the bazaar but trying to wring the last iota of enjoyment as the stalls are being packed away.

'Youse'll be turned back,' the nay-sayer said. 'Or worse.'

They hurried down Talbot Street, no longer strolling as they had been, and turned on to Gardiner Street. On any other day of the week street walkers would have been abroad here, congregating on the footsteps and brazenly showing off their wares, the windows of the lower floors thrown open so the passer-by could see their squalid boudoirs on display. But it, too, was eerily unpeopled, except that lying in the middle of the street, where the people should have been, was a horse. A black carcass, a bloodied hole in its haunch, glittery with flies. Its dead eye seemed to observe them. Valentine hung back and Mrs Beaver took the lead.

'We'll go as far as Abbey Street,' she said sensing that each stage of this journey would have to be negotiated for Valentine was waxing nervous. They made it almost as far as Butt Bridge before they were stopped. A couple of soldiers were lodged there behind a barricade of sandbags laced with wire.

'Move back,' one of them yelled, waving his rifle at them. 'Move back, I tell you. There's nothing to see here.'

But he was wrong. All along Abbey Street, the once erect buildings and fancy shops were full of gaping wounds. The floors above the shops had sagged in places, the masonry like the roughed-up lace on the tail of a petticoat. When she looked up, fine parlour rooms on the upper storeys were exposed where the glass had all been shattered. Curtains billowed raggedly. The houses left standing were reduced to nervous wrecks as if they had suffered from the jitters of war. Mrs Beaver had heard reports of war from afar – her eldest, James, was in colours and the newspapers were full of dispatches from Verdun – but nothing prepared her for the ruinous complexion of it on the streets of Dublin. She had never been a gawper by nature but there was something about this wreckage that mesmerised her. Despite all the evidence of ruin, there was barely a sound. This must be what the Great Silence is like, she thought, this dreadful peace. While she was thinking this, a vast boom emanated from Sackville Street making the very ground under their feet shiver. It was answered by the puny rat-a-tat-tat of gunfire. For the first time, Mrs Beaver was afraid.

'Come on, Mam,' Valentine said and grasped her hand.

They clung to the hems of the buildings, ducking from one doorway to the next, their journey punctuated by sporadic firing, which though not close, made them dive for any shelter they could find. In one such respite, they shared their billet with a young man in a dusty grey suit and muffler. A second boom rang out.

'Dear God,' the young man muttered, 'they're trying to blow our lads to kingdom come.'

From the way he said 'our lads', Mrs Beaver knew he was one of *them*, the insurrectionists.

'If I were you, young fella,' he said to Valentine, though the two boys were of an age, 'I'd take my mammy off home. This is no place for ladies nor civilians.'

He blessed himself then and darted out of the doorway. As he did, Mrs Beaver noticed the dull glare of gunmetal beneath the flap of his coat. All went deathly quiet again and she and Valentine were about to venture forth when a single shot rang out. The young man halted and staggered forward. He seemed to rise, levitate almost, his arms aloft in supplication before he folded decorously and fell. Even his cap stayed in place. He lay quite still, his eyes closed as if he were in slumber.

That could be my James, lying there, Mrs Beaver thought, but her son was out beyond in a foreign field, fighting for his country – where this boy should be, by all rights, instead of joining himself to this villainous mayhem. But her righteousness only lasted a moment. In the lightning flash of the gunfire, she saw another one of her errors. How could she have let James go, when she should have lain down before him to stop him, to spare him *this?* The young man twitched and groaned, his fingers groping blindly.

'We should do something for him,' she said to Valentine.

'And get our heads blown off?'

'Still and all,' Mrs Beaver said thinking again of James.

'Still and all nothing, Mam.'

And while they were debating thus, the young man died, Mrs Beaver was sure, his life quenched out before their very eyes.

If she had been in thrall before, she was paralysed now. She had always imagined battle as a continuous and logical barrage, organised and stately. But no, it came in waves like the sea rushing to the shore, but unlike the tide, it was impossible to predict. The next report of rifle might be for her, or worse, her poor son whom she'd dragged into the middle of this danger instead of shielding him from it. So rooted to the spot had she become, that Valentine had to prod her to get her moving again. They crouched and began to make their painful way like crabs scuttling in the dirt, their eyes fixed at street-level. The thunder of field-gun and patter of rifle-fire continued at their backs. On Mecklenburgh Street they squatted in the porch of an ale house and Mrs Beaver, thankful of the glassy calm, closed her eyes. But Valentine would not let her rest.

'Come on, Mam, come on, would you?'

Reluctantly she opened her eyes and knew immediately something had changed. She blinked twice not sure if she had conjured up what she saw. A piano. Had it been there all along? Or had God rolled it on to the stage while her attention had been distracted? It stood in the gutter at the other side of the street, canted to one side. Against instruction, Mrs Beaver straightened.

'Stay low, Mam, stay low,' Valentine hollered at her.

But something reared up in Mrs Beaver. She had been low long enough.

It was a Broadwood, an upright Broadwood, intact in all this ruin, offering itself to her. Indian rosewood case, inlaid panels and candle sconces, the lid open to show a perfect set of teeth, a music holder with a scrolled inset in the shape of a treble clef. She laid her hand gingerly on it. The wood was silky to her fingertips and she felt a rush of the sublime.

'Mam!' Valentine shrieked.

She knew that she should follow him but she couldn't move. She wanted this so badly it made her throat ache. Valentine sprinted back and tugged her by the elbow.

'Come away out of that,' he said. 'Leave it be. It's looters' leavings. Some gurrier will be back for it, you can be sure, and we've had enough strife for one day.'

But she could no more have left it than she could have abandoned a child.

'Here,' she said, looking hurriedly around her, 'you catch it by the other end.'

'What?'

'We cannot leave it here like this. It'll only get destroyed.'

He looked at her aghast.

'Are you mad, or what, Mam?'

She *was* mad, maddened with desire, or greed. She was not even sure of the difference. Who knew what had taken hold of her, a respectable fifty-year-old widow eyeing up a piano in the middle of a battlefield and wanting it for herself.

'Are you going to let your mother struggle with this alone?' she demanded.

Her voice came out shrill and panicky to her own ears. But it galvanised her son. He put his shoulder to the piano and none too gently began to push. The strings let out a timorous screech. With Valentine at one end and her at the other, they loosed the piano from the rut which had obviously defeated their thieving predecessors and with enormous effort, they levered it on to the kerb and got it rolling on its brass casters. Valentine set his shoulder against it and began to push. Mrs Beaver pulled from the front as if leading a reluctant beast. Every so often she would halt their progress. The strings would issue a celestial sigh of relief. She would lift the lid and check the shivering keys. Then she would throw her shawl over the top. It looked pathetic as if she thought this would disguise what they were at.

'Ah Mam, give over with the inspections or you'll get us killed,'

Valentine shouted at her. 'Or bloody banged up in a polis cell.'

His mother let the oath pass, a sure sign she was not in her right mind. She was forever chastising him for rough language. Twice he was sure he heard a policeman's whistle but it was only the casters shrieking for want of oil.

'We are like Sisyphus with his burden,' his mother said between gasps of exertion. Valentine Beaver loved his mother, but sometimes he wondered if she was a bit soft in the head. As they heaved and pushed, he kept a scouring eye out on every side-street they passed for signs of the law. As if reading his mind his mother said: 'If we are challenged, we will say that I am the Principal Teacher at the Model School in Marlborough Street and this here's the school piano that we are trying to save from the ravages of war.'

The notions! As if anyone would mistake his tenement-thin mother for a professional lady. One look at her dour, service-able skirts, her speckled grey hair all awry and escaping from the grasp of a gap-toothed comb, her front tooth cracked where his father had given her a belt once, would give the game away. They rumbled their prize on. As they progressed, they had to halt several times for his mother was quite out of puff and it is heavy labour shunting a piano. The casters were wayward and apt to follow their own direction. No more than his mother. Each time they stopped, sweat pouring from his brow, he would beg, 'Let's leave it here, Mam, and be done with it.'

But her only reply was to lean into the haunch of the damn

piano as if she were involved in birth labour.

They were not stopped, not by anyone in a uniform that is, though they got some queer looks from the few citizens they passed. As they travelled his mother seemed to grow bold, a haughty jib to her jaw, so by the time they'd made it to the Five Lamps, he swore she would have cowed any challenger with a mere look. He was never so glad to reach Brady's Lane with all the doors thankfully shut for they would have faced the third degree had the neighbours been about.

'Mam has entirely lost her wits,' he declared as they struggled to push the Broadwood over the threshold. 'She made me lug this yoke all the way from Mecklenburgh Street! '

'Where's the bread?' Babsie enquired, arms folded in indignant fashion across her chest.

'I'm hungry,' Baby John wailed.

But Mrs Beaver ignored both lamentation and rebuff.

Once inside she examined the piano for signs of damage. It was a wretched and undignified way to treat a precious musical instrument, akin to violent assault, but it seemed to have escaped unscathed. She beckoned to Babsie and John to help her put the piano in place under the four-squared window that squinted on to the street. She stood back to admire it. Her very own piano, the sum of every fine and noble aspiration she had ever nurtured. She pulled up a kitchen chair and dredged up from memory Mozart's *Rondo Alla Turca*. Her ruined fingers knew their way about though her swollen joints were rusty. She stumbled through to the end, her children clustered around her as if at a recital, but they were surly with puzzlement. This gaiety of their mother's was a mood they did not know. When she had finished she eyed them fiercely, an expression they were more familiar with.

'If anybody asks,' she warned, 'not that it's anybody's business, you can tell them this is your mother's inheritance, do you hear?'

'A likely story, Bella,' her brother said coming upon the scene, for in her haste to get the piano safely housed, Mrs Beaver had left the street door open.

Babsie stepped away from the piano. There'd be fireworks now, the girl thought. Her Uncle Jack and her mother were always at loggerheads. Like chalk and cheese, that pair. Her mother, proud, Protestant and loyal to the Crown, her uncle a Labour man, a nationalist, a spouter of Irish, even. And Godless with it, her mother would say. Babsie was surprised to see him for she was sure he would have been mixed up in the rising. Skirmish, she corrected herself.

Her uncle was forever talking revolution, the workers throwing off their chains. She knew for a fact he'd been off drilling with the Citizen Army.

'Are you not out with them?' she asked him.

'Ah no, Babsie . . . this whole business,' – he jerked his head towards the street – 'it's a bloody folly.'

Her mother's hands had fallen to her lap. Like Babsie, she was waiting for the lofty condemnation that was sure to come. No matter what he thought of the rising, he would not approve of looting. He stood on the threshold of the cold room – no fire lit, no food on the table,

'Don't mind me,' he said, 'play on.'

Her mother went back to the keys, reprising the Turkish tune. When she was done, Uncle Jack clapped his hands and let out a whoop of admiration. Then he began to laugh while Babsie and Valentine exchanging perplexed looks.

'What's the joke?' Baby John asked.

'Bella fiddles while Dublin burns,' Uncle Jack said finally, still spluttering with laughter. Her mother made no response to the mirth at her expense.

'Paradise regained, Bella, by hook or by crook!' Jack tried again.

'By crook,' Valentine said, scowling.

But even then her mother refused to be riled. She returned to her playing. A different tune this time, more sombre, a dead march tempo. Babsie flounced into the scullery to put the kettle on. It would have to be third-hand tea now from the last pot they'd brewed. Really, her mother was the giddy limit. Send her out for tea and she comes back with a blessed piano. And then she sits down and gives a recital!

'The *Moonlight Sonata*,' her mother announced.

Valentine knelt before the hearth and tried to rouse a spark from the ashes. Baby John's stomach grumbled. Mrs Beaver shut them out. Hang them all! Even her brother, once so beloved, trying to bait her on the doorstep. She concentrated on the creeping left hand, like the steady arpeggio of time. Once, she would have favoured the yearning right. She closed her eyes and let her creaking fingers lead her blindly back, back to the beginning of their story.

ELYSIAN

MISTRESS OF HER

CIRCUMSTANCES

Her mother, big as a house, was at the washboard in the scullery when her waters broke. She let out a piercing shriek. Bella Casey, two floors up, at the piano in the drawing room, paused, her hands frozen above the keys. It was a Chapell upright with turned columns and panels of fretted silk in the top door, with the name Elysian carved in gold above middle C. At fifteen, Bella was squeamish in matters biological and irked at being kept from school. Especially since Aunt Izzie had agreed to be on hand; she had been a nurse tender and knew a thing or two about bringing babies home. But Bella's mother was nervous of this birth; she had lost the two babies before to the croup.

Bella, truculent, had spent the day trying to master the *Moonlight Sonata*. When she heard her mother first cry out, she sat for a few moments praying that this chalice might pass.

'Bella!'

There was no mistaking the summons a second time. Bella rose and made her way downstairs, full of dread. Her mother stood by the Belfast sink, hands doused in blue, clutching her belly and moaning like an Arab at prayer.

'Get your Auntie Izzie,' she commanded through gritted teeth.

Aunt Izzie was somewhere in the upper reaches of the house.

'Go,' she said again as Bella stared at her mother and realised how very small she appeared and how very large the creature inside her must be and it drumming to come out. She had shot up that winter and found herself being able to look down on her own mother – a queer sensation.

'What ails you, girl?' Mother all but roared. 'Go, would you?'

Soon her mother would be felled like a tree, petticoats up about her and her privates all on show. There wouldn't even be time to lead her to the bed where Izzie had laid newspaper to spare the linen. Bella wanted to flee. Luckily Aunt Izzie bustled in at that moment and took charge.

'Water, Bella, if you please,' she barked, 'and plenty of it'.

'That girl is useless,' Bella heard her mother say as they set to about their sordid struggle. Mother yelling and Aunt Izzie shouting until their voices bled into one and then slowly, inch by bloodied inch – the head emerged, not like a child at all but like some. . . some *thing*, angry and inflamed, with Mother at one end clenching around her prize and Aunt Izzie at the other ignominious end trying to take it from her. And it was as if Mother wouldn't let go and so the pair of them tussled like a pair of dogs over offal until Aunt Izzie won and Bella's brother Jack was delivered on the floor of the scullery. Bella, blood-stained, sudsmeared witness, felt she had birthed the child herself.

He was born with a caul. It was like a veil that covered his eyes. Straight after the birth, Aunt Izzie placed a sheet of paper over the baby's head and peeled the caul away with her fingertips. The next day, rising prematurely from her childbed, Bella's mother dispatched Izzie off with instructions to go down to the Seaman's Mission on the Quays and sell it off. Bella's father had already refused though he was in the way of going there whenever a big ship was in port to do his proselytising. His title at the Church Mission on Townsend Street was clerk but he was much more than a keeper of accounts. He taught Bible study on Sundays to working men and in the evenings he would often tramp around the docks with pamphlets culled from the tracts of the Reverend Dallas. The one who had 'saved' Pappie. Though Bella found it hard to believe, her father had been born a Romanist. He had devoted his life to repaying his debt to Reverend Dallas, despite the aggravation it caused him. On his rounds, people would spit at him and call him a souper. Ragged children – egged on by their mothers – would run after him in the street and chant

'Go way, you dirty pervert.' For that is what those ill-educated roughs called evangelicals. But her Pappie suffered their insults in silence. A soft answer, he would say, turneth away wrath.

Aunt Izzie came back with two guineas for the caul. A certain Captain Boyle, bound for the Cape Horn, had purchased it believing it would save him from shipwreck and drowning.

'It's akin to Popery believing in such charms,' Pappie had said, scowling as Mother pocketed the money.

But then he cheered.

'Now, David Copperfield,' he mused, 'he was born with caul and didn't he turn out well in the heel of the hunt?'

But so was Hamlet, Bella was about to say, since Pappie was calling on literature as witness. But she held her tongue. It didn't do to boast idly of knowledge.

Jack did not fall to the croup like the two before him for Mother watched him like a hawk. She rubbed tallow on his chest at the rumour of a cold. If she heard even the ghost of a cough she'd be off down to the apothecary on Talbot Street for a tuppence worth of squills. But in the end it was his eyes that came to scourge him. From the age of five he was tormented with trachoma and this led on to conjunctivitis. She and Mother tried to ease his pain with zinc and rosewater and poultices of tea-leaves. They took turns dousing his head in a bucket of cold water while trying to make sure his eyes were open – a certain cure, or so they said. He must have been the most baptised child in Ireland. And to add insult to injury, they had to bandage his eyes for left to his own devices he would have rubbed them raw. So the poor mite was often plunged into darkness. It was a strange cure, Bella thought, being made blind to prevent blindness. Her mother was at the end of her tether with him. Until she heard tell of a Dr Storey at the Ophthalmic Hospital by the back of Trinity College. He prescribed Golden Eye ointment which it was Bella's job to apply underneath the child's eyelids. The battles she had with him! She almost had to rope him down. Bella cared for all her brothers, of course she did. She was the eldest, she'd minded Mick and Tom and Isaac, she'd organized them and bossed them about, tied their shoelaces, wiped their noses. But she *loved* Jack. Maybe it was because she had seen him being born? That she had known him before he had opened his sticky eyes to the world, before he even knew himself? Or was it that she was tied to him by love and pain, in equal measure?

Bella had gone as far as Fifth Standard in the Model School when Miss Arabella Swanzy suggested she go on to be a teacher. Miss Swanzy was the head governess of the Teaching College and called in person to press upon Bella's mother the advantages a profession would bestow on a girl in her circumstances. That was how she put it – 'her circumstances' – even though Miss Swanzy was shown into the good room in No 85 and was plied with tea from the silver service. Mrs Casey was impressed with Miss Swanzy's regal bearing and afterwards remarked on how clever she appeared.

'Miss Swanzy said you'd have something solid with the teaching. You cannot be dismissed and the position takes a pension.'

It seemed Miss Swanzy had said all the right things, Bella thought. Her Pappie was already converted. He had always taken a quiet pride in Bella's achievements. Her mother was more impressed with the financial prospects though she nearly had a fit when she looked at the list of apparel Bella would need for the College.

'One Shawl or Wrap, Two Hats, One Jacket or Mantle, One Ulster,' her mother began, her tone laced with indignation.

'Two Dresses, Two Outside Petticoats, if you please, Six Pairs of Drawers.'

She paused there, for effect.

'Four Bodices, Two Pairs of Gloves – One Outdoor Woollen, One Indoor White, Formal With Pearl Detail.'

She paused again.

'I ask your pardon! Pearl detail, did you ever hear the like?'

'Now Sue,' Pappie interjected.

'Is it some class of Swiss Finishing School we're sending her to?' Mother went on, undeterred, and Bella feared her fate might be decided on the strength of a pair of blessed pearly gloves. 'Sure this will cost a holy fortune!'

'If this is what our Bella needs to get ahead, than that's what she must have,' Pappie said with the kind of firmness that put a stop to Mother's grousing.

'I only hope said pair of gloves will help her find a husband,' she said, adding with a little touch of spite, 'Miss Swanzy, I see, is on the shelf.'

On Bella's first night in the college, Miss Swanzy ordered that baths be drawn.

'I don't know what this is all in aid of,' one of the other students said as they stood, two by two, with their towels and soap bars on the corridor.

'Some of these girls,' she said looking straight at Bella, 'will never see a bath when they get out. '

How dare she, Bella thought, cataloguing in her head the appurtenances of home. The running water in the scullery, their own privy and two reception rooms with lace curtains tied with crimson cord, a horsehair sofa, a portrait of the Queen at one side of the mantel and a picture of Lord Nelson on his way to Trafalgar Bay on the other. But this haughty specimen could see no evidence of any of this in Bella; she saw only a scholarship girl, a charity case.

'Excuse me, Miss Collier,' Mildred Purefoy said before Bella had time to open her mouth. (It was the rule that the students should not use their Christian names with one another. It breeds informality, Miss Swanzy said.) Mildred was a Quaker, tall and beaky, who tried to be a peacemaker. 'It doesn't do to make such uncharitable judgements. We are all equal here, and more importantly, we are all equal before Our Maker.'

'Don't be preaching God to me,' Prudence Collier snapped

back. She was an ugly girl, Bella thought, ugly in nature if not in looks. 'You, who goes neither to chapel or to church.'

'Let us at least act like ladies, then,' Mildred pleaded, ignoring the taunt.

Of all of them, Mildred was the closest to that exalted condition. Her father held a high position in the Belfast and Oriental Tea Company and she would go on to be a governess to a double-barrelled family in Kildare.

'Hark at her! Ladies, is it?' Miss Collier tossed her brassy curls.

The simmering row might have escalated had Miss Swanzy not intervened ushering Bella into a narrow cubicle. As she filled the bath and disrobed she felt a cloud of disappointment descend, mingling with the steam rising from the claw-footed bath. As a girl without sisters, she had hoped to find amiable companions among her classmates. Instead, on her first night, she had provoked bitter disagreement, without even having her own say in the matter.

'A teacher,' Miss Swanzy would intone, 'must be morally above reproach.'

Not something that troubled Bella Casey for her head was full of books. Carlyle, Molière, Racine, Joyce's *Handbook of School Management*, the pedagogical teachings of Pestalozzi. She was relieved that her interest did not run to young men. Once or twice, she had been invited by Mabel Bunting or Iris Dagge, to pair off with a friend of their young men, for a foursome was more respectable than two alone. But since she was only brought along as gooseberry, she had no thoughts of romance for herself in these expeditions. She would often listen to the girls at the College talking, sighing over this fellow or that, wondering if they'd worn a brighter dress or a different pin in their hat whether they'd have been noticed by some swain or other. Romantic speculation would run through the dormitories like a high fever, particularly before College socials to which the male students from Kildare Place were invited.

These were strictly supervised affairs, with Miss Swanzy on patrol for indiscretions, but even there Bella had never met a young man who was worthy of the kind of fascinations that kept her classmates up all night. She wondered if she was deficient in some way. The Kildare Place students reminded her of nothing more than her brothers and their pals. Mick and Tom often brought friends home, but for their own entertainment, not for Bella's benefit. They were in the habit of returning in high good humour from the pub and carrying on as if home were a wing of the tavern. The Bugler Beaver was a face that appeared many times. She remembered the first time, for unwittingly she'd made a show of herself.

She had been roused well after midnight by the sounds of revelry coming from the kitchen and thinking it was only her brothers carousing, she went to quieten them. They had an invalid in the house. Pappie was confined to bed after taking a fall at the Mission in which he'd hurt his back, but did those boys take a blind bit of notice of that? No, they carried on regardless. Bella stormed into the kitchen, dressed only in her night clothes, her hair all down, ready to give them a piece of her mind.

'For pity's sake, boys, can't you pipe down?' she started in a well-worn litany of complaint before she realized there was company in. At least she had her good cotton gown on and had taken the trouble to throw her Ulster on over it, so she was half-ways decent, if a trifle eccentric-looking in this strange mix of the bed-chamber and the street. Her feet were bare and for some reason that was the first thing the Bugler looked at as he rose to greet the tousled apparition before him.

'And who's this charming maid with the nut-brown hair?' the Bugler asked, quoting a parlour song she recognised.

'That's my sister, Bella,' Tom said a little sourly.

'The scholar, is it?' the Bugler enquired. 'You're going to be a teacher, I hear, Miss Casey.'

'Oh give over, Nick, with your Miss Casey,' Mick interrupted, 'our Bella has enough airs and graces as it is.'

This was her constant tribulation – trying to hold her head high at the College among those who would look down on her, while being accused at home of having ideas above her station. But despite Mick's surly interjection, the Bugler sounded impressed and that, in turn, impressed Bella.

'Are we keeping you up, Miss . . . Bella?' he asked contritely.

His expression was half-admiration, half-mocking. His dark hair, she noticed, was glossy in the candlelight and his manner, even in the midst of drinking, full of a kind of courteous mischief.

'Not at all,' she said in a complete reversal of what she meant to say. 'I just came for a drop of water.'

Nicholas Beaver was a handsome man, she had to admit. The kind you'd follow with your eyes on the street if you were a certain kind of girl. Not that Bella was *that* class of a girl. He was tall, well-built, with a fine pair of shoulders. His Spaniard's hair and moustache gave him a foreign look, though his eyes were the colour of gunmetal. The streets of Dublin were fairly thick with uniforms. Full of themselves, Bella thought, just because they sported braided finery they thought they could cock their hats at any girl they pleased and she'd come running. But not Bella Casey; not everyone who wears a tricorne is Lord Wellington, she would remind herself.

'Well, boys,' the Bugler said having the grace to look shame-faced, 'I suppose it is time that good people were in their beds.'

Bella watched him go, feeling like a scold.

The young men from Kildare Place who came for the socials were much the same. Either raucous and harmless like overgrown cubs, or they were the opposite, too earnest and dry without an animating spark. One of them, Bella remembered, a certain Charles Bentham droned on in her ear for an age about some Hottentot sect led by a Yogi, if you please, that believed that God was not a personage as *we* all believed – he said it contemptuously, including Bella in this company – but existed as a presence in every living thing. She had never heard such a preposterous notion and was surprised that any so-called Christian would be espousing such shocking suppositions. And to think this young man would soon go forth to tutor young minds . . .

'He does go on so,' a young woman in the company said conversationally when Mr Bentham was called away. 'He might be my cousin but he could talk for Empire.' She introduced herself as Lily Clesham.

Bella had a hard time understanding Lily at the start for she spoke in a soft, complicated way. She was from somewhere out west, Galway or Clifden or somesuch. Bella had never had a close association with a country person before. There weren't many country people on Dorset Street bar the cattle drovers who used to usher their beasts down to the bull ring on fair day and leave in their wake steaming heaps of . . . what Bella referred to as Thomas Brady, to be polite. It repulsed her, to be truthful, to see those wild-eyed animals skeetering and flailing about, slithering in their own muck.

'So, you are on the Long Course,' Lily said, 'and on a scholarship!'

Out of others' mouths this might have sounded snooty, but Lily was genuinely admiring and Bella immediately warmed to her.

'And you?' Bella asked.

'I'm training with the Irish Church Mission in Clonsilla.'

'My Pappie works for them!' Bella rushed in, pleased to be able to boast a connection, 'nothing official you understand –

he's a book-keeper – but he's pure devoted to their work.'

'Well, that's something we hold in common,' Lily said smiling. 'My father's a clergyman so they're both in the business of
saving souls.'

She invited Bella to sit and soon they were trading informa-
tion as if they were old friends. Once Lily got her certificates
there was a position waiting for her in one of the ragged schools
run by the Church Mission in Galway, close to her father's rec-
tory at Ballyconneely. Bella would remember the name though
she never saw the place, except through Lily's eyes, who viewed it
through a rose-coloured mist.

'Oh Bella,' she would say, 'you'll have to come and see it for
yourself.'

Lily was always homesick, always hankering after the stone
house on the brow of the hill with the view of the island. Omey,
it was called. But when she said it, Bella saw O May like a declaration of love in a Shakespeare sonnet. Maybe it was Lily's poetic
way of talking, but Bella had never felt that way about any place.
She was proud, of course, of the home she'd come from. But she
didn't love the streets and the houses all about them, the stuff the
city was made of, not in the way Lily loved the rocks and trees
of Ballyconeelly and its wild tormented sea. The granite prow of
Trinity College, the stout majesty of the Custom House, the fine
houses of the gentry on Fitzwilliam Square, these were places of
which you could be justly proud, but she couldn't, in conscience,
say she loved the cracked pavement stones or the slimed cobbles

that she walked on daily, or the shuttered-up pawn shops or the dim little dairies or the tenement houses with their rickety children and the smell of Thomas Brady in the yards seeping into your nostrils. She couldn't say she loved *them*.

Unlike most of the girls, Lily did not come to the College shindigs on the look-out for a sweetheart. No, she had already met a certain Mr Frederick McNeice and she told Bella there was an understanding between them. So when Bella and Lily met at these do's, it was one another's company they sought out. In time, they would not depend on organised socials to meet, but on Saturdays when they were both free, they would stroll around the Green and if they had a shilling to spare take tea at the Imperial. If not, they would brew up in the College kitchens and retreat to the deserted dormitory, for most of the girls would be out on passes. There they could while away several hours undisturbed, stretched on Bella's bed, the curtains drawn around them.

'It would not pain me much if I were to follow in the footsteps of Miss Arabella Swanzy,' Bella confided in Lily. She had found in Lily someone with whom she could hypothesize about her future without sounding presumptious. 'She has an office of her own and a title after her name. I don't think less of her because she has never wed.'

'All the same, Bella, if you were to marry, who would you choose?'

'If I were to marry . . .' she replied. 'I would want someone respectable, someone elevated and refined, a schoolmaster perhaps, or a clergyman . . . .'

But in truth, it was Lily she was thinking of. She endlessly compared herself with Lily – and found herself wanting. Lily was charitable where she nursed resentments. Lily's nature was to be rich in hope whereas she found herself surrendering to the ugly persistencies of doubt.

'Yes,' Lily said dreamily, 'a heart's companion.'

Some impetuous urge overtook Bella and she planted a kiss on her friend's lips. Lily turned a grey gaze on her; a flicker of doubt crossed her features. Bella cursed her unruly impulsiveness for, clearly, she saw now, it had been to Mr McNeice that Lily was referring.

'Some day, Bella,' Lily said gravely, 'all of your gifts will be recognised.'

But privately, Lily was not so sure. Although she and Bella were of an age, she'd always felt motherly towards her friend, on account of being motherless herself, perhaps. She confided in her young man.

'Do you think Bella's unstable, is that it?'

'No, no,' Lily replied, already feeling she was betraying her friend. Fred was a dear man, but he was clumsy in female territory, a tentative traveller. A time would come after the babies came when Fred would become afraid of her changeable emotions, her down-thrown moods.

'Maybe she's a little in love with you,' he offered, trying to chivvy her out of her sombre mood. 'And who would blame her?'

'No, no, it isn't that either,' Lily said, pushing away his compliment. 'It was just so unexpected. Bella is usually so guarded, so proper, and then to be so suddenly at the mercy of her emotions. I worry for her.'

'Oh come now.' Fred was tiring now of this talk about a woman he had never met. 'I'm sure she's well able to fend for herself. Hasn't she had to strive to get this far?'

But that was just the trouble, Lily wanted to say. Bella's striving seemed to come at the expense of her heart, a heart that seemed given to inflammation on being granted the most commonplace of kindnesses.

THE UNDISCOVERED

COUNTRY

She was Principal Infant Teacher at St Mary's School on Dominick Street, the first of her class to secure a position. Take that, Prudence Collier, she thought. The position came with living quarters and though they were modest and high up in the attics, Bella was extremely proud of her two rooms. True, you had to stoop by the three low windows to look down on to the street, but it felt safe up there, both fortress and haven. There was one big room with two windows facing west which housed a plain deal table and chairs, one large armchair, a rag rug thrown over the bare floorboards and a small fire grate. In the corner there was a little pantry with a stone sink. Oh yes, there was running water and a privy below in the yard. The bedroom was pokey enough with an iron bed wedged under the third window but there was a little locker beside it – for keeping her drawers and other unmentionables – and a pine press where she could hang her clothes. She brought her own homely touches to the place, lace curtains for the windows, an eiderdown for the bed, a brand new kettle and a pair of small framed prints – *The Flower Girl* and *The Gleaners* – which she had bought from a dealer in Francis Street. She completed the effect with some books from home – the three volumes of Shakespeare she'd won for gaining high honours in Final Standard, and several of her Pappie's Dickens to take the bare look off the place.

In the mornings Bella would travel down from the eaves to open the street door and for a few moments before the throngs of children arrived, she felt quite the lady of the manor. Though some of the houses at the far end of Dominick Street had seen better days – Dublin was like that, pockets of finery in a threadbare fabric – it was still an elegant address and bore itself proudly, or so Bella fancied. Even St Saviour's at the top end was a handsome edifice if you could get past the crowds of Romanists filling bottles of what they called holy water from a butt on the southern side of the chapel. The street rolled gently away towards Great Britain Street. At that hour there was only the odd dray cart or milk float to disturb the peace and so it was easy to imagine herself as mistress of this great house. Sometimes though, in the evenings, hers seemed like a high lonely state. The schoolroom way down in the basement was far distant. The floors in between with their fine stuccoed rooms – including even a ball-room – were empty and pregnant with shadows. But she had little time to consider the ghosts that might haunt the place; she was too taken up with her new duties. Even after the last of the children was seen off the premises, the desks had to be cleaned and dusted, the slates and chalk put away, the schoolroom fire tamped down. Then there was the record-keeping. Sometimes, Miss Quill, who taught First and Second Class in the neighbour-ing room, would stay on after hours to check stationery orders and fuel requisitions with Bella, but Miss Quill lived out and by 5pm each evening, Bella was alone, often plangently so.

She was standing at her teacher's desk, set into a raised platform overlooking the empty classroom, when the Reverend Archibald Leeper paid his first visit. There were a hundred things needing doing that day. The desks were all askew, the stove door was wide open and billowing smoke into the room. She was not used to its vagaries yet; it was always too hot or too cold, the children either scalded or shivering, provoking their piteous chilblains and all manner of running fevers. The older girls in First Class could be relied on to feed the stove but the infants couldn't be permitted to go too close to the fire.

'Miss Casey,' the Reverend Leeper commanded.

He was standing in the doorway of the schoolroom, his fingers steepled to his lips. She didn't know how long he had been there, or whether he had overheard her contemplating her chores, which she was in the habit of whispering aloud when she thought herself alone. The Reverend had been on the Board of Guardians that had interviewed her for the position, but like all men of the cloth, he seemed to fade into his canonicals and she had not taken much account of him, bar remembering a thin pale face, a hank of limp tawny hair on his brow, a bony hand extended into the dim hallway when he opened the door to her.

'Follow me, if you please,' he had said as they trod through the gloom and down a back-stairs. Her eyes, she remembered, had taken some time to adjust to the ill-lit interior from the brash glare of the July day. As if sensing her discomfort, he had turned to her on the stair and said, 'Watch your step.' She should have heeded.

'Reverend Leeper,' she managed to reply now when she had recovered from her startlement.

He ambled into the room. On his way he picked up a slate that had been tipped to the floor in haste when she had rung the afternoon bell. He placed it in her hands like a rebuke.

'I am dismayed, Miss Casey, to find that so early in your probation you have been negligent in your duties,' he said.

Bella tried to quell her alarm. What had she done? What had she not done? He paced the floor, his arms behind his back like a constable and refusing to look her in the eye.

'You will recall at your interview,' he went on as if reading her thoughts for though he left pauses in the conversation they were not meant for the listener to interject, 'that your listed duties included leading the church choir. But you have not deigned to grace us with your presence.'

He made a barrack-room turn and halted.

'With your fine musical training from the College and your lovely voice, so amply demonstrated at your interview, may I add, it should be no burden to you . . .'

'On Sunday, is it?' she asked.

'The house of the Lord is open daily, is it not, Miss Casey?'

He made her name sound like a deprecation.

'Choir practice on Tuesday evenings and Saturday afternoons, and the weekly services I don't need to tell you about since you are such a devoted parishioner.'

He smiled at her, but it seemed sickly and insincere. He was not a healthy man, she saw now. He had the pallor of an invalid as if he never saw sunlight, his scalp pale beneath his thin hair. His eyes were so deep-set beneath a bony brow that it was hard to tell what colour they were rightly. He had to keep on moistening his meagre lips as if they were parched. He seemed prematurely aged though he was not much past thirty, she guessed.

'We will see you so, Miss Casey,' he concluded brusquely, 'seven-thirty service. Don't be late.'

And that is how it started, with a call to worship.

She was up at cockcrow the following morning and setting out by seven, her crimson cape thrown around her and her boots ringing out on the cobbles of Coles Lane. The malty whiff of the brewery singed the air. Seagulls wheeled and clamoured.

The Reverend Leeper was already in situ when she climbed the narrow staircase to the gallery in St Mary's.

'Miss Casey,' he said testily, 'we have been waiting for you.'

But I am not late, she thought, but he was already half-way through his introductions. There were two ladies, Miss Florence Horner, a seamstress by trade with a fine voice and Mrs Mabel Lecky who could hardly carry a tune but who boomed a lot, as well as three pupils from the Model School, Grace Winter, Muriel MacHenry and Gertrude Sargent, a giddy trio who had to be constantly called to task. There were two gentlemen, the brothers Orr, Henry and George, who worked as chandler's clerks and though well into their forties, showed no signs of committing themselves to the state of matrimony. They did everything together and any woman taking one of them on would have the other to contend with, too. Maybe that's why they were still unclaimed, Bella thought, notwithstanding they were respectable gents who were well turned out and changed their collars daily. But when you addressed one, they answered in unison as if they had never shed their childish brotherhood, like those twins tied at the hip who travel around with the circus.

'Your mission is to lead the choir, Miss Casey, conduct them and expand their repertoire,' the Reverend intoned, 'so that they'll be ready for christenings and confirmations, complines and evensong.'

Bella struggled through the early morning service. How much easier it was to instruct infants than full-grown adults whose wills were set and whose dispositions not so malleable. She was aware all the time of Reverend Leeper's listening ear below and braced herself for the reprimand that was bound to come.

'You have a very sweet voice, my dear,' he said after the choir had dispersed. She found herself unaccountably blushing. She did not expect compliments from the Reverend; indeed there was something unseemly about his flattery. Shouldn't he be preoccupied with the welfare of her soul rather than the timbre of her voice? It caught her off-guard.

'Thank you, Reverend,' she said.

They were standing in the portal of the church. The street, which had been dawn-blushed and silent when she had entered, was now agog with activity. The ring of a tram, the gay whistling of porters trundling crates of fruit from the markets, the footfall of clerks hurrying to their offices. She was mindful of the clock. She had a roomful of infants waiting and not so much as a sup of tea taken. And yet, the Reverend Leeper held her there, engaging in frivolous small talk. A silence fell between them that, laced with unease.

'Well, Miss Casey, off with you now. Have you no duties to attend to?'

A hot flare bloomed on her cheeks but this time it was injustice that inspired it. She felt corrected for being courteous, as if her politeness was some kind of needy appetite for praise. The Reverend was like light and shade, she thought as she hurried away, like a spring day when the sun is shy about coming out from behind low cloud and when it does, it shines but weakly and you know soon that it will be eclipsed again.

For several weeks the Reverend Leeper's conduct followed the same pattern. He would scold her for being late or for failing to keep the choir together, even for wrong notes that Mr Cecil Anketell would coax out of the organ (the wrong note came more easily and sweetly to him than the right one) as if she could, somehow, control the old codger's short sight and his hazy notion of the rudiments of music. Mr Anketell was as wheezy as his instrument. When he pulled on the stops, Bella was not sure if it was the organ or his own chest that was barking. Often he would forget which hymn number the choir was on and be off with 'O God of Bethel, by whose hand' when they were pursuing 'Lead Kindly Light'.

'Miss Casey,' Reverend Leeper would call out from the body of the church. 'The choir and the organist are not meant to be in competition.' As if the disharmony were all her doing.

It never seemed to occur to him to admonish Mr Anketell. But she resolved, for the time being at any rate, to keep her trap shut, as Mick and Tom would say. Nonetheless, she grew to dread the words 'Miss Casey' from the Reverend Leeper's lips for they always heralded either a complaint or some unexpected declaration of concern.

'Miss Casey, what time do you call this?'

'Miss Casey, you look a little flushed this morning, I hope

you're not coming down with a fever.'

'Miss Casey, perhaps you'd stay behind when choir practice is over. I need a word with you about school matters.'

School matters?

She waited among the silent pews while the Reverend Leeper divested himself. The Ten Commandments were inscribed in gold script under the stained-glass apse window and she found herself reading through them as if to examine her own conscience. It seemed the church walls spoke. There was a strange gloom in an empty church after evensong, not altogether unpleasant, but she came to associate its silence with her own apprehension. Sometimes she thought the Reverend Leeper deliberately made her wait to augment her nervousness, to give her more time to fret. But that could not be; a man of God would not be so petty.

School matters?

Bella could think of no reason why he should want to question her about her classes. She had followed strictly the tenets of her training – cultivate a humble, teachable disposition, avoid all negligence in personal appearance, let your manners be cheerful, sober and decorous. In fact, if there had been a complaint, it was that she was too conscientious. On seeing that she had pinned a map to the blackboard showing all the Crown's Possessions in red, Mr Braithwate, the schools inspector, had remarked that it was rather ambitious to try to teach geography to infants.

'Miss Casey,' the Reverend Leeper began, emerging from the shadows, making her start even though she had been hovering for ten minutes, anticipating his presence. 'I'll be needing to see your log books and records tomorrow evening in the school-room, if you please.'

Bella felt a stirring of mutiny. This was the Canon's job and he had taken scant interest in the books, throwing only a hasty eye over them when he came to instruct the children in Scripture.

'The Canon usually. . .' she began.

'The Canon is indisposed, 'the Reverend interrupted, 'so I'll be taking over some of his duties.'

Her heart sank. The elderly Canon had baptised her – and all the Caseys – at the font in St Mary's. She had always looked on him as a kind of fatherly guardian; she could not imagine ever feeling that way about the Reverend.

'Tomorrow then,' the Reverend said, 'at five.'

Bella turned to go and as she did, he summoned her back.

'Miss Casey?'

She faced him, full of spite within, and not even caring if it showed in her face.

'I have to say the colour red becomes you. Gives a fine glow to your cheeks.'

He smiled his wet smile, expecting some grateful acknowl-edgement. But Bella would not give him the satisfaction. As she hurried off, though, she cursed the blessed crimson cape. Next time she would travel without her cloak.

In preparation for the Reverend's visit, she spent a good hour slaving over the entries in her books to make sure they were up to the minute. She had kept the school stove lit even though it would mean cutting back on coal over the next few days. The children would have to go without so that the high and mighty Reverend Leeper might keep his feet warm.

'You must understand, Miss Casey, that it is vital the accounts be kept up to date, in case an inspector might call.'

But that is the inspector's business, she thought to herself, not yours. The Reverend paid particular attention to the Fees Outstanding.

'The sooner these parents pay, the sooner you'll qualify for your increment,' he said as if she had never spoken.

'If you'll pardon me, Reverend Leeper, should we not give leeway on late payments to those families in distress. . .'

She had stopped feeding the grate by this stage in the hope that it might remind him that he had warmer places to be, such as his own hearth, where a wife waited.

'It is your future I am thinking of, Miss Casey.'

He laid a hand on her forearm. She felt a strange charge, even through the thick serge of the coat she had thrown around her shoulders to cheat the chill. She had never stood this close to him before.

'Now,' he said with a click of his heels, 'it is time to inspect the teachers' quarters.'

'I beg your pardon?'

'It *is* part of the school premises, Miss Casey,' he snapped.

'The Canon has never . . . '

'I am in charge now and I insist upon it,' he said testily. 'The teacher's accommodations must be kept to the same high standard that you clearly keep in your schoolroom.'

There it was again, a rebuke lying down with a compliment.

Bella locked the schoolroom door and led the way up the back stairs. As they ascended – it was black dark now – she tried to make an inventory in her mind as to what state she had left the place when she had hurried out that morning. Might there be a petticoat lying in sight, or worse? But surely the Reverend would not want to see the bedroom? What business would he have in there? Afterwards, remembering what she had thought on the stair, Bella wondered whether even contemplating such a lewd proposition had somehow directed events. At the head of the stairs, she opened the door and stood back to let the Reverend Leeper enter. He stood rather imperiously, silhouetted in the window through which the faint glimmer of gaslight could be glimpsed. She hurried into the scullery to light a candle for she knew there was no paraffin for the lamp. She realised how nervous she was when it took her three strikes of the match to set the flame aglow.

'Well,' he said looking around as she bore the candle tremulously toward him. 'That's much better.'

He looked around him. 'It is spartan, but it's clean.'

She felt herself bridle. Would he have preferred trinkets, cheap china pieces, swathes of damask on the windows, a tapestry footstool, an overstuffed armchair? He prowled around, inspecting her books on the shelves she had made up out of an old orange box and stained to look like oak, and paused over her two framed prints. As she brought out the candle and set it down on the table – a little leafed one that Mother had bequeathed her from home – he roused himself from his intense examination of her possessions, deemed so meagre, and turned his gaze on her. In the candlelight his face seemed cadaverous, his bleared eyes sunk in deep hollows. He stood for several minutes inspecting her – that was the only word for it, as if she were on the parade ground.

'Well, Miss Casey,' he said finally, 'may I remark how pretty you look in this light.'

He advanced towards her and took both of her hands in his, then turned the palms upwards as if he might read her fortune.

'Oh Isabella . . .' he murmured.

It was so long since anyone had used her full name that for a moment, Bella failed to recognise herself. And she was so used to Miss Casey this and Miss Casey that, that she was lulled in a strange way.

'I have been longing for this moment . . . ' There was a small, pulsing comfort in his touch as he caressed her hands. 'You must have felt it too, surely.'

What Bella felt was a sensation of unmooring, as if she had drowsed at the theatre and woken suddenly to find herself at a different play. A melodrama of the romantic kind. And she was a player who did not know her lines.

'Of course, we must be chaste and pure in our affections . . .'

She tried to squirm her fingers free, but he held them firm.

'Grant me a hearing, Isabella, dear.'

Stupidly, she was still waiting for him to speak of the school accounts and she did not wish to give offence in any way in case it might colour the outcome. She was waiting for this soft and foolish Reverend Leeper to give way to the stiff and formal version she was used to.

'Our love must be like that of brother and sister . . .'

'Love?' she heard herself say, though once it was out of her mouth it sounded contemptuous.

He leaned forward and planted a chaste kiss on her cheek. His lips trembled as if his heart were in his mouth.

'Hush now,' he whispered as if her discomfiture had nothing to do with him. Then, swiftly, he made for the door where he paused again.

'Oh and Miss Casey?' She did not turn to face him so he spoke to her back. 'I will be checking the school logs every week until the end of term. I have to say, your book-keeping leaves a lot to be desired.'

After his departure, she stood rubbing the spot on her cheek where the Reverend had brushed his lips. It was the only way she could convince herself of what had occurred. Then when she had convinced herself, she gave into fuming. Why, she berated herself, was she so slow to anger? To think that for all these months while she had been labouring to gain the Reverend's approval, he had been nursing his untoward desire and waiting for his moment. He had thoroughly ambushed her, as surely as if he had crept up behind her on the street and demanded monies. But what troubled her more was that she had somehow played a part in the wickedness herself. Hadn't she let him hold her hand, caress it, without a word of protest? How could she have been so dim-witted, so acquiescent? The truth was that she had given into a vapourish female kind of weakness, like one of those silly ninnies at the College who prated on about their beaux. Was she, in the end, no better than they were? Every flurried thought led to a new question. How could she face the Reverend in the schoolroom or the church? What to say? And what more might he demand of her? But no, she reassured herself, he was a clergyman. Anyway, if there was any more trouble, couldn't she set her brothers on him? Mick and Tom would sort him out in a flash, clergyman or no. But that would involve admitting what had already taken place, which she could barely admit to herself. And what exactly could she accuse him of – a declaration of love? Hardly a hanging offence. And she could not deny the thrilling flattery of having become, with no effort of her own will, an object of devotion even if it was the Reverend Leeper for whom, heretofore, she had felt only a baffled repulsion. He might have been her superior – in the school, at church – but in this matter he was but a slave to his carnal thoughts. And he a married man! Bella had seen his wife only once, a slender thread of a woman with a defeated look.

'Poor woman,' Miss Quill had told her, 'God has deigned that she never carry a child to term.'

Bella had thought Mrs Leeper merely pale and wan; now she wondered how much of her demeanour could be laid at her husband's door.

She decided to tell no one of the encounter, either at home or abroad. Perhaps after his transgression, the Reverend would govern his instincts and honour his promise of renunciation, she thought. But the opposite was the case. His protestation of love seemed to open a door. It did not make him any more tender in his official dealings with her, but it heralded a campaign of creeping liberties. He brushed against her seemingly by hazard in the schoolroom one day after Scripture class. He accosted her in the basement hallway by the teachers' press when the children were gone, and pressed his reluctant embraces upon her. He would often crush her to him urgently – in the classroom, or on the stairs – then release her, pushing her away. It seemed he drew her close only to repel her more violently, as if he was testing himself against her. He acted as if it was she who had steered his hand to her bodice or forced him to caress her face. One evening, after choir practice, he went further, planting a kiss on the nape of her neck in the dark of the gallery stairs as they were descending. She did not say anything because when she turned around to speak, he only issued his customary warning.

'Watch your step, Miss Casey.'

She fretted that it was something in her that had encouraged his bewildering conduct. She examined her conscience but she could not think what it was. For all her education, she was not schooled to deal with this. A match girl would have been better able to swat him away with a loud reproach and a careless laugh. But she with her Teacher's Certificate and salaried position could resort neither to vulgar directness nor feigned nonchalance. She tried to avoid him, but it was no easy task with his constant visitations, the checking of her records, the choir rehearsals and all the other little businesses of the school that required his say-so. With each passing month she felt more frantic, more desperate to extricate herself. But how could she do that without losing everything she held dear – her position, her respectability, her reputation?

Her vigilance was so taken up with the matter of Reverend Leeper that she failed to realise the import of other changes about her, of a far graver nature. It was over a year since her Pappie's fall at the Meeting Rooms. (He had overstretched himself hanging a banner for the Harvest Festival and had crashed to the ground crushing something in his spine.) But he had gone into something of a decline, which the doctors couldn't explain. The Mission had had to let him go, and though there was some compensation, the family could no longer afford to live on Dorset Street and had moved to a more modest address at Innisfallen Parade, a terrace house at street level. They still had all of their own furniture, though, including the Elysian, which consoled Bella. Home would always be where the piano was. But it was here that Pappie really began to fail. His face grew gaunt, his hand turned to claw. He spent much of his time sunk in the armchair in the front room before a low fire. Afterwards Bella would wonder if some other illness was afoot. Had her father, in the midst of stout health, been growing the contagion of his own death? As the months went by, he no longer had the strength to stand upright and Mick and Tom moved his bed downstairs into the front room. Mother set up a pallet on the other side of the fireplace and she kept the grate stoked all night for Pappie felt the cold keenly. But despite all these portents, Bella only realised the gravity of his illness when he called her, Mick and Tom to his bedside.

'You know I'm for the dark,' he said, his voice rasping.

Mother had propped him up high on a bank of pillows to help his breathing.

The boys shuffled. Bella could feel tears welling up but she determined not to give in to them, though she had full cause to, thinking of all the times she had been consumed with trifles of her own when he had been busy preparing himself to meet his Maker.

'I want you three to take care of your mother since I will not be here to do it.'

Then Bella understood the finality of this summons.

'And in the case of Isaac and Jack, to look out for them especially for they will not have the benefit of a father, as you have had.'

He stopped to take breath and in the noisy silence of him drawing in enough air to continue, Tom had crumpled to his knees at the side of the bed weeping with a terrible clamour in big manly croaks. A lump was blossoming in Bella's throat. She gripped the iron foot of the bed and bit down on her lip to stop it trembling.

'See to it, Bella,' Pappie went on, for it was a struggle for him to speak and he was determined to get to the end of his piece, 'that Jack gets to school every day. We don't want him ending up as a dunce. I know I can't depend on this pair of blackguards in that regard.'

That really set Tom off. So much so that Mother had to hurry into the room and steer him away.

'Come here,' Pappie said then to Bella, almost in a whisper.

He reached out his waxen hand.

'You're a good girl, Bella, and you've made your father very proud.'

And then she could hold her tears no longer. Out they came in a childish spurt and she was all set to confess about Reverend Leeper for she knew she was not worthy of his blessing. But she stopped herself; it would have broken his heart to know that she had been besmirched even in the smallest way. Better that he go ignorant in his pride, firm in the knowledge that she was a good and faithful daughter. If he had lived, perhaps all manner of things would have been different. But without him, there was no one to think the best of her, and so she began to fall in her own estimation.

A FINE SILK SHAWL

Pappie was buried on a tender day in September with some sun, a little blustery wind and a pale sky filled with racing cloud. It was a fine funeral with three carriages, twenty-six cabs and six side-cars. The undertaker and his assistant wore silver-buttoned long coats of Prussian blue and black top hats, the horses – one black, one roan – were kitted out in embroidered head-dresses with black plumes.

Once inside the gates of Mount Jerome, Bella and Mother alighted from the carriage. The wide avenue petered out into narrow pathways between the green-furred gravestones, and they made their way on foot to the spot where Pappie would be buried. Mick and Tom and two men from the Mission shouldered the coffin along with two of the hearsemen. It tilted to one side on account of Mick being smaller than the others, Bella noticed, but she countered this with the thought that Pappie would have been proud of the boys at that moment for they looked like the men he had wanted them to be, stiff and serious in their good suits, and sober. But as soon as the Canon had said his piece – *dust to dust, the way we all go in the end* – and the gravediggers had begun to shovel the clods of earth over the coffin, she knew her brothers' minds would turn towards diversion.

It came in the person of the Bugler Beaver, whom Bella spied once the coffin was lowered, moving through the crowd in his gay scarlets.

'Sorry for your trouble, Miss Casey,' he said and bowed a little like a real gentleman.

He took her gloved hand in both of his. He, too, was wearing gloves – spotless white ones – and even though their flesh did not meet, Bella felt a certain intent in his touch. This much she had learned. The recognition came as a soft shock; she could no longer count herself innocent.

'What's that fella doing here?' Mother said *sotto voce* as the Bugler turned away.

'To pay his respects to Pappie,' Bella whispered harshly.

'Sure, he never even met your father,' Mother said.

Mick collared his military friend, clapping an arm across his gold-encrusted shoulders and muttered urgently. 'What about a jar with Tom and myself in The Bleeding Horse?'

'Now now, son,' Mother said.

Mick scowled. He took the Bugler aside and there was some urgent whisperings between them, some male hugger-mugger afoot.

'Bella?' Mother called.

She was climbing into the carriage and settling herself on the seat with Jack on her lap.

Presently Mick joined them, lumbering aboard reluctantly and Tom followed him. The carriage took off with an enormous lurch. Through the window, Bella watched as the figure of Corporal Beaver, standing alone by the graveside, receded from view. The other mourners had scattered so her last sight of Pappie was of the Bugler, standing guard at the open grave.

It was a desolate sensation returning home to the darkened rooms with the blinds down, the clocks stopped. It seemed to Bella as if the house held its breath, the floorboards waiting for Pappie's tread. Only his belongings were still in residence – his jacket hanging on the hook of the parlour door; his books by the bedside. He had got only half-way through Trollope's *The Way We Live Now*, she noticed, thinking how poignant that he would never know now how the tale finished. His Bible lay on the counterpane. She opened it and riffled through its pages. In the inside back cover he had inscribed the marks from her report cards at the College. Her 52 out of 60 for penmanship, her 56 for spelling, even her poor 28 for grammar. It made her heart seize and she shut the good book quickly so as not to be reminded. Of his absence; of her own promise.

She set to and made an early tea. Mrs Tancred, next door, had left some eggs and they sat down to eat in a silence as solemn as the Last Supper, broken only by Isaac who remarked there wasn't much eating in an egg, not for a man. He was all of twelve but he had developed notions of himself, particularly with his father gone. They were the only words exchanged between them. Bella was glad of it – it seemed an offence to chatter. When they had finished and Bella was stacking the plates, Jack came up to her and nuzzled into her side.

'When is me Da coming home?'

Of late, being distracted, Mother had let him pal around with that Connor boy, a Catholic of decidedly rough manners who called his own father just plain Da.

'Who's looking after me Da?' he persisted. 'Why aren't you up in the room looking after me Da?'

She hated hearing Pappie being reduced to the level of Mr Connor, a common labourer.

'Oh Jack, will you stop it before you give us all a headache,' she snapped at him.

'Bella!' Mother said and whisked the child on to her lap.

'He's only making us all feel mournful with his lonesome whingeing,' Bella said trying to justify being short with him.

They each lapsed into their own thoughts after that. Jack fell into a drowsy sleep; Mick lit up his pipe; Tom read the newspaper. Then somewhere in the distance a church bell chimed the seventh hour. Mick and Tom hauled themselves out of their stupor and donned their greatcoats.

'We're off for a quick drink,' Mick announced for both of them. That's the way it was with those two. Mick rowed out and Tom got carried in his wake. He halted at the door. 'A word outside, Bella, if you please.'

She followed them out into the hall.

'I have something for you, Bella,' he said, 'though I'm not sure it's at all suitable.'

'What? What do you mean?'

'I have a little *billay do* for you,' he said, plucking a letter from his inside pocket. 'From an admirer.'

She blanched. The Reverend, she thought immediately. Had it come to this that he could worm his way into the middle of their grieving? Then she shook herself; it couldn't be. Could it?

'What admirer?' she asked, making to snatch the note from his hand. Mick winked at her and feinted a few times.

'Ah, Bella,' he taunted as the pair of them danced around the letter, 'don't you know that a certain bugler is sweet on you?'

Fear gave way to relief.

'Give it over here,' she cried, 'and quit your teasing.'

'What's going on out there?' Mother called out.

'Give it over,' she hissed, 'before we draw Mother down upon us.'

Mick surrendered the letter.

'You'll have to open it straight away – he'll be wanting an answer.'

She fixed in her mind the picture of the Bugler Beaver in the graveyard in his jaunty regimentals, standing guard beside Pappie.

'Bella?' Mother called.

'You can tell Corporal Beaver, the answer's yes,' she said though she did not even know the question.

She shut the door behind the boys and leaned up against it, still holding the unopened letter. Bella was written on the outside (no more Miss Casey, she noticed) in a steady, robust hand with no curlicues, the hand of a practical man. It wasn't cramped like a clerk's or illegible like a doctor's. It could have been the script of a teacher so well-modulated was it, but it had a confident flair, an impatient progress, the letters sloping forward as if each one was rushing to embrace the next. She opened the envelope and unfolded the note.

'Dear Bella,' it read. 'Slip out if you can. Am having a jar with Mick and Tom in Nagle's but can make my excuses and meet you at the Rotunda Rooms at 9. Say you'll come. Nick.'

There wasn't much to it, though quite what she had been expecting she couldn't rightly say. It sounded terse, a command rather than a request. But those last words – say you'll come – betrayed an urgency that twinned with her own. Was *this* the way out?

She sat in the parlour till going on half past eight. Mrs Tancred was in residence and looked like she might stay the whole night.

'Mother,' she said quietly, using words she'd been rehearsing for over two hours. 'I'm going to slip out for a breath of fresh air before it gets dark. Maybe take a turn by the canal.'

Before she had a chance to reply, she turned to Mrs Tancred and used her sweetest tone. 'Would you sit with my mother a while longer, Mrs Tancred, for I wouldn't want her to be alone on this of all nights.'

'Gladly, Bella, I'd be happy to.' She beamed at Bella munificently for Mrs Tancred was the kind of woman who was never happier than when she was being considered as indispensable in the affairs of others.

'My head is throbbing,' Bella said by way of explanation, 'after the exigencies of the day.'

'I know, I know, Bella, it's been a long day for all of us,' Mrs Tancred said, clutching her own temples in sympathy. 'Sure your mother is dead on her feet.'

Mother sat with her head bowed. Bella was not even sure if she was awake or asleep.

'Is that alright with you, Mother?'

Mother made no reply. She wouldn't say anything derogatory in front of a neighbour. As Bella put on her hat and threw a shawl over her shoulders, she added, 'I won't be long, Mother.'

'Oh, please yourself, Madam,' Mother replied tartly, 'for you do always.'

Well, Mrs Tancred thought, the hide of Missy, off out to see a young man on the very night of her father's funeral. Oh you couldn't pull the wool over her eyes. A breath of fresh air, a stroll by the canal, is it? The only business done there was of the unsavoury kind, in the shadow of the bridges. Not that she'd accuse Bella Casey of that. But Mrs Tancred, mother of three daughters, knew well when a lie was being told. She had a nose for it. What amazed her was that it was Bella Casey making those ramshackle excuses. She'd always been a girl for the books, never gave her mother a day's worry and now, all of a sudden . . .

Guiltily, Bella made her way down Dorset Street, looking over her shoulder as she went for fear that – what? – Mother might be following and learn her true intentions. It was ridiculous, she knew. Perhaps it was the ghost of her father she feared would appear, doomed for a certain term to walk the night. But Pappie had died in a state of grace; he had no need to linger. She turned the thought on its head. Perhaps Corporal Beaver's declaration of interest coming at this moment was due to Pappie's intercession? There, she felt better. She was glad to reach the illuminated streets and the sounds of revelry on Rutland Square. There might have been rowdies spilling out on to the street from pubs and wine lodges but they left her alone. Maybe it was out of respect for her mourning garb.

The season was on the change and the nights were drawing in so it was verging on darkness. She could feel her heart thumping faster than was usual but it wasn't romantic fervour, but the subterfuge that agitated her. Small doubts niggled at her – was Corporal Beaver's manner a mite oily, his looks on the flashy side, his eye a tad gamey, his manner too charming to be entirely sincere? But she countered with herself, wasn't she settled now, with a year's teaching behind her and an increment on the way? Wasn't it high time for her to be considering her marriage lines? But what swayed her most in this argument with herself was the Reverend. A few days' respite from him, even if it was to mourn for her dear Pappie, had convinced her. She had to find a way to escape from his avid clutches. Without Pappie, the breastplate of her armour against the world had been removed. Even though he had known nothing of her predicament, she felt weaker without him. Anyway, it was too late to turn back now for the Corporal was already there, standing under a halo of golden lamplight.

'Is it yourself, Bella?' he asked simply as she approached as if they had met by chance rather than by assignation.

'Yes,' she said, 'it is.'

'I knew you'd come,' he said.

How, she wondered, how did he know? Was there something about her that spoke so loudly of easy virtue when that was not at all her nature? What made him so sure that a respectable daughter, such as she was, would venture out and her father not cold in his grave? But she banished these disputatious thoughts. She was here, wasn't she?

They strolled down Sackville Street as light ebbed from the ashen sky. Corporal Beaver was attentive to a fault, steering her with the faintest touch to her elbow and prompting her into conversation with a gentle but confident air.

'You are now a fully-fledged schoolma'am, the boys tell me,' he said.

It gratified her to know that he had been following her progress.

'Yes,' she said for she could think of no way to elaborate. She should have pressed him for some details of his occupation at this point but she found herself miserably mute.

'How do you keep them all in check?' he asked. 'Bad enough to keep the barrack-room in order, but a squad of snotty children!'

'We try to keep their noses clean,' she retorted.

'Touch-ay,' he said winking.

The humour seemed to lubricate their exchange and though she had been shy at the start, the words began to flow when she spoke about her work.

'Lead by example, that is what Mr Pestalozzi, the great educator, would say.'

'Pestalozzi – would he be an Italian now?' the Corporal asked. He drew the eye out of Italian, she noticed.

'No, no, he was Swiss,' she replied. 'In each child, Pestalozzi said, is a little seed that contains the design of the tree so the educator must take care that no untoward influence disturbs Nature's march of developments. Before a child learns words by rote, he must understand and so the teacher must show the meaning of the word in a practical way.'

'So you demonstrate . . .' he said.

'Exactly so!' She was excited that he was so quick on the uptake.

'Like the great generals,' he went on, 'with their battle plans.'

'From the known to the unknown, that's how Pestalozzi put it,' she said. 'Life shapes us and the life that shapes us is not a matter of words but action.'

The Corporal was silent and Bella feared she had lost him. She had committed the sin of straying into abstraction where Pestalozzi would insist on the concrete. So she went on to describe the schoolroom in Dominick Street with its smoking stove and clouded windows. She chattered on about the motto she penned on the blackboard each day – *A Healthy Mind in a Healthy Body, A Place for Everything and Everything in its Place, Inaction Begets Misdeeds, A Mended Woollen Smock is Better than A Silken Robe That Has Not Been Paid For* – for even small children, she told him, must have something to aim for, some higher ambition to lift them out of whatever brute circumstances they might find themselves in.

'You'll have to show me,' he said.

'Show you . . .?'

'This cushy school you teach at,' he replied. 'When I was a lad, the leather was our teacher, which didn't make me partial to book learning.'

'Well, you have a fine hand, so your education wasn't wasted on you.'

He halted in his tracks and looked at her abashed.

'Truth is, Bella, I didn't scribe that note myself. 'Twas your Mick penned it for me, for I wouldn't trust my own penmanship with a teacher.'

It was her turn to colour. Imagine, she had not recognised her own brother's hand! But then, a girl does not expect a love letter from her brother. No wonder Mick had been sniggering before he surrendered the note for he knew already what it contained.

'But I dictated it,' Corporal Beaver went on, 'so the sentiments are mine, all mine.'

He laid a hand at her waist to emphasise the point. 'Tell me more about this Pestalozzi chap.'

And so she prattled on as they ambled towards the river. Past Nelson's Column, past the tram timekeeper in his half tall hat calling out his litany of destinations – Palmerston Park, Sydney Parade, Howth – past the Happy Ring House.

'Oh look at me going on so,' she said, 'it must be the grief talking. Pappie, God rest him, was always keen to hear of my doings . . .'

She found her voice trailing away, remembering a particular Sunday evening when she had come home from the College to relieve Mother in the sick room. Pappie had been steeped in slumber that night and she remembered thinking her vigil had been fruitless. To her shame, the change in him, his very frailty, had made her wary of him. Anyway, she was stuck in her books, swotting up on Joyce's *Handbook of School Management*, on which Miss Swanzy was threatening to examine them the following week, and she was beside herself for fear she'd fail. She had been hard at it when Pappie cocked open an eye and said softly.

'Fetch down the Shakespeare, Bella, there's a good girl, and give us a bit of *King Lear*. I do love the way you read that.'

And what had she said to him?

'Ah, not now Pappie, sure amn't I too busy with my own books?'

A thankless child, sharper than a serpent's tooth.

The tears came in an undignified squall at the memory. The Corporal moved quickly, folding her in his arms, there on the street, and he let her cry until she had wept her fill on his golden-crested shoulder. When she was sated, he fished out of his uniform pocket a large handkerchief and tilting her chin towards the light, he mopped her damp face like he would have a child's.

'People will think I've got you into trouble,' he said finally.

She was too embarrassed to look at him. In the Casey household water drops were considered women's weapons and she had turned Corporal Beaver into a comforter when she had determined to be bright as a sovereign. He took her arm and led her into the portico of a shop and retrieved a silver hip flask from his tunic. How capacious those uniforms are, she thought, and so taken up with decoration you could hardly imagine they could hide such deep pockets which seemed on the surface thin as pursed lips. Tossing his head back, the Corporal drank deeply. With a satisfied sigh, he wiped his mouth with the back of his hand.

'Care for a drop, milady?' he asked holding out the flask to Bella. She saw at closer inspection it was made of plate.

She shook her head.

'My god,' he said, laughing. 'A Casey that doesn't take a drop?'

Alcohol had never passed her lips, but now she was being offered a flask on the street! If Reverend Leeper were to see this . . . But perhaps this is what he did see, some laxity of morals she barely knew in herself. But no, she would not let the Reverend be the judge of her.

'Ah, go on,' the Corporal said, 'it'll be a comfort to you.'

Bella thought of Pappie – there was no escaping him on that day – and felt the sprouting tears again. So, to create a diversion, she took the flask and drank. It was cold as she washed it around her mouth, but when she swallowed it, it burned her up as if someone had set her alight. It brought scalding tears to her eyes, but at least this time, she could blame it on the spirits.

'There, there, girl,' the Corporal said as the whiskey inflamed her breast and she coughed and spluttered.

He clapped her back and then his mouth was on hers, and it was Nicholas Beaver she was imbibing. The taste of him, even without the whiskey, was intoxicating and as their inflamed breaths mingled and his tongue found its way into the arched vault of her mouth, it was as if her whole body had been roused from slumber.

'Bella, Bella,' he whispered as they drew apart. 'Did anybody tell you, you're a fine silk shawl in a crowd of cotton?'

*

As she pushed open the hall door of Innisfallen Parade, she prayed that the household would be abed. She stole into the parlour, remembering that only yesterday in this very room they had shut the wooden door on Pappie. She remembered the hearsemen driving the screws home, each one with a grinding squeal, as if the wood refused the brass. It seemed like another age, so distant was that scene – the black-plumed horses, the clods landing on the coffin lid. The fire was almost out and there was no sign of Mother or Mrs Tancred. She expected to hear Mother's voice call out from the back room, but instead another voice greeted her, the wretched whimper of a child torn from sleep. Jack, bleary with some night-horror, stood in the doorway rubbing his eyes.

'Where's me Da?' he cried in a bewildered tone.

'Your Pappie's gone to Heaven,' Bella said softly.

'Ma says he's in the ground; she says he's in Mount Jerome.'

'Mother's right, my pet.'

'Won't me Da be cold out there?'

'Your Pappie's quite safe,' she said refraining from using the Da word.

'But what happens when it rains?' he asked, agitated again.

'Pappie's body was buried in the ground, but his spirit is where rain or wind can't touch him, his spirit has entered the Great Silence.'

She gathered the child up in her arms to dispel whatever demons had woken him, burying her head in the crook of his little neck.

'Bella, you're hurt!' he said.

'Hurt?'

'Look, look,' he said pointing to her throat.

She rose and looked at herself in the mirror over the mantel. There was a strawberry bruise where Nicholas Beaver had left his mark. She smarted with shame that she had come into such a squalid reckoning of her womanhood on this of all days.

'Are you going to die too?' the child asked, frantic.

'No, no, my pet, that's just a little scratch. Don't you know your sister would never leave you? Sure who'd look after Jack Casey if I were not here?'

And that, finally, seemed to comfort him.

THE ORNAMENTAL BIRDCAGE

The following day she returned to her post. The Reverend Leeper appeared at dinner-time as she was supervising the children in the yard.

'Miss Casey,' he said, 'Accept my deepest condolences on your loss.'

'Thank you,' she managed to murmur. When he was being benign, she found herself softening towards him.

'You have been sorely missed, my dear.'

She regretted instantly her concession. The endearment seemed brazen; the possessive added as an insult.

'Isabella . . .' he breathed leaning in to her, out there in the middle of the playground in front of all the children. She would not look at him.

'Mavis, if you please!' she called out. Mavis Tallant was

engaged in a tussle with Essie Beale over the slate for piggybeds. Both girls looked at Bella in dumb surprise for it was unusual for Miss Casey to interfere in schoolyard disputes.

'Hand it over, Mavis,' Bella repeated loudly. 'It's Essie's turn.'

The child slung the slate to the ground so violently that it came skeetering towards the Reverend, landing at his feet. He took a step back.

'Mavis!' she scolded loudly, though, secretly, she had never been so glad of a gratuitous show of spite.

'Really, Miss Casey, you must learn to take a firmer hand with such vile behaviour. Come here, girl.'

Mavis reluctantly came forward. If truth be known, she was a dull-witted child, pasty and cross-eyed. Bella would never manage to teach her her alphabet, let alone master reading; she would be another recruit for the candle factory.

'Hold out your hand, young lady, till Miss Casey punishes you.'

He nodded to Bella expecting her to have a cane about her person whereas it was gathering dust in the dunce's corner. The intercourse between teacher and children is imposed otherwise than by blows, so says Pestalozzi, she wanted to quote. She never used a bamboo on her charges; the fool's cap, maybe, or the shame-bench, but never the birch.

'I will see to the reprimand later, Reverend Leeper,' she said. 'Off with you now, Mavis, and behave yourself.'

The September sun suddenly withdrew, leaving spatterings

of shadow, the schoolhouse chimney embalmed in the yard. Obscurely, Bella knew that there would be a penalty for defying the Reverend over Mavis. Perhaps it was that which prompted her, or was it the secret armour of Corporal Beaver, or the insidious appropriation of her name in public, but whatever it was, she found herself saying without having had a notion of it a minute earlier.

'If you please, Reverend Leeper, in the future, I think it better if we confine our conversation to school matters.'

He looked at her quizzically.

'For the sake of the children,' she added pointedly. And with that she loosed her grip on the tongue of the school bell and raised a din so loud that even if the Reverend had had an answer, it would have been drowned out.

She was on her hands and knees cleaning out the schoolroom grate that evening when he came upon her.

'Miss Casey!' he commanded.

She clambered awkwardly to standing, but before she could properly right herself, he grabbed her by the shoulder and spun her around as if she were a child's top. The dust pan she had in her hand went flying; the brush fainted at her feet. They stood in swirls of fine ash, flakes of it falling on his shoulder speckling his clerical black, the rest of it settling on her hair.

'Dust thou are, Miss Casey, and unto dust thou must return,' he said and for a moment Bella thought it a kind of absolution, as if he were calling a halt to the terrible turbulence between them. Then he caught her roughly by the arms and kissed her hungrily. If his previous approaches had been timid and tainted with shame, this was a gesture oiled with pride. It was only after he had settled himself, tamping down his meagre hair, sweeping away the residue of the ashes from his shoulder caps, that he spoke.

'You must realise, Miss Casey, that the way you spoke to me in the yard this morning has tested me beyond the limits of endurance. You see now the fruits of your challenge to my authority. You have forced me to defile the chasteness of our association.'

He paused, but it was only to draw breath for he was quite worked up now. His eyes narrowed with contempt.

'You have provoked me,' he seethed. 'You Jezebel!'

He backed away as if she were contagious, then with a tug at his collar and cuffs, he was gone.

How had she inflamed him so? Was it drink that had spurred him on? A weakness for the drop might have accounted for his stormy changes of mood though she had never got the whiff of drink from him. She had seen enough of Mick and Tom's excursions to the ale house to know that men fired up with alcohol can become easily riled. She had witnessed many's the argument at home after closing time about Parnell and Home Rule and the like. Indeed, she had joined in for she had strong views on Ireland's 'gintleman leader' who, it was reputed, had made a show of himself by casting an untidy eye on Mrs Kitty O'Shea.

'He should have more respect for himself,' she remembered saying.

Not to speak of his talk of breaking the link with England when God-fearing people were loyal to queen and country and proud of it.

'Oh we all know, Miss High and Mighty, he has no right to be making a fool of himself over a woman, married or no, Bella. We all know your views on the topic,' Mick had barked at her. He could get woefully wound up over the slightest difference of opinion, but though he might have ranted and raved about matters political with a few drinks on board, it had never made him amorous, if that's what you could call the Reverend's state. Were men's appetites so unstable, Bella wondered. Could her sober teaching dresses showered in chalk, and her hair bunned and pinned and her unpolished lips undo a man so that when he looked at her, what he saw was a brazen temptress?

Her second meeting with Corporal Beaver was in broad daylight, for which she was glad. He had made an arrangement to *rendez-vous* – he liked to use such words, she noticed, for their military ring and as a nod to her acquaintance with French – outside the Penny Bazaar on Henry Street. She was still in mourning but the weeks that had elapsed since Pappie's death made this assignation seem less furtive than the first. She felt entitled to wear her scarlet patelot over her inky dress to brighten the effect for the Corporal would surely come in his ceremonials. She worried over what she would say when she met him again, fearing that the memory of her spilt tears might create awkwardness. But, she reasoned, he had issued the invite to meet this time, and he was waiting for her at the doors of the arcade. He was always on time. The army training, she supposed.

'Bella!' he called to her as she approached and he took her hand. It was flesh on flesh this time. She felt reassured. They were just stepping inside the covered arcade when her name was called again.

'Miss Casey!'

The Reverend Leeper stood before them. In a moment, the expedition turned sour. Must he taint every last thing that was hers, hers alone?

'Miss Casey,' he said again and nodded stiffly at the corporal.

'May I introduce Lance Corporal Nicholas Beaver,' Bella said, 'of the King's Liverpool's.'

'Corporal Beaver,' he acknowledged, though Bella fancied he lingered on the rank to make a point.

He seemed disconcerted. Was it such a surprise that she might have a young man of her own? Or that he was as prepossessing as Corporal Beaver? Even if she were never to clap eyes on Nicholas Beaver again, he had done her a favour by his very handsome presence.

'And where are you serving, young man?' the Reverend asked as if the Corporal was an errant child.

'Wherever I'm sent,' Corporal Beaver replied in what Bella thought a churlish manner. 'It is in the nature of a soldier's life.'

But what he said was true even if it sounded graceless. He was often on the move. He had recently returned from Belfast where his battalion had to quell riots on the streets over all this Home Rule business. The Reverend looked down and noticed her hand clasped in the Corporal's. Good, she thought. And even though it was awkward, she wanted to linger over the encounter if only to impress upon the Reverend that she had a protector to hand.

'Well, Miss Casey, I hope you enjoy this lovely afternoon, despite your recent bereavement,' he said finally, squinting up at the sun which had made a fitful appearance in a pillowy sky. 'I must be on my way for I am in the midst of my sick visitations.'

He seemed intent on cataloguing his good works for their benefit, Bella thought.

'Oh and Miss Casey, don't forget this evening's choir practice.'

He doffed his hat then and went on his mirthless way.

'I've no time for those God-wallahs,' Corporal Beaver said when he was out of earshot. 'Always trying to make a chap feel small.'

How quickly he'd got the measure of the clergyman, Bella thought, though his obvious lack of piety alarmed her. But then did 'God-wallahs' like the Reverend Leeper deserve anyone's respect? He, whose said devotion hid a pageant of lies.

They entered the Bazaar, a long high room with beams of mottled light streaming through the high windows in the gallery.

There was a throng of strollers and browsers, and she and the Corporal stopped here and there, while Bella fingered an embroidery or picked up an ornament or one of the other assorted trinkets that were on show.

'What is it like,' Bella asked him, for the Reverend's questions had put her in mind of it, 'the army life?'

'It's an uncertain one, that's for sure. A chap never knows where he might end up,' the Corporal replied, 'so he learns to make a home of where he is.'

'Still and all, it must be a doleful thing, to be parted from your family,' she said.

'I was only fifteen when I signed up so you could say the barracks is as close to any home as I know,' he replied.

'And what about your mother and father?' she asked for he had made no mention of them. All she knew of him was that he came from the county Waterford.

'Da was in the colours, but he'd been pensioned out an invalid. He wasn't out a year when he passed. My mother said it was the army as what ruined him, but I think it was the grog that done him in, not the soldiering.'

Did him in, she said to herself silently.

'She was dead set against me going, but it was bred into me, you could say, for every morning we rose to the sound of soldiers drilling in the barracks yard, answering to the reveille . . .'

'All the same, it must be lonesome,' she said.

'Ah, the boys do their best to make even the dreariest barracks room cheery. At Christmas time we even makes our own decorations – paper chains and wreaths made out of holly.'

Make, make, she wanted to say. She decided there and then that if something came of this liaison, then a few lessons out of the Excelsior *Grammar Book* wouldn't go astray.

They had come to a stall of little brassy ornaments and figurines arranged in tiers on a red velvet drape. There were little monkeys and tiny thimbles and miniature boxes, but her eye lit on a silvery birdcage, constructed as intricately as a cathedral, but small enough to fit in your palm.

'Oh look,' she cried and lifted it up.

'No bird I know would fit in there,' the Corporal scoffed. But Bella ignored him. She loved the delicacy of this pretty item with no other function than to please the eye.

'It is a thing of beauty all the same,' she said.

'If you're so taken with it, you should have it,' the Corporal said. 'You can have it as keepsake, Bel, for you'll not be seeing much of me in future. We are to be posted to Queenstown.'

She felt her heart sink and it showed in her face.

'There you have it, Bel, that's the army life for you.'

The following Monday evening the Reverend called to her quarters, standing at the threshold while she guarded the entrance.

'I see,' he said in even tones, 'that you have found another on whom to lavish your affections.' Lavish – those luxuriant words he used! 'Am I so easily forgotten?'

She tried to answer, summoning up false reason.

'But Reverend Leeper, as you said, we cannot . . .'

'Exactly so, Miss Casey.' When he reverted to formality she knew she was in for punishment.

'But to flaunt your young man in front of me like that, it speaks of cruelty.'

'Cruelty?' she repeated.

'Don't play the innocent with me, Miss Casey,' he said, 'when you are only out to torment me.'

Then he stormed off, clattering down the staircase like a fugitive being pursued. But he came back, as she knew he would. Twice that same week and more persistent. He would stretch out to caress her cheek, or breathe her name greedily into the shell of her ear. She remained flinty during these onslaughts. But it hardly seemed to matter for even in her silence, he saw, or fancied he saw, coquetry. Or if not in her muteness, then in the curl of her hair or the hem of her dress. Sometimes, he would get fierce in his affections and pinion her to the wall, pressing his lanky weight upon her so that she feared she might be subjected to the ultimate degradation. After such an episode, weeks might go by and, labouring under some new regimen of his own devising, he would stay away. But these lacunae were almost worse since they were filled with a terrible imminence. Each knock on the door could be his, each step on the stair. His behaviour ran its course like an unpredictable illness, a high temperature, a flushed brow, a derangement of the senses followed by a dormant phase of easeful slumber, a calm convalescence. But Bella never knew what stage in the cycle he was at, or what pitch of agitation he might have reached while absent. And then, just as she was beginning to despair, a chance event in the world of men offered a reprieve. Mick and Tom enlisted.

Mother saw red.

'I'm sure your Beaver put them up to it,' she said to Bella in surly tone. How quickly he had become *her* Beaver, when, alas, he was no such thing.

'Prancing about in full fig,' she said, 'and filling my sons up with notions.'

As if the Corporal had seduced them into the ranks.

'If they were officers itself,' Mother raged, 'but in the ranks along with porter-swilling RCs!'

In whose company they'd hardly stand out, Bella thought, but kept her lip buttoned.

She understood why Mother was fretting. She was depending on the boys' pay packets to keep her head above water. They had both joined the Post Office, Mick as a telegraph clerk and Tom on a district route. Such positions might not have answered the ambitions Pappie had held out for them – he had paid for drawing lessons for Mick in the hope that he would go on to be an architect. But at least the boys earned steady money and army pay, by comparison, was downright measly. Mother would be left with only young Isaac's office boy's wages to keep them all afloat.

'If you could see your way to it, Bella,' Mother said in a whee-dling tone, 'to have us in your quarters then it would ease our lot.'

It was a strange reversal for Mother to be depending on her and it was a pleasant sensation to be in the position of offer-ing salvation. And for it be seen as a great favour. In other cir-cumstances she might have resented the invasion, but Bella saw immediately the advantages of the new arrangement. If there was one thing likely to deter Leeper's advances (she refused pri-vately to call him Reverend), it was a fierce mother and two noisy youngsters. Foiled, she thought victoriously.

'Of course you must move in, Mother,' she said luxuriating in the *noblesse oblige*. 'It will be like old times.'

THE VENUS ROOM

wo women in the one kitchen was not a recipe for harmony, Bella was to discover. She was grateful for Mother's
housewifery, a hot meal on the table, a welcome fire in the grate,
and she was happy to be surrounded by the cherished items of
home – Pappie's chair, the table they had supped at as a family,
the painting of Trafalgar – even though crushed into her two
small rooms they gave her quarters the aspect of an overstocked
warehouse. The most treasured piece, however, had not made
the journey. The Elysian had to be sold off for it was impossible
to hoik a piano up the narrow staircase to Bella's quarters. But
despite the presence of these familiar tokens, and the clamour
of Isaac and Jack that made the place feel full, it never took on
the hue of home. Perhaps, without Pappie, there would never
be home again, Bella thought. She could have talked to Pappie

about Balzac and Dickens, but her conversations with Mother could not roam far beyond household linens and the price of turnips. Even in concerns she and her mother could have shared, disputes were quick to arise. She would try to interest Mother in her worries about a roomful of infants in smocks and petticoats. Illness nested among them – chesty coughs settled like a damp fog in their number, rashes spread, scabs multiplied. But Mother considered such talk an imposition.

'Haven't I my own to worry about?' she would snap when Bella would fret aloud about Norman Symonds or Herbert Pratt.

One evening they nearly came to blows over a minor mishap. Bella had cleared a space at the table to do some preparation for her classes. She had propped a copy of *Geography General-ised* against a jug and taken down a volume of the *Popular Ency-clopaedia*, laying it open at Galileo. Miss Quill had been kept away with a severe case of bronchitis – probably picked up from one of her charges – so Bella had had to throw open the folding doors that usually separated the infants from First and Second Class and teach all of them at once. It was bedlam, running back and forth between them trying to keep all gainfully occupied. Bella had been trying to teach the older ones about the planets, their names and their movements but had found nothing in Miss Quill's desk that was of service to her. As she was poring over the *Encyclopaedia* (she was buying the entire volume on the instal-ment plan from a travelling salesman), Jack sidled up to her.

'What are you doing, Bella?' he asked.

'I'm reading about the planets and the stars,' she replied.

'What is the stars?'

'What *are* the stars, Jack?' she began, for despite being now under her tutelage, his grammar owed more to his playmates than his book learning. But that aside, it was a good question and Bella had no ready answer. How would Pestalozzi instruct children about the heavens? He would use everyday objects, Bella, she said to herself. Pestalozzi never failed her. Beside the jug was a pair of oranges. She picked the oranges up and one in each hand, she traced the trajectory of the earth and the sun on the cloth. She scattered a spoonful of sugar across the navy calico.

'These are the stars,' she said.

'Mind, Bella, mind,' Mother said crossly, 'that cloth went on fresh this morning.'

'Leave us be, Mother, I'm showing Jack something important here,' Bella muttered. 'About the planets.'

'Oh excuse me pardon, your ladyship,' Mother cried. 'Is the stars more important than keeping the place respectable? A house don't keep itself, I'll have you know! Some slavey has to keep it so, when there are some too high and mighty to lift a finger!'

And with one flick of her hand she swept away the heavens.

But these were minor irritations when compared with the reprieve she enjoyed from the Reverend Leeper. With Mother and the boys in residence, he stopped making evening visitations to her door. Jack had started in the infant class. He was like a lucky charm keeping the Reverend at bay. She encouraged him to stay in the schoolroom after hours so she could do her tidying and records without fear of interruption. At the church she devised another way to stymie him. She feigned a friendship with Mrs Lecky, the foghorn of the choir.

'Mrs Lecky,' she would say at the end of practice, 'could you help me gather the hymnals?'

Or she would offer to walk her home after evening service for Mrs Lecky, though a stout matron, was of a nervous disposition and lonely with it. Mabel Lecky would not have been her natural choice of companion, but Bella had learned from teaching that there are adults, no more than children, who bask in the attention of being singled out. Mrs Lecky was one such. In truth, she found Mrs Lecky tiresome. A widow who'd worn the weeds for nigh on twenty years, she spoke of her husband as if he had dispensed the wisdom of the Sermon on the Mount.

'The late Mr Lecky always said there's nothing like a spring day to lift the spirits, wasn't he right, Miss Casey?'

In time, Bella found herself railing inwardly against the sheer number of the dead man's commonplaces. But she shamelessly employed Mrs Lecky's appetite for a ready ear. She might have had to suffer long monologues about Henry Lecky's dining habits, his interest in plant propagation, the indignity of his gout, but it was a small price to pay to sidestep the Reverend Leeper.

It was to be three months before Bella saw Corporal Beaver again.

When they returned, the First Liverpools were stationed at Beggar's Bush Barracks only a mile or two distant and the Corporal took to visiting occasionally.

'It's himself again,' Mother would announce if it was she who answered the door, not granting him the civility of a greeting or a name.

In his company, Mother would often be silent and shoot glares at him. Bella knew she blamed the Corporal for the disruption of her domestic arrangements and the fact that her two boys were beyond in barracks in England. Without saying a word, she made her disapproval clear and the Corporal couldn't fail to notice.

'Have I done something to upset Mrs C?' he asked.

'Don't mind her,' Bella said, 'she's only being sour.'

But she found herself inventing excuses to get away from her mother's baleful presence. Despite the obstacles thrown in her way, she determined that she must keep him sweet. If the weather was fine, they would go for a stroll down Dominick Street and do a couple of rounds of Rutland Square, although she suspected the Corporal might have preferred an alehouse snug. As she had promised, she took him to the schoolroom.

'Is that where you stand?' he asked, climbing on to the teacher's pedestal.

'Very rarely,' she told him, 'for in the teaching of infants there is no good insisting that you perch on high. Already we tower over them!'

He laughed and she put her fingers to her lips for fear, somehow, that they might be overheard. The imminence of Reverend Leeper oppressed her even at times like this on a Saturday afternoon when she knew he would be off on his sick visitations. But she knew if he came across them here, he would berate her for an 'unwarranted intrusion on school premises'. (So accustomed had she become to his tyranny that she could speak his language in her head.)

One day she took the Corporal to view the Venus Room two floors above the schoolroom for indeed that was a spectacle. It had been a ballroom once when the house on Dominick Street had been a private residence. The ceilings were encrusted with intricate plasterwork, with gilded brows done by the master stuccodore Robert West, as she told the Corporal. Overhead there were garlands and fat fruits, the raised wings of birds. Two shimmering chandeliers hung from the ceiling. The walls of the ballroom were mirrored, as were the entry doors, so when you were inside, it was like being inside a silvery cage. The maple floor made a sweet warbling when they stepped on to it for it was high sprung for dancing.

'Care for a turn?' the Corporal asked in that amused way of his. Bella never quite knew if he was in earnest or mocking her.

'Here?'

'Well, it *is* a ballroom. The plasterwork is all very fine and good, but it was meant for dancing. I daresay no one has stepped out here in an age. Don't suppose that dryballs of a curate would allow it.'

Bella let the soldierly language pass since it pertained to the Reverend and she would not make any defence of him. The Corporal held out his arms and he provided the music, though he had neither drum nor fife. He hummed the tune of a waltz, 'Over the Waves', as they circled around the echoing ballroom seeing themselves reflected in every surface – his braid matched by the encrustations of the room – so that it appeared that the place was sprouting with couples and the room full. He swept Bella around in a generous arc and her breath was coming in a quick rush.

'We could be at a Castle Ball,' she said breathlessly to him, a trifle embarrassed even as she said it, for it reminded her of something witless Prudence Collier from the College might have said.

'Ah now, steady on, Bel,' the Corporal said in a chastising tone and he came to a halt so that they stood, their arms still raised, frozen in thin air. The crowds in the glass fell away. 'The nearest a chap like me will get to the Castle will be on sentry duty outside.'

The spell of the mirrors was broken.

Was it her giddy talk of Castle Balls that frightened him off? Or had he tired of Mother's cool welcome? Whatever the reason, it was after the visit to the Venus Room that his appearances began to be fitful, to say the least. Bella wondered whether it was just the association with the family that Nicholas Beaver enjoyed, some fond remembrance of comradely times with Mick and Tom that had kept him coming to Dominick Street. Or had he found a prettier, more accommodating girl who was keeping him away? If only the Corporal were her fiancé itself, but the understanding between them was nowhere near that advanced and Bella could see no way to make it so.

THE STRIKING OF ALFIE

BAXTER

'Isabella?'

Soft and low. So soft and low Bella thought she could pretend not to hear it. She hurriedly quenched the candle and sat in the darkness. She had been darning a pair of stockings – her boots were forever cutting through her hosiery. She sat, needle poised, afeared that he might hear its silvery movement. She held her breath in the miserable hope that receiving no response he might be discouraged and go away. He rapped again, a little louder and mouthed her name again. Even the thought of his lips brushing up against the grain of her door made her quail.

'Isabella,' he urged.

She laid down her needle and clenched her fists and begged God and the darkness that he might go away. But it was all in vain. It was as if he smelled her yearning – not for him but against him – and took possession of it. He rapped again, this time with blunt authority.

'Miss Casey,' he said in his most stentorian tone, 'I command you to open the door at once. I have urgent business to discuss on behalf of the School Guardians. I know you're in there and I will not desist until you answer.'

She went to the door and inched it open a fraction.

'It's very late, Reverend Leeper, and a most inconvenient time,' she whispered. 'My little brother is abed, he's been feverish all day and I fear a visit would only wake him.'

'Do not resort to falsehoods, Miss Casey, it ill-becomes you.'

He knew then. It had not taken him long to get a whiff of her new solitude. After six months, Mother and the boys had moved out, having heard tell of a house in the East Wall that was going at a reasonable rent. It was a pleasant little cottage with a garden out front, a neat front parlour and a yard with private facilities. The neighbourhood was peopled by a motley assortment of trades-people, sailors and ship's captains, the steady tramp of the blow-ers to the bottling plant, gaggles of girls off to shift work at the match factory, mechanics and shunters employed at the railway yards. It being farther out of the city than her other addresses, you could catch the whiff of the sea there clearly and the wind had a way of whistling at the gables as if eager to be on the brine itself and not tangled up in narrow enclosed streets. It might not have had the grandeur of Dorset Street, but the house in East Wall was cosy, or at least Mother would make it so. Despite the rancour between them, it had made Bella forlorn to imagine the burst of spring cleaning that would accompany their arrival as Mother busied herself with the settling in. There would be the washing of the windows, the beating of rugs, the hunting down of fleas in the upholstery and ticking . . .

'Let me in, if you please, Miss Casey.'

The Reverend pushed past her and sniffed. The air was singed with the smell of the just-guttered candle. He stood, as if paralysed, with his back to Bella.

'It's no good, Isabella,' he said finally and turned around with a defeated air.

The reiteration of her name encouraged a new dread. His officious self Bella could deal with, but this frank softness frightened her.

'These past months have been an agony for me, as I know they must have been for you. But you are a dutiful daughter as I have been a dutiful husband.'

'Reverend Leeper,' she interjected.

'No, no, no, Isabella,' he said raising his hand, 'it must be declared. I have prayed, nay I have stormed heaven but . . . ' Here he paused again and a strangled groan emanated from him like a door in need of oiling. 'But I am a man of the flesh, a weak man . . . '

He made his move then, not like a weak man at all, and mana-
cled her in a fierce embrace. His whole frame trembled, but not,
she sensed, with weakness but with power. He groaned again as
if holding her thus was a pain to him.

'Reverend Leeper,' she said, desperately trying to wrestle free.

'Darling Isabella, don't fight against it. It is too powerful for
either of us.'

He pinioned her wrists behind her as he plastered her cheeks
with greedy, moist kisses. She tried to avert her face, but he
clasped her jaw in his hand and crushed her mouth like some
soft, ripe fruit between his fingers.

'You little vixen,' he snarled, 'are you trying to madden me?'

'No,' she cried, but her feeble nay counted for nothing.

He placed one hand on the nape of her neck and the other
in a vice grip around her waist and Bella could feel all the fight
in her seep away. She thought of her neat teacher's quarters, her
schoolroom below with the mottoes on the blackboard, her years
at her books when other girls were running around only interested in getting ring-papers for themselves. And she thought of
her Principal Teacher's salary, forty pounds a year all in, and to
her shame, she yielded.

Dawn had spread its icy fingers through the casements before
she could rouse herself. She had lain slumped all night in the
place where she had been broken into, her blouse ripped from
shoulder to waist, buttons orphaned on the floor, her skirts and

bloomers down around her ankles, her feet still shod – the only innocent part of her. Her hair, matted and snagged, fell over her bare shoulders. She clutched at the remnants of her chemise to cover the nakedness of her breasts, remembering how he had scrabbled at them as if he wished to peel back the very skin that clothed her. There were scrape marks on her arms – for all the world like she'd tangled with a thorn tree – where his talons had dug in. She must have slept, but it felt more like a withered waking, her nerves alive with a kind of readied startlement, for fear he would return. She had curled into a ball against the skirting, sinking as low as she could. Her limbs grew stiff, her blood ran cold as a step-mother's breath. Her skin was like veined marble where it had been scraped and torn, her mouth smarted. Her breasts, when she dared to look, were blood-bruised. Finally she managed to haul her body – for it felt separate to her like a heavy weight, a dead thing – into the bedroom. She lay gratefully on the unmolested bed and slept fitfully for an hour or so, still in her desecrated clothes, until a distant clock chimed seven. Then she rose and painfully made her way down the back stairs to collect water in a pail. It boiled laboriously on the hob – everything seemed to take an age as if time had dropped to a slower march. She drew out the tin bath and poured the water in. She sank into it gingerly and scrubbed every inch of skin until it was red raw. Then she heaved herself out, creakily, for she felt as old as a crone troubled with rheumatics, and covered herself hurriedly so that she would not see the mutilations or be reminded of the ones she couldn't see.

*

That morning, Miss Quill had decided that the children's heads must be scoured for lice. As they worked through sixty crawling heads in the downstairs hall, Bella's limbs ached beneath her costume with their new brutish knowledge. But there was no manifestation on her face as to what had befallen her. She thanked heaven that Jack was no longer among their number – he had passed on to St Barnabas School for Boys – for she doubted she could have dissembled in front of him. She executed her duties in glassy rote. But the children knew no different. Their calls and demands were just the same. They had to be taught to sing their tables and count their abacus. Somehow, she struggled through the morning. By the afternoon she was sufficiently composed to forget herself for long stretches at a time as if her tasks were being performed by another. All might have proceeded as normal had Elspeth Parker not raised her hand after the lunch break. She was a cheeky one, often sent as an ambassador when others were not bold enough.

'Yes, Elspeth, what is it?'

'Is it true, Miss?'

'Is what true, Elspeth?'

She leaned up to Bella conspiratorially and whispered in her ear. 'Are you going to be married, Miss?'

She felt her cheeks scalding. As if the child could divine the terrible disgrace she was nursing beneath her sober dress and tamed hair.

'What's that, Elspeth?'

'Are you going to get married, Miss?' she asked, brassily, this time.

The class tittered.

'Don't be impertinent, Elspeth Parker. Now back to your desk, if you please.'

'Me and Bessie . . .' she started.

'Bessie and I . . .'

'We saw you stepping out with a solder, Miss.'

There was another ripple of amusement. How cruel they seemed in that moment, not innocent at all but malevolently knowing.

'He was all dressed up. My brother says he was a lancer.'

Tears suddenly sprouted. She had not wept throughout her ordeal. There had been a dry tempest of shame, but no tears. Now, there was an abundance of them, so much so that she feared she might drown in them, so without further ado, she rapped the desk with her cane and dismissed the class early. Leaving the stove lit and the schoolroom in disarray, she fled to her rooms and wept until she could weep no longer.

It was in this state, blurred and sodden with grief that Leeper found her. In the grip of her distress, she had left the door of her quarters ajar. She raised her head from her cradling arms. What a sight she must have been, her face blotchy and ruined, her cheeks feverish and damp.

'Have you entirely forgotten your manners, Miss Casey? Or do you no longer stand when your pastor enters the room?'

Slowly, disbelievingly, astounded by her own docility, Bella rose to her feet, while rubbing fiercely at her face with the sleeve of her dress and trying to hush her weeping hair.

'I am appalled . . .' he began, then stopped. He dropped his eyes as if the sight of Bella distressed him. As well it might, she thought. But, once again she was mistaken. 'I arrive to find the door to the street thrown wide, the schoolroom deserted, slates thrown on the floor, the fire still alight. The whole place might have gone up in flames.'

'I was feeling poorly, Reverend Leeper,' she said dully.

'You can feel poorly on your own time, Miss Casey,' he said, pulling out his fob watch and tapping the glass ostentatiously. 'It is not yet half past the hour and already your charges are milling about on Great Britain Street. Unless I am greatly mistaken, three o'clock is the hour when the infant classes let out, is it not, Miss Casey?'

'Yes Reverend,' she replied. She must, on no account, aggravate him.

'I consider this a gross dereliction of duty,' he said. He had walked to the window, still clutching the watch and studying its face intently. Then he strolled back and stood on the hateful spot, the place where . . . in her mind's eye she could see a version of her ruined self still lying there.

'Sit, Miss Casey,' he commanded. She sat, gratefully.

'Not only,' he continued as if he had the speech all arranged in his head, 'not only have you deserted your post, but you have allowed your pupils to roam the streets like urchins. What would have happened if an inspector had called today with neither pupils nor teacher in evidence on the premises? What would he have made of that?'

He paused. Now, Bella thought, now he will make some reference to the loathsome events of the night before.

'It pains me to say this, Miss Casey . . .'

Now, she thought again, now.

'But your display last evening of what I can only describe as animal lust, I found both deeply shocking and downright degrading. You lured me into an intimate association with no consideration for my elevated feelings, which I had declared to you in trust. Knowing that you have been a torment to me, Madam, your conduct is inexcusable.'

His face was on fire, his brow beaded. But then his voice softened.

'I believe you are not the kind of teacher who is fit to be in control of young, uncorrupted minds, but . . .'

He raised a hand as she opened her mouth to say something, but that is far as she got. All her impulses seemed laggardly and slow.

'. . . in view of your unblemished record so far, I will not take this matter any further. But should there be any repeat of such wantonness, the Guardians will have to be informed. And believe me, Miss Casey, there will certainly be no reprieve then.'

She could scarce believe her ears. How had he turned events on their head so that *she* had been cast as the wanton one, a – she hesitated to say this even in the sanctuary of her own thoughts – a whore. How?

'I will be keeping a strict eye on you, Miss Casey,' he said with such force that his spittle flew. 'And should there be even the hint of further impropriety, as God is my judge, I shall drive you out myself.'

He snapped his watch shut and lodged it in his pocket. Then he marched out and down the stairs like an executioner who had delivered a harsh but just verdict.

This, then, was the worst. Not the night previous, although memories of that would come jaggedly and unbidden as she laboured through her days. The scene seemed engraved on her eyelids so that even when she lay down to sleep, the crush of his body against hers and the awful pulse of his appetite invaded her dreams in lurid and sudden bouts, shocking her into wakefulness, her heart drumming and her brow soaked. She was condemned to relive her undoing, night after night. Meanwhile, the Leeper (she refused to call him Reverend), while keeping his distance in person, was on the warpath about the school records. Knowing he might swoop at any time to check on her books made her sick with anguish. She could not concentrate on even the most menial duties. She would make terrible mistakes – once entering Fees

Withheld in the wrong column, which meant she had to tear off the offending folios and redo a whole week's entries. There were blots and stains on the ledger, the latter from her frustrated tears, the former as if the pen, in sympathy, wept. Anticipating Leeper's judgement of her work seemed to heighten her capacity to blunder and sometimes the results were so blotchy in presentation, and patchy in nature, that had one of her pupils handed it in, she would have dismissed them as lazy and slovenly. But the more he castigated her – *Miss Casey, what, pray tell, is this figure here? Miss Casey, where are last week's attendance sheets?* – the more inept she became. He turned her into a dunce in her own schoolroom.

She found her temper shortening, even with the children. One day when little Cissy Roberts pestered her once too often could she please go to the lavatory, she was so consumed with getting through her appointed lesson unobstructed that she ignored the child and the inevitable happened – a large pool on the schoolroom flags. Another inadvertent victim was Alfred Baxter. Alfie was a dim-witted child, soft and fat. He was slaving over his headline template and having trouble with his p's and q's. Poor child, he always turned them backwards. Bella remembered halting before him. He was bent over the page, his little tongue edging out over his bottom lip in avid concentration.

'What did we say about the P, Alfred?' she asked.

'P goes right, Miss.'

'And Alfred, which is your right hand?'

The stupid child raised his left.

Looking down at the unseemly page in front of him, the unmitigated mess of it and Alfie's trusting face so full of sunny certainty gazing up at her, Bella felt a surge of anger. She had the teacher's pointer in her hand; she had been using it to point at the alphabet inscribed on the board.

'Hold out your hand,' she ordered. Alfie looked up at her. Confused. Always confused.

'The other one,' she barked. She raised the pointer and brought it down hard.

She would never forget the look on the child's face. Not of pain though she had succeeded in making him howl and had brought up a red weal on his little palm. But of betrayal. Like many of her pupils, Alfie felt the belt at home. Bella was acquainted with his father, a brooding bully of a man, whose children would run into mouse-holes to escape him. There would be many actions she would take in her life that she would be ashamed of, but if there was to be a Judgement Day, Bella knew that this transgression – the striking of Alfie Baxter – was the worst.

MANOEUVRES

The blow brought Bella to her senses. She might not have been schooled in the uncouth lessons of biology, but she had missed her monthly and she knew the import of that. She had seen this happen once before at the College. To her *bête noir*, Prudence Collier, no less. One minute Miss Collier was in the full bloom of love with Her Neville – which Bella saw in capitals so partial was Prudence to repeating it – the next she had been sent down in disgrace. Neville Cardew was a scrivener's clerk at the Custom House; he was going to climb the ladder of Her Majesty's Service, reaching such heights that he might well move into the Vice-Regal Lodge and be running the country any day now, according to Prudence. On she wittered, imagining herself already as the wife of a Castle functionary. Then at the height of her fancy, she disappeared, on account of what Miss Swanzy called a family emergency. When Bella had reported this to Lily, she had guessed immediately the true reason.

'I fear,' Lily said, 'that the family emergency might be of Prudence's own making.'

'Whatever do you mean?' Bella remembered saying, still the greenhorn.

'Oh Bella, her family took her before her encumbrance began to show,' Lily said as if explaining some complicated lesson to a child.

'Poor Prudence,' Bella had said then, without thinking. For Prudence's absence would improve her daily life no end. There would be no more sniping, no snide remarks. But she *had* been sorry, sorry for the loss of the fine life Prudence could have had, the good education gone west, the prospects of betterment banished. And she remembered what Lily had said, a rueful valediction.

'One slip, Bella, is all it takes.'

It was time to make haste.

The Liverpools, she discovered, were to play on the bandstand on the Carlyle Pier the following Sunday. On the pretext of taking the air on the pier at Kingstown she donned her style and walked as far as Merrion Square to catch the tram. As arranged she met Clarice Hamilton at the stop. Clarrie had been at the Model School with her but had failed to reach Final Standard. Instead she was sent to train up under Madame Felice, the milliner's on

Wicklow Street. Bella had lost touch with her until she had visited the shop one day shortly after she had started work and was ordering a hat – a dove-grey toque, she remembered – and who was serving behind the counter but Clarrie Hamilton.

'Oh yes,' Clarrie had said after they had done their catching up. 'Mrs Faylix has been very good to me though she's a bit uppity if you ask me. Not French at all but she likes to drop a bit of the *parlay vu*.' This all delivered in loud tones in the body of the shop. Clarrie had never been what you'd call discreet. 'She's from Newfoundland Street, if you please.'

Their acquaintanceship had persisted from that day, and on certain occasions – such as this one – Clarrie's brand of brave jollity was exactly what was called for.

'Aren't you the dark horse, Bella Casey?' Clarrie cooed when Bella told her of her plan. 'I never imagined you'd take a fancy to a soldier!'

She nudged Bella in the ribs – she had always been robust in her expression and not at all lady-like. Poor Clarrie was no oil painting. She had a long angular face, a tall awkward build and decidedly big feet.

'Don't worry, Bella, if we run into him, I'll make myself scarce.'

She gave Bella a rum wink, delighted to be in on the conspiracy.

'Sure isn't my auntie sick and I must visit her, isn't that what I'm to say? Oh, I *love* this,' she said as they mounted the tram.

Bella was glad of Clarrie's uncomplicated company as they drove out to the sea. The day wore a blue bonnet that matched her own, though up on the upper deck it was so windy they had to hold their hats on their laps. The sea when they came upon it was frilled with white. Clarrie chattered on beside Bella, commenting on what people wore – the ladies' hats in particular – but also threading her own ambitions for the day into the conversation. Wouldn't it be great if they were to bump into Lance Corporal Beaver? How thrilled she was that she might be the agent of such an assignation, and wouldn't it be just the ticket if he were to have a soldier companion with him?

'They always have a less handsome friend,' Clarrie said.

Rather sadly, Bella thought.

The regimental players were filing up the steps to take their places as she and Clarrie hunted for a free seat among the white timber deckchairs scattered on the green. Clarrie snaffled two and positioned them to the side of the bandstand so as to enjoy an unobstructed view.

'Which one is he?' Clarrie hissed in her ear. Bella surreptitiously pointed.

'No wonder you're in such a tizzy, isn't he a darling man? So tall and don't you just love the get-up of him? And look, look,' she said and pointed out something Bella had not noticed. 'He has a tattoo there on his left wrist. I hope he hasn't got another girl's name embroidered there for that would be hard to wear. I thought it was only sailors as had tattoos, though I suppose since he's in colours, that's what you might call a military tattoo . . .'

Bella could see those around smiling at their expense for Clarrie had a voice that carried. Because she was rambunctious by nature, it was sometimes difficult to be sure if people were laughing with her or at her. But, whichever it was, she brought a touch of gaiety even if, sometimes, it was at her own expense. Luckily the band struck up then – *The Radetsky March* – and the rest of Clarrie's monologue was drowned out.

Sitting there in the benign mid-summer sunshine with half the world streaming by, arm-in-arm, and the other half gathered around the bandstand tapping their feet to the merry music and children skipping to the beat or rolling hoops, the day rinsed and clean, the sea sparkling and everyone in their Sunday best, it was easier for Bella to believe that some good might come of all of this. Though, inwardly, she quailed.

'I'm sure he'll come this way,' Clarrie said excitedly in a pause in the music. 'Give him a wave.'

But before Bella had a chance to respond, Clarrie shot up and raised her own two arms like a woman drowning, so that the Corporal would have to have been blind to miss her. He waved doubtfully at the apparition that was Clarrie, only relaxing, Bella thought, when he saw that she was not alone. At the first break in the performance, he laid down his brass and made his way through the scatter of chairs towards them. Bella braced herself. Not alone had she to charm this mercurial man, she had to ensnare him. She wasn't equipped for this. Then she thought of her condition and quelled her doubts. Needs must. At least, she had already felt the quickening of desire for the Corporal and wasn't it better that she felt some stirring for him, than nothing at all? It raised her above some stylish-dressed pusher on the street with an eye for a uniform. Still, what she was planning required a dimming of her heart in deference to her intellect. She had to bend this man to her will. She had to feign the innocence of the barefoot girl she had been when they first met in the kitchen of Innisfallen Parade and have him wed her before she began to show. Turn him into a keeper, as Clarrie had said, but she only knew half the story. Bella was soiled merchandise – that is what Clarrie would have said had she known for she did not put a tooth in things – and from now on she would have to act accordingly, until she could don the habit of a wife.

'Bella Casey!' the Corporal announced bold as you like – almost as loudly as Clarrie trumpeting in her ear.

Bella showed a cherry smile, courtesy of Clarrie who had pinked her lips on the top of the tram.

'If it isn't Corporal Beaver!' she replied taking up his tone of bravado. He did look a treat in his dress uniform, a red coatee with blue-roll collar and cuffs, his black breeches trimmed with white, a yellow rope across his chest on which his bugle was slung, his buttons and his epaulettes all golden gleam. She saw the enormity of the task ahead of her and felt her own inadequacy in the face of it.

'Enjoying the music?' the Corporal asked. 'That last one was our regimental quick march, "Here's to the Maiden".'

'Oh, Clarrie and I were just taking the air, as it happens. The music was a pure bonus,' Bella said.

The Corporal smiled.

'This is my friend, Clarice Hamilton,' Bella said. Clarrie extended her hand in her forthright way.

'Oh look,' she said to Bella, 'it only says MOTHER.'

She was back to the tattoo, a garland of indigo at the Corporal's wrist, which had always been eclipsed by cuffs or gloves before. He had the grace to look confused.

'Any news of those brothers of yours?'

'Oh they're doing fine,' Bella replied. 'As far as we can make out, though Mick is forever being confined to barracks or put on latrine duty. For what he does not say.'

'For unspecified misdemeanours, no doubt,' the Corporal said with a wry smile.

Clarrie was still hovering, against all instructions.

'And how's Jack?'

'He's quite the grown-up now going to big school at St Barnabas. I don't see as much of him now that Mother and he have moved away.'

A salient fact Bella was determined to smuggle into the conversation.

The Corporal played with his dress gloves. Bella fixed on his tattoo, the letters cast in red, entwined in what looked like thorns. Go, she urged Clarrie with her eyes, go.

'I don't suppose I could interest you in a turn on the pier,' he asked finally when Clarrie insisted on standing there, mute. 'It'd be a pure disgrace to have come all this way and not enjoy the scenery.'

'Indeed,' Clarrie agreed heartily.

'Perhaps your friend would like to join us?'

Time for the sick auntie line, Bella thought, come on, Clarrie. How often had they rehearsed this!

Just then another soldier appeared, another Liverpools' man, broad and plain-looking, years older than the Corporal.

'Ah Nick, me old compadré,' he said and clapped his hand on the Corporal's shoulder. 'Aren't you going to introduce us?'

'Clarice Hamilton,' Clarrie interposed and shook his hand in that manly way of hers.

'Vizard,' the squat man replied and his plain face broke into a wreath of smiles. 'Corporal James Vizard. Charmed, I'm sure.'

The newly introduced pair moved ahead while Bella dawdled behind with the Corporal.

'I've been thinking of the first time we courted,' the Corporal was saying as he and Bella strolled towards the glaring brine. 'That evening of your father's funeral, God be good to him.'

Bella blushed to think of it. Pappie was never far away, much and all as she might wish it in this particular instance.

'Oh,' she replied, a mite too hastily she feared, 'but we have met several times since then. There was the bazaar and sure haven't you paid your respects in Dominick Street, too?'

'Ah yes,' he conceded, 'but I don't count those. Don't get me wrong, I'm very partial to Mrs C and all, though I think she's on the outs with me for me for leading her darling boys astray.'

'Oh no,' Bella lied.

'Ah, Bel,' he said. It was the first time he had used her name in that candid way, the way a sweetheart might. 'You know what I'm driving at. We were always in company, is all I'm saying.'

He halted and took her arm, placing it in the crook of his.

'But that first night on Sackville Street,' he said 'you were quite the spitfire.'

How strange that he should remember her forwardness when what she recalled of the evening was her tears. She summoned up all of her false courage.

'And can be again,' she said and reached up and kissed him full on the lips in broad daylight so as he could not be in any doubt.

She wore her blue chenille with the leg-of-mutton sleeves, her black garibaldi jacket with the military braiding and her two-tone boots with the Louis heels. She put her hair up in a French twist and donned her straw boater with the polka-dot band. She chose a corner booth in Bewley's at the solemn back of the noisy café. Wan afternoon light streamed in as she unpeeled her gloves and laid them on the marble-topped table. Her new boots were pinching. On top of that, a pebble had lodged itself between the sole and her stockings, and all through the encounter she was aware of it, a tiny irritant, a chafing presence. She was early, deliberately so, and was hoping that the Corporal would not be too late for she would have to guard against someone else asking to share the table. A young woman alone in a café could attract the wrong sort of attention . . . The minutes ticked by and she felt most singular, despite the shelter of the maroon-coloured upholstery and the wood-panelled walls. The waitress didn't help, coming up to her and licking her pencil ostentatiously and with a stern jib, standing over her with a peremptory 'Yes Miss?' – as if Bella were some kind of street-walker looking for a free sit-down. Bella was about to tell her that she was waiting to be joined by a gentleman, when the Corporal arrived. He was a vision of gold and crimson, the flurry of the street still about him. He included the waitress, Bella noticed, in his broad smile of greeting.

'Apols,' he said, 'for the delay.'

Bella rose immediately and held her two bare hands out to him.

'Nicholas darling,' she said in her most cultivated tone for the benefit of the little waitress.

'Bel,' he said doubtfully.

But it had the desired effect. Vanquished, the waitress, who had tried to make her feel so unworthy, took the order and slunk away.

'Sit, sit,' Bella said for she knew she must take charge at once. And the Corporal sat, obedient as a scolded child.

'Well, well,' he said, 'the schoolmarm is never off-duty, I see.'

'We'll take tea here and then . . .'

'And then . . .?' He arched his eyebrows sardonically.

'Then, Nicholas Beaver, you can escort me home and if you're very good . . .'

*

She excused herself once they arrived at Dominick Street and went directly to the bedroom, asking the Corporal to wait. She lifted her hat carefully from her head and shrugged off her jacket, placing both on the chair by the bed. Her fingers trembled as she undid her boots. She unhooked her stockings, thinking how carefully she had donned these items not three hours before. She looked at herself in the mirror before she went on, but she didn't linger on the reflection. Instead, she took a deep breath and readied herself for the performance.

'Can you help me with this?' she asked going to the portal of the bedroom with her back turned. She loosed her hair, baring her nape. The blue chenille had a finicky row of buttons down the back. The Corporal came up behind her and made his way down, undoing each cloth-covered bulb until he reached the seat of her spine. When he was finished she freed her arms and peeled the bodice of the dress away so that it swaddled her waist. She could feel his breath on her neck as she stepped out of the skirts. Once she didn't have to face him, she could do this, she told herself.

'And now the corset,' she said, sounding to herself like a teacher, going through the alphabet of her apparel.

He deftly undid the lacing – men must have more practice with these, she thought – and she lifted it away, letting it slide to the floor. The whalebone made it stand, not fall. It was like her last piece of armour. Swiftly she stepped out of her petticoat which sighed at her ankles. Now there was only her pantaloons and chemise. He needed no further commands to help. The chemise got tangled around her face and for a moment she was swathed in white, breathing in muslin. If she could have stayed in this cocoon she would have, but he whipped it off and threw it to the floor, impatient now, she could sense. Still she could not face him. He fingered the drawstring on her pantaloons.

'Turn around,' he said.

And on his knees, he drew them down.

Before Leeper, Bella had thought her innocence of the brutish intimacies of congress as a kind of refinement. A superior state. Mother had never spoken of the act or gone into the sordid Facts of Life. The mystery of the passions of men and women remained that – a mystery. The only glimpses Bella had had was down on the canal bank in the dark or among the low talk of drinkers let out on the street at closing time.

'Bel, Bel,' he kept on saying as though cajoling her, when persuasion wasn't necessary. Surely he must have noticed how readily she submitted. There was no struggle this time. When he fell upon her his weight seemed a nestling and her own abdication was like the unfurling of a sail, an airy thing, not a despairing surrender as before. She'd only known violent storm; now she learned that there could be gentle passages too, glassy lagoons where stillness gave way to piercing spears of red-lined pleasure, her own unexpectedly so, and so soon after . . . no, she would not think of that. She tried to block out the memory of Leeper's bestial howls, as Nick went about his careful excavation. Yet, when the time came, he was so silent she was not sure that it was done. It was a moment of fierce solemnity, like a bridal vow, she thought. As if he sensed, somehow, the gravity of their union. (Years afterwards, he used to wax lewd about that first time – the convict and the soldier learn to do it quiet, he would say.) His ardour for consummation matched her own, it seemed, the only difference being that hers was full of avid calculation.

'I thought you would look down on the likes of me,' he said afterwards as they lay together in the becalmed sheets.

'But you have travelled further and seen the world.'

'Well, England,' he conceded, 'Gibraltar and the Isle of Man.'

'Further than I've ever been.'

'And where would you go, Bella Casey, if you had a magic wand?'

'I'd go to Paris!'

'Ooh-la-la!' he mocked.

She did not proceed with that line of talk. She didn't want to come over as high-faluting. Though it was hard to see how she could be accused of that in this state, her hair in riotous tumult and her breasts wantonly exposed and Nick fondling them.

'How are my two girls?' he whispered to her nipples. He peered at her between the hills of her flesh. It became a joke between them, her breasts his offspring, until he had daughters, that is.

'I had you down for prim and proper, Bella Casey, but look at you now, stretched out like a strumpet . . .'

The word made Bella flinch. A Jezebel, according to Leeper and now a strumpet. But from Nick's lips, it was said with mischief not venom. In any case, with all her wily machinations, she could hardly deny it. She could barely recognise herself – where was the girl who'd been too high-and-mighty to trouble herself with young men, who'd considered herself above all that? The girl who'd told Lily Clesham she would only consent to marriage to a schoolmaster or a clergyman? The girl who swore she'd never strike a child in her charge?

'A penny for them,' Nick said when she made no reply.

She roused herself. She could not afford to lapse into self-recrimination. She must finish this performance and persuade with it.

'Don't my thoughts merit silver?' she asked brightly.

Nick guffawed loudly and rolled her in his arms.

'You do too much thinking, Bella Casey. In future,' he warned all mock-stern, 'you'll leave your thinking cap behind when you lay down with me.'

And then it was Bella's turn to smile. His joking words had betrayed him. She had, it seemed, manoeuvred Nick Beaver into seeing a future with her.

THE ART OF NECESSITY

Although she knew it not to be true, Bella liked to think it was on one of those balmy full-leafed summer nights that Susan was conceived. Was it a crime to refashion the fabric of the facts, a nip here, a tuck there, in order to arrive at another truth? The truth of one's best intentions. She had courted disaster purposefully with Nick several times by then. What did she care for her good name since it had already been taken from her? And she had to be sure. When she *was* sure, she sent a letter to the barracks, asking Nick to come, for even after the conjugal intimacies they'd enjoyed, his appearances were mercurial. She hoped she would not have too long a wait. The task at hand was predicated on time and she was nearly three months along now. She kept her distance from Mother lest her eagle eye might light on Bella's roundening. She invented a story that her bicycle was punctured and hoped that this might pass as explanation for not visiting. It troubled her, all this dissembling, how one lie begot another, however innocuous.

The worst part of the business altogether was that there was still no word from Nick. She tried to be the pattern of all patience as the leaves began to fall and the mellow month of September gave way to October. The infants brought polished conkers and chestnut cones to school and they made a Harvest Table. She looked at the children more closely now, appraising each one as if he were standing in comparison to her own. Would he be dark like little Jack's friend, Georgie Ecret, or angelic like Thomas Bryson, or frankly loud like Hubert Weir? Such dreamy meditations were a way to stem her rising panic as the weeks went by and there was only silence from Nick. Even Miss Quill was beginning to suspect something, she feared. Had she heard her early morning retching, for often she would have to run to the lavatory before class? If she knew what ailed Bella, she might report her, for Miss Quill was most upright in matters pertaining to the efficient running of the school. She sent another note, this one more peremptory than the first, so that if Nick did not know the nature of her indisposition, he must surely recognise the urgency of her appeal.

After another month had gone by without so much as a word, she decided she must take action. One Saturday, wearing her charcoal grey cambric dress the low buttons of which were already straining, and her most sober hat, she made her way to Beggars' Bush Barracks.

'Yes, my love.'

The soldier who threw the door open had lately finished his lunch. The crumbs were still on his tunic, which he didn't trouble himself to brush off. He had a cockney accent, cheeky, disrespectful.

'And now, my darling, what can we do for you?'

He swung out from the lintel; from the brown inside Bella could hear the sniggering of others unseen. She did not know how many more were in there but they made enough noise for an entire company.

'Looking for a soldier, is you?'

'I'm here to see Lance Corporal Beaver of the King's Liverpools, First Battalion,' Bella said drawing herself up to her full height.

'My, my, hark at this, a lady for a lance corporal!'

There were guffaws within.

'And does her ladyship have an appointment?'

He was standing in the doorway his arm across the jamb as if she might try to storm the place. He was a bunty man, able to exercise his authority over her only because the guardroom door was atop a few stone steps.

'I mean, does 'e know you're coming?'

Boots thumped on the floorboards within as if they were viewing a chorus girl at the Tivoli. Was this the type of company her Nick favoured? Was this the sort of smutty talk that passed for conversation among his ilk?

'First Liverpools, is it?'

He dipped behind the door and drew out a large ledger. He ran his fingers down the columns then he looked up at Bella regretfully.

'No, Miss, you won't be seeing no lance corporal today, so if it's ring papers you is after, you're out of . . .'

Is that how she appeared? Some desperate doxy chasing a uniform? How dare he!

'Excuse me, I'll thank you not to be so pass-remarkable.'

'No need to get uppity with me, Miss. We get a lot of your sort round here looking for their due. Or they'd settle for a fuzzy-wuzzy some of them, the state they're in.' He then beat his buttoned tunic with his fists like some primitive baboon and let out a halloo. On such yahoos the honour and dignity of the Empire relied.

'If it were up to me, my darling, you could 'ave the entire regiment, but Liverpools ain't here at present.'

'What do you mean?' she asked suddenly fearing that Nick had been posted to some far-flung parts.

'Manouevres, my sweet. Bet your Corpoal Beaver knows a thing or two 'bout that. Manoeuvres is right.'

There was a music hall roar from inside.

'Run along my darling, for there'll be no fun for you today. The Liverpools are in the Curragh on musketry and won't be back this way till December. Hope you're sure of him, so, for he'll have been gallivanting with those wrens down there. They lives in ditches and offer up their services to all and sundry. You'll have to find another, my pet. May I introduce myself? Private Terence Stackpoole at your service, Ma'am!'

He clicked his heels together and bowed extravagantly.

'December?'

'Are you hard o' hearing or something?' He leaned his coarse face towards her. 'Now, sap, sap, before I set the dawgs on you.'

His companions duly set up a raucous barrage of barking and with that uncouth racket ringing in her ears, she was dismissed.

Violet Quill was perplexed. She'd noticed a change in Miss Casey she couldn't account for. She and the Infant Teacher enjoyed only the most formal association, but it had always been cordial. Unless one of them was indisposed, the folding doors between their two rooms remained closed and they maintained separate kingdoms. She knew nothing of her young colleague's life beyond the classroom and being burdened with the care of her elderly mother in Harold's Cross, she did not linger in school after hours but had to rush home to the sick room. Their conversations for the most part ran to comments on the weather or discussions about ordering fuel and stationery. Miss Casey was twenty years her junior and Miss Quill felt acutely the restrictions of her own closeted life. What did she know of dances or entertainments? Not that there was any complaint about Miss Casey's conduct in that regard. No, no, no, quite the contrary. She was a serious, conscientious girl. But lately Miss Quill noticed the tremor of argument in her demeanour. Just yesterday, she had come across her bent double over the schoolroom stove.

'Is everything all right, Miss Casey,' she'd enquired.

'Yes, yes,' Miss Casey replied, though she staggered to a chair and sat heavily.

'Are you sure, my dear?' She allowed herself the endearment. Her elderly mother, a cranky invalid, couldn't abide sweet talk, so Miss Quill had to practise using such intimacies. She felt Miss Casey's brow, for her life as a tender made her vigilant about fevers.

'Oh look at you,' she said, 'you're quite done in.'

'Really, Miss Quill, just a little stitch in my side.'

'Once that's all it is,' she said.

'What do you mean?' Miss Casey said, rather sharply.

Miss Quill felt rebuffed, as if there was something unseemly about her concern.

'You must be careful, Miss Casey, even strong healthy young women like you can fall prey to the consumption.'

'Oh I'm sure it's not that,' Miss Casey said.

The invincibility of the young, Miss Quill thought as she turned away, but she would not offer the hand of friendship again.

As Bella's waist thickened, her hearing seemed to multiply. She strained after each scuffle at the hall door, desperate that she might miss Nick if he paid a visit. She would often race down the three flights of stairs, convinced it was him, only to throw the door open on an empty street. When he finally arrived, so great was her relief she fell upon him on the doorstep, her arms clinging to his broad shoulders and her tears dampening his saucy tunic. Their breaths mingled in the frost-bitten air.

'My, my, Bel, that's quite a welcome for a chap.'

She disengaged immediately, relief giving way to dread for now indeed was the moment of truth.

'Well,' he demanded cheerfully, 'aren't you going to let me in? Or are we to conduct our business out on the street?'

She stood back and let him pass. He moved ahead of her, all clank and swagger. She followed with considerably more deliberation. When they reached her quarters, he sat magisterially at the table and surveyed her.

'Got your letters,' he said, 'so what's all the mystery?'

She stood before him, wringing her hands, not wanting to begin her dolorous confession for it was clear from his demeanour that he had no inkling. She did not know where to start or how to prepare him. She didn't want to blurt it out all at once when he was hardly in the door.

'I'd have come before but we were posted to the Curragh on training.'

He rattled on about the bleak accommodations in the Curragh, confined to barracks mostly except for long tramps on the plains, forced marches and a great deal of square-bashing.

'Miserable spot if you ask me, in the back of God-speed, with too much nature for my liking and nothing in the way of entertainment for a chap bar a few dingy taverns and the natives are less than friendly, crowd of ragamuffins, surly and full of backchat. Why this one yokel threw down a challenge to me and Vizard. You remember Vizard, your friend Clarrie was quite smitten with him, not for his looks I'll be bound, but he's a steady type and an all-round good . . .'

She felt she had to stem the flow of talk.

'Nicholas,' she said with something of the schoolroom for he stopped immediately.

For a minute they were both stalled in an attitude of hideous silence.

'Nicholas,' she began again.

'What is it, Bel? Spit it out, girl.'

'I have something to tell you . . .' Now that it had come to it, she couldn't bring herself to utter it. She tried a different tack.

'Do you notice anything different about me?'

'What's this Bel, fishing for compliments? You look just dandy to a man who's been on short rations.' He rose and moved to embrace her. 'Why don't we get reacquainted?'

He swung her round which made her feel quite dizzy and she had to raise her hand to get him to stop.

'Please . . .'

This was no way to behave, to be so free and easy with his gestures as if all he needed to do was to appear and bob's your uncle, as he would say. When all this time she had . . .

'Is it your time?' he asked. She was aghast at his familiarity with a woman's biologicals and to talk about it openly!

'For God's sake, Bella, what the hell is it?'

He was riled up now – how else to explain his taking the Lord's name in vain? She drew a deep breath.

'I'm with child,' she said.

'Oh holy God,' he said, 'Sweet suffering Jesus!'

'Nick!'

He fetched out his flask and took a deep draught.

'How long?'

'Nearly four months.'

'There's a woman I've heard of . . .'

She raised her hand to stop him.

'Down there by Reginald Square, some of the boys have used her, very discreet and reliable . . . I'm sure I could scrape together a few bob . . . .'

How quickly he had reached for such a dastardly solution! As if she would even consider . . .

'It's too late,' she said, 'for that.'

He held his head in his hands.

'What are we going to do?' he asked, addressing the floor.

Here was the moment of truth. There was only one thing to be done. If she'd had dreams of a suitor dropping on one knee, then she would have been sorely disappointed with this betrothal scene. Luckily, she had not.

'You're going to have to marry me,' she said.

BATTERSEA, LONDON, 1935

She had married a man who had destroyed every struggling gift
she had had when her heart was young and her careless mind was
blooming. He had given her, with god's help, a child for every year, or
less that they had been together. Five living, and one, born unsound,
had gone the way of the young and good, after being kept alive for
three years till it grew tired of the dreadful care given it, leaving her
to weep long over a thing unworthy of a tear or a thought . . .

Seán lifts his hands from the keys and rips the sheets unmercifully from the mulish typewriter. Half the page stays on the
roller forming a jagged horizon, the other comes away in his
hand. He crumples it into a ball and flings it at the wicker

waste basket, narrowly missing it. He takes his glasses off and snaps them shut. With that gesture, he is back in the world again. A strange slippage occurs when he writes. It's not that he's unaware of the passing of time. From his desk he can hear the mantel clock, its ticking magnified in the silence of the deserted flat. It isn't that time slows up, exactly, but that the light of other days seems to creep in, making the present seem odd, dislocated. He is five floors up. He can distantly hear the sound of children, playing in the park opposite. At his window there is a wan sky aching to be blue and a weak sun, tumorous behind cloud. Inside, though, the airless gloom of the past holds sway as if what he's written has bled not onto the page, but into the very room, fogging and clouding it. He cannot shake it off, the spell of it.

He is trying to write the story of his life, a portrait of the artist as a young man. But before the artist, there was the child, the father of the man. Long before he had been Seán O'Casey, scribe and playwright, he had been Jack Casey, the boy with two mothers. There was the woman who had borne him, who had, as far as he was concerned, blown the very life into him; her sheer will-power had sustained him as if the cord between them had never been severed. And then there was Bella. All airiness and wingéd ambition set beside his mother's defiant certainties. What a beauty she had been! Something marbled about her skin; her scent, the cool blue of lavender. He can see her, in his mind's eye, heading off to the teaching academy; dove-grey skirt, crimson cape, brooch at her laced throat, and his childish heart agape. *That* Bella cannot be resurrected. When he tries to call her up, it is the wretched Mrs Beaver who appears, the charwoman with the ruined hands, her palm always outstretched for coin, as if every penny *weighed*.

Raising Bella is like trying to polish silver. He rubs and buffs and polishes but what he comes away with is grime. He remembers as a child watching his mother buffing the tea service in the good room in Dorset Street. Once a month she would fish these yokes out of the sideboard in the front room and go through the sacred ritual. Exotic as chalices, they were, and twice as ceremonial. Were they even meant to be used, he wonders now. He remembers only one occasion. The chief cook and bottle-washer of the teaching academy was coming to visit, to discuss Bella going on to be a teacher. What a palaver that was – you'd swear it was the Queen of Sheba deigning to call. Bella had talked his mother into serving a silver tea. As three-year-old Jack Casey, still in petticoats, he had imagined the tea itself would sparkle. He was crushed to discover that the tea was the same tobacco hue as always.

The silver service was the stuff of treasure. Buried treasure, mind you. Never on show, pushed to the back of the sideboard. Exposure, his mother said, led to tarnishing.

Cleaning it was a filthy job. Swathed in a butcher's apron, his mother would set to, hands mittened in newsprint, face clenched in sour disdain. She muttered to herself as she worked – a kind of peeved narration; was that where his writing started? – as if she could bully a shine from the duck-billed jug or the urn-like sugar bowl. Whether it was her words or her sweat, the end result was a surface so high it would give you back your own reflection, though the teapot's belly was more fun-palace mirror than candid looking-glass.

It is one of his few memories of the large corner house on Dorset Street, three storeys of high ceilings and draughty landings. Any other impressions of it came through Bella. Fifteen years older than him, she seemed to have lived a lifetime before he came along. She would talk of their first home as if it were some kind of Elysium.

'Pappie was the named leaseholder there, you know,' she would declare as if this gave his poor Da some elevated rank. He could have told her that a leaseholder was no more than a jumped-up servant enslaved to a greedy landlord.

The provenance of the silver service was a matter of complicated pride. 'Oh yes,' she would say, 'it was a wedding gift from the Archer side of the family.' His mother's people from Chambers Street, more prosperous than the Caseys, were prone to looking down their noses. That must be where Bella got the notions of grandeur. He remembered some years ago dining at Lady Astor's and thinking how Bella would have loved it. It was a snazzy affair where the food was borne in on enormous silver platters. He'd contemplated nicking one

in Bella's memory. She'd always considered him light-fingered
and the idea of posthumously proving her right appealed to
him. (He was light-fingered though not in the way she'd suspected; he was a pick-pocket of the imagination.) How he'd
have smuggled it out would have been another question. His
greatcoat had been taken by a wing-collared flunkey at the
door and he'd have needed a satchel to stow one of these
monsters away.

Bella loved to inventory the treasures of No 85 – the
veined fireplace in the front drawing room, the leafed mahogany dining table, the Chapell piano. A memory comes to him
of pewter-coloured light, a high window, a brocade drape.
He can feel the furry flock of it against his cheek. Or is that
Bella's dress, made of some purple stuff? She is at the piano,
her hands travelling languidly over the keys like a woman in
a Vermeer. She hummed when she played as if enraptured by
some secret music in her head rather than the embroidered
pages in front of her, while he squatted at her puckered hem,
working the brassy foot pedals with his dimpled hands. A tiny
puppet master, fingers in the dirt.

She was sister first, then nurse and teacher. When he and his
brothers came down with scarlatina, it was Bella who ferried
broth to them. The boys were pitched into the one room so
as they would all come down with the dose at once. Enforced
infection. Bella was the only one of them free of contagion.

She'd had scarlatina as a child, though it was difficult for him to imagine that she had once been as poxed as they were. He remembered laying his fevered head on her breast and hearing through the pin-tucking of her bodice a silvery ticking. He imagined *this* was the sound of Bella's heart. It was only afterwards he realized it was her teacher's pin watch with the upside-down face he'd heard.

The watch marked time in the infant school. Muzzled light of a basement room with the mottled wainscot and the row of hooks for the children's coats, fumes from the fire's pot belly. Bella's drawings on the wall – A is for Apple, B is for Ball – her mottoes on the board – *A soft answer turneth away wrath*. She passed between the rows of desks, a rustle of skirts fine-dusted with chalk, the pointer in her hand, though he never saw her use it. In that, she was like his father who had never raised a hand in anger. As a boy, he was parent-proud of Bella. His sister, the Teacher. Even when the other children teased him he didn't care. He nursed a kind of devotion for her then, heart-scalding and helpless, that shamed him now as a greying man because it smacked of unrequited love. Made him out to be a fool. He shook himself; he would not dwell on it. Back to the fumy schoolroom . . . the reverend who taught Bible enters the class. Long string of misery he was. The plangent song of tables ceases. Bella raises her hands, palms up, and thirty smocked infants shuffle to their feet.

'Good morning, Reverend Leeper.' Greetings chanted as mournfully as evensong.

Bella constantly deferred to him. It was yes Reverend Leeper and no, Reverend Leeper, and three bags full, as she scurried to do his bidding. Maybe she nursed a fancy for him, because he was always complimenting her, making the children complicit in his flattery.

'Aren't you the lucky pupils to have such an accomplished teacher as Miss Casey?' or 'Miss Casey has done a fine job teaching you your hymns.'

Bella would blush and shake her head as if they were a courting couple. If only she had chosen someone like him . . . instead of the bloody Bugler, strutting about with his peacock swagger and a great welcome for himself. No, no, he wouldn't squander his time on that waster . . .

He sits, scowling, before the empty typewriter, fingering the pages, snagged and wrinkled by the force with which he's whipped them from the roller. When had it become so hard? It was not the first time he'd written about Bella. He'd put magpie variations of her in his plays. Dressed her up as flighty Nora Clitheroe, the nervous new bride in *The Plough and the Stars* and dressed her down for earnest Mary Boyle in *Juno and the Paycock*. He had used her prim righteousness – and those challenging breasts – for Susie Monican in *The Silver Tassie*. Her unaccountable heart he'd given to Minnie Powell.

But he wasn't writing for the stage now. There was no wand of drama, no costume of disguise to depend on. Now he was reduced to the facts of life and feet of clay.

A memory comes of Bella in her righteous prime. Remember that business with the dog when she was flinty as an executioner? His brother, Isaac, had picked up the mongrel, a stray he called Joxer. Wouldn't the squireens in the dreaming spires just love it that a dog was behind one of his best characters? Joxer, the man, followed Captain Boyle around as slavishly as that dim, faithful mutt had shadowed Isaac. Isaac was his favourite brother, five years and two dead boys between them. They would go off down by the canal and spend hours throwing sticks for the dog. The creature must have been the runt of the litter, God knows, for he was a low-slung creature like a baby carriage with bockety wheels.

One day, Joxer went off on an adventure of his own and bit a child on Fontenoy Street. The irate father of the child came to the house to complain, accompanied by the hapless dog who had led him straight to their door. Bella answered and showed Mr Kirwan into the front room where his father was permanently stationed. He was sick then. In his memory, his father would always be ailing. Some words were exchanged and Mr Kirwan exited. When he was gone, his father ordered Isaac to fetch a sack from the coal hole.

'Now, you know what you have to do.'

Snivelling, Isaac scooped up the luckless Joxer.

'Bella, go with him. See that he does as he's bid. And take Jack with you,' Da ordered.

He had no idea what was in store. They all set off, Joxer tripping busily at his feet. When they got to the bank of the Royal and turned down on to the towpath, Isaac halted.

'Ah Bella, don't make me do it, please don't make me do it.'

'Say goodbye to Joxer, now, there's a good lad, and let's get this business over with, Isaac,' she said.

Isaac gave the dog a hug then bundled him into the bag. Bella lifted two large stones that lay in the scuffed grass near the bank. While Isaac held Joxer, wriggling in his hessian shroud, Bella loaded the stones into the bag and tied the knot fiercely.

'Please Bella,' Isaac begged.

'It's not up to me to grant a reprieve.'

How stern she was then about her father's business. Isaac handed the struggling bag over and Bella slung it into the scummy water. Joxer set up a terrible yelping. They could hear his muffled death-throes as the bag sank into the dark.

'Why are we leaving Joxer in the water?' he asked.

'Because Joxer has done a bad thing and must be punished,' Bella said.

Then his father died, or they took him off. That's how he remembered it. He was sent off to Mrs Tancred's at the end and was having a high old time, so death was preceded by spoiling. Mrs Tancred had eggs every second day and bought him a hap'worth bag of aniseed balls at the dairy. But while he was away, they'd made his father disappear and in his place a waxwork was lying stiff on a bed of satin as if some ghastly trick had been played. When the time came to screw down the coffin lid, he was fetched in from the street where he was admiring the black-plumed horses and the crested carriage.

'Time to pay your last respects to your father, now,' Mrs Tancred said, catching him roughly by the arm and dragging him inside. She prodded him forward.

'I don't want to go near it,' he said. This thing in the box was not his father. He made to run, but Mrs Tancred caught him in her ample grasp; gone now the dispenser of sweetness. He fought against her.

'Put him down, Mrs Tancred, if you please,' Bella said quietly.

'I don't want to, Bella,' he said, catching a hold of her mourning skirts.

'You don't have to,' she said. 'Just touch the side of the coffin so, and that'll be your goodbye. And I'll give your poor Pappie a last kiss from you.'

She brushed her lips on his forehead; then she bent over the open casket. That's when she became father and mother to him.

He plays with his spectacles but doesn't put them on. Without them, everything softens, mystifies. Out of the mist, she comes to him, cycling on a Shamrock Cycle, bought new from the factory. A gleaming black frame and shiny silver wheels that make a ticking sound. She pedals fiercely, her brow knotted, her skirts as ballast. She comes to a halt before him with a squeal of brakes, her booted toe decorously set on the kerb. She taught him to cycle on the footpath outside Innisfallen Parade. The bike was much too big for him and he had to stand up on the pedals while she steered from behind, her hand on the saddle springs.

'Don't let go,' he cries into the wind, as he wobbles and weaves, his sticky hands trying to find purchase in the rubber stocks of the handlebars.

'Look ahead of you,' she admonishes, 'look where you're going!'

He puts his glasses back on, settling them on the bridge of his nose, just in time to avoid the fall.

The Queen's Jubilee was Bella's idea.

'Jack would love the spectacle, Mother,' she said, 'and isn't it history in the making?'

History, he thinks, history is our undoing.

He remembers his childish excitement, walking through the milling throng. Women in their Sunday best, youngsters straddled around lamp-posts like roosting crows, trying to get a better view. The crowds were four-deep along the procession route. They were crushed almost to extinction on Dame

Street as the dignitaries rolled by. His mother and Bella had to crane their necks to catch a glimpse when all he could see were backsides.

'Let's try to get to the front,' Bella said.

'I hope you haven't led us into danger,' his mother replied as they squirmed through the crowd, each one manacling him, a wrist apiece.

'Ah Mother, sure isn't it all good-humoured and no sign of those ruffians who threatened to spoil the day.'

The ruffians would become *his* crowd, who wanted to break with the Crown. But that is later, much later. He mustn't contaminate his story with afterthoughts for if he can't find himself as a child, how will he ever find Bella?

She is there, one minute holding him by the hand, and the next gone, the connection broken, his hand flailing in thin air as he is lifted off his feet. Unmoored, the ground sickeningly receding, his boots skeetering and rasping on the cobbles but finding no purchase while the crowd swells and surges, as if a great wind has swept through them. He's clawing at coat-tails but there is nothing to cling on to. Beneath him, he can hear the scrape and shuffle of hobnails though he can find nowhere solid for his own feet. He raises his eyes to the blue pocket of sky that was there a minute ago, but all he can see are ballooning banners, and in his ears, the smacking stammer of bunting, a blaring brassy din.

'Bella!' he manages to cry out as he begins to sink.

'Mind the child, lads, mind the child,' someone says. Then suddenly he is being scooped up. His mother elbows her way in, freeing up a necklace of air. She catches him and hoists him on her shoulders. He is above the crowd that almost closed over him.

'I have you,' she says examining him fiercely for marks, 'I have you now.'

And then Bella is by their side, all breathless.

'Look, look,' she says.

She's pointing at the soldiers filing past, a blaze of colour, a regiment of crimson and white, the chestnut sheen of horses, the fluttering of plumage.

'See, look, it's the Liverpools,' she says, jubilant.

'Where did you get to?' his mother demands. 'The child was nearly trampled to death while you were busy having your head turned.'

'There he is!' Bella says.

He follows her finger, peering intently. He's always afraid he'll miss something on account of his eyes.

'There's who?' he asks.

'Corporal Beaver, of course! Doesn't he look a picture? Wave to him, Jack, so that he may see you.'

But they all look the same to him. Then one detaches himself, a brash-looking fellow with shoulder taps and a bugle, who delivers a saucy wink in their direction. Bella hallooes and waves back. Something childish within him curdles.

*

'Mother says you have a puncture,' Isaac said. 'We've come to mend it.'

They trooped into the gloomy hallway of Dominick Street. Leaves scampered in behind them. Bella tried to whoosh them out with her foot.

'The Reverend will be on to me about that. The hallway, Miss Casey, must be kept spotless at all times,' she mimicked. 'It is the portal of the school and must speak of cleanliness and Godliness and not reek of the tenement.'

She danced with the whirling leaves.

'Oh bother, let them blow in,' she said. 'What difference does it make now?'

Now.

She took Isaac out into the yard where the forsaken bicycle was slung against the wall with a front tyre as flat as a pancake.

'I think it must be a slow puncture,' Bella said with some deliberation, 'for I always avoid sharp glass on the setts.'

'Sure, what would you know about punctures, fast or slow?' Isaac scoffed. He flicked the pedal shaft around with his foot. It whined unmercifully. 'And you haven't been too busy with the oil neither.'

'The smell of it makes me bilious,' Bella said.

'What you need, Sis, is a man about the house,' Isaac said with the air of an expert. 'What about his nibs, the drum major?'

There he was again, the Bugler Beaver.

'Would you prefer I'd wait for Nick who would gladly do it for nothing,' Bella said.

Nick, when had the Bugler become Nick? The devil incarnate.

'You know the drill, Jack, a pair of forks and a basin of water,' Isaac said throwing off his jacket and rolling up his sleeves as if he were a field surgeon about to perform an amputation.

'It doesn't take two to do the job,' Bella said, 'Jack's coming with me. We'll put the kettle on and when the job is done you can come up for tea and gur cake.'

He was torn. He liked to be a party to whatever capers Isaac got up to. It was Isaac who would bring the stage to him; amateur theatricals at the Coffee Palace, loud rehearsals in the front room. Without him, there might never have been a Seán O'Casey.

'Oh,' Isaac sang, 'who's the little sissy boy?'

'There'll be plenty other punctures to be mended,' Bella said, 'but there mightn't be shop-bought cake the next time you call.'

She took his hand in hers. As they climbed the stairs to her quarters she began a kind of plain chant.

'Remember the day ...' she started and recounted how she had seen him come into the world, how she'd rocked him to sleep, bathed and bandaged his eyes, taught him his alphabet. She made it into a soothing litany, a crooning lullaby. He'd thought it strange then. Now he saw it as a kind of valediction. Lest he forget. And he hadn't, had he?

The day she came home with the announcement, he had listened in at the scullery door. A boy could learn more from eavesdropping, particularly with Bella and his mother. Pregnant silences often fell when he was between them. His mother was baking currant bread and had just put the cake in the oven so the sweet pungency of rising dough swelled in the house.

'You are to be married, Bella, is it? And when is the happy day?'

He knew from his mother's tone that this was not good news.

'We were thinking March.'

'So soon? What's the rush?'

'The Liverpools are to be sent to Aldershot . . .'

'If your father were here to see this day . . .'

'Don't bring Pappie into this,' Bella said in a beseeching tone.

'What about your job? And your pension? Is all that going to be thrown over for a little drummer boy?'

'I can teach after I am married. Anyway, won't Nick look after me?' Listening outside the door, he pictured Bella, a glittery hardness to her eye.

'As he has done already?'

There was some movement from within, the stifling of tears, he was sure. Bella seemed to be forever dissolving these days.

'And you can stop your snivelling right now, milady, for

you'll get no quarter from me. To think that you have the gall to march in here and expect my blessing, is it?'

'Mother, please . . .'

'And what about your music? And your French? They'll be of no use to you when you're plain old Mrs Beaver.'

'I don't know so much about that, after all isn't Nick something of a musician himself?' Bella shot back.

'A few rattles on a drum and a couple of bugle calls?' He could see his mother's curled lip.

'A girl should give up a lot for love,' Bella said.

'Seems to me, milady, you already have.'

There followed weeks of staccato argument. Bella rehearsing her defences. 'He'll steady after marriage' or 'It's not the learned that always make a woman happy' while his mother clattered at her chores, making her own pronouncements. 'He drinks too much.' Or 'You weren't brought up to give yourself to a man like him.' They were like angry birds, pecking over the same stretch of winter ground.

When the time came he played wedding attendant though he was forbidden to attend the ceremonials. On the morning of the wedding, while Bella arrayed herself for the bridal, his mother stayed in bed with the door firmly shut. The house seemed empty with Mick and Tom away in colours and Isaac at work. So it was left to him to haul out the tin bath and set it down in the parlour. He helped Bella fill it to the brim, staggering beneath the weight of the big cauldron boiling on the stove.

'Like the witches in *Macbeth*,' she said as she hefted down the pot to fill the bath. 'Off with you now, while I go through my ablutions.'

When she was done, she called out to him, skulking in the hall, to bring the towel. When she rose from the waters, he caught a glimpse, damp flesh, globe of breast and tufts of . . . like Botticelli's *Venus*.

'Turn your back and shut your eyes,' she commanded, 'till I have myself covered.'

He inhaled the waft of perfumed soap, heard the chafing of the towel against her skin, the shrug of her chemise and the flounce of petticoat, the laborious fastening of stays.

'Alright, you can open them now.'

She was barefoot still. It excited him, as if he had seen her naked. She rolled on her stockings, one leg hoiked on the chair, and then the other.

'Fetch me my dress,' she said, 'and don't be standing there gawping. It isn't polite.'

It was an Empire line, indigo blue. The fabric chattered at her neck and whispered at her hips as she pulled it on. Next her hair had to be tamed, the only unruly part of her, if you didn't include her heart. She let him brush it, static sparking from his hundred strokes, before she deftly plaited it in a barley twist at her neck. She lifted her hat from a milliner's box that read Madame Felix, the letters in raised gilt so you could read them with your fingers. The hat was made of soft crimson with a single white feather. Using the mirror over the mantel, Bella tilted it this way and that until she was pleased with the effect. She powdered her cheeks, then coloured her lips with a slash of vermilion and smiling coquettishly at herself, she caught his eye in her reflection.

'What do you think?'

But what did it matter what he thought? None of this was for him. Her mind was racing ahead to her wedding day, and the night that was to follow with Lance Corporal Nicholas Beaver. 'Cat got your tongue?'

She stooped to lace the silk ties on her beaded ivory shoes. She threw her coat on, placed a scent bottle of lavender in her muff and put on her pearly gloves, the ones from the Teaching College.

'Something old,' she murmured. 'Oh, but I've nothing borrowed. Can you lend me something, Jack?'

What had he to give her? He rummaged in his pocket and drew out a farthing he'd kept back when his mother had sent him for the messages. He placed it in Bella's gloved palm. It left a little smudge from the grit of the street.

'So you see, you'll be at my big day, after all, no matter what Mother says!' she said loudly for the benefit of the closed door.

*

The day after the wedding, the newly-weds came to visit. Bella was still in her wedding finery, the Bugler in his dress-up gear.

'Sit down, Corporal Beaver,' Ma said.

'It's Nicholas, Mother,' Bella said. 'He's one of the family now.'

Tea was poured. The remnants of the good china had been brought out, the silver service having been long ago pawned.

He remembered sidling by the door but he wouldn't set foot in the room. For though it was the same Bella standing there, in the same clothes he had seen her don the day before, she had been altered, somehow, by the wedding he hadn't seen. Overnight, she had a wifely tilt, like Mrs Tancred, as if the sister in her had been chased away. It made him shy of her. He'd had another bout of his eye trouble and was wearing a bandage over his left brow. Who would bathe his eyes now, he thought, or apply the Golden Eye ointment?

'Is it your eyes, pet, are they troubling you?' Bella asked. 'Why don't you shake hands with Nicholas, for he's your brother-in-law now.'

The Bugler rose.

'Put it there, Sonny,' he said, offering his hand. Seeing Jack's piratical tourniquet, he added. 'Me and Bel will see to it that from now on you'll not go short of anything.'

Bella and I, he thought, expecting Bella to correct him. She made no exceptions for bad grammar. But there was no word of reprimand for the Bugler. Reluctantly, he offered his hand. The Bugler crushed it so firmly he heard his own fingers crack.

'Don't fret about that, Mr Beaver,' his mother said icily, refusing the Bugler his rank, 'I'll see to it that the boy is provided for, thank you very much. For it's a poor thing to have to depend on anyone.'

But they had always depended on Bella. Hadn't they lived with her, shared her quarters above the school on Dominick Street? Hadn't she given him the benefits of her book learning, her Shakespeare, the movements of the heavens?

'We were thinking of going out to Bray,' Bella said. 'We thought it would be nice for Jack to come along. Wouldn't you like, that, Jack?'

'I don't know if it's suitable,' his mother said, 'with a pair of honeymooners.'

'The fresh air would do him good, for his lungs and such.'

'There's nothing wrong with his lungs,' Ma replied.

'We haven't much time, Bel,' the Bugler said. 'If we're to catch the next train.'

You have all the time in the world, he thought savagely.

'Anyway, his eyes are too bad altogether,' his mother said.

The conversation went on above his head.

'I don't want to go,' he announced to silence them.

Bella knelt down and caressed his cheek. 'Wouldn't you like to go on the train and see the sea? And there'd be donkey rides and all.'

'I don't want to see the old sea,' he replied, jutting out his lower lip.

'Of course, you do,' Bella coaxed. Then she whispered into his ear. 'Don't you want to come and paddle in the pools that are left when the tide goes out? Just you and me.'

Even then, he only half-believed but he nodded his assent.

'There,' Bella said, casting a victorious look in Ma's direction, 'that's more like it.'

'We should be off ...' the Bugler said.

'He can't go looking like that,' his mother said, 'look at the state of his hair.'

'Like the quills of the fretful porcupine,' Bella said. *Hamlet*, he recognised now, though not at the time, when no one understood, particularly not the Bugler. Even at ten he read better than his brother-in-law who could manage the newspaper but only with his lips moving. A clean collar was fetched. Then his mother took out a brush and attacked his hair.

'Stand still, would you?' his Ma said as he squirmed and let out a yelp. 'I hope, Bella, you'll be able to keep him in check on the train.'

'Nick will hold his hand, won't you, Nick?'

'Only if he's a good boy,' the Bugler said. 'All I can say is that he's the fortunate fellow to have a sister like you, Bel.'

Bel. That was not her name. Her name was Bella. Beautiful bees, eloquent elles. Bel was hard and sharp and flat. Dolorous as the call of church or schoolyard. Overnight, the Bugler had stripped her name of music.

When they got to the station, the Bugler peered through the porthole of the ticket office and slid the coins into the scooped hollow set into the wood like the bowl of a silver spoon. The clerk peered over his spectacles and spotting him said. 'And will you, young fella, be following your Da into the colours?'

But he's not my Da, he was about to say, when Bella did not put the clerk right. He felt tears brimming. *I will not cry, I will not cry.*

The Bugler palmed the tickets and led them down on to the platform.

'Which carriage?' the Bugler asked. But he would not play *that* game. He would not be diverted from his pain.

No sooner were they settled in, than the train gave a terrific lurch and let out a dry squealing retch. The carriage juddered catching them all unawares, throwing the Bugler and Bella together. The Bugler nuzzled into Bella's neck.

'And how's my little wifey?' he whispered.

'Give over, Nick,' she said, 'not in front of the child.' As if he couldn't see, as if his being there made no difference at all. The Bugler sighed extravagantly and leaned back against the seat, holding Bella's hand firmly in his lap. As if he owned her.

'Look,' Bella said when they reached Booterstown, 'at the birds wheeling over the marsh.' But he only saw flecks of smut, tossed about by the wind.

'I told you,' he said, 'I didn't want to come.'

She stretched out her hand to touch his cheek, but he drew back. If she touched him again, he would surely bawl.

'Oh let him be, Bel,' the Bugler said. 'There's no pleasing him.'

When they arrived at the beach, he wandered away almost at once while the Bugler and Bella sat on a bench on the promenade. He would not be a witness to any more of their canoodling, Nick whispering in her ear or pressing his hand on her thigh. The tide was almost as far out as England. He sloshed through puddles. His boots were letting in and he could feel the damp seeping into his soles. It was too cold to go paddling barefoot as Bella had promised. And there were no donkey rides either.

'Oh,' she lamented, 'it's out of season.'

Her every promise dwindled into falsity.

He stood on the dappled shore, with the seagulls crying out their grievances and even the sea seemingly withdrawing from him and felt solitary and disowned. The courting couple were like distant smudges on the promenade but no matter how far he travelled he couldn't create enough distance to reduce them to nothing. He squatted by some rocks and felt low, as beadily evil as the slimy ochre wrack at his feet. A crab scuttled from its hiding place, cocky in its ox-blood armour.

He saw red. He reached for a large flat stone, smooth and silvered, and so heavy it took two hands to lift it. He raised it high, and brought it down. Once, twice. He heard the crack of the creature's carapace and the sudden collapse of its claws.

'That's for you, Bugler Beaver!' he muttered. 'Damn you!'

The oath satisfied him.

When he lifted his eyes, a shadow had fallen between him and the weakling sun. He shielded his eyes with his hand to escape the glare and in the dark cave his fingers made he could see that it was Bella. Had she heard? He didn't care.

'Come along now,' she said and offered him her hand. But he wouldn't take it.

The next day the Bugler was gone, posted with his regiment to Aldershot.

A week after her wedding, the little gate of Hawthorn Terrace squealed, serving as a herald of Bella's approach.

'What is it now?' Ma muttered to herself as she went to the door.

That was the way of it once Bella had taken up with the Bugler, her every appearance was twinned with trouble. Bella brushed past his mother and made her way into the front room, sinking gratefully into the sofa. She moved heavily these days as if she were carrying the weight of the world. It was only when she was with Nick – *her Nick*, how her lips pressed on the possessive – that she was gay, as if she had found with him the girl she had never been.

'What is it, Bella? What?' Ma repeated, all panicky.

'I was called in by the Reverend Leeper,' Bella began.

'What has he done to you?' his mother demanded.

Bella hesitated, bit her lip.

'What in God's name is it?'

'There was a meeting of the Guardians. The Reverend led the charge, berating me for my 'atrocious' record-keeping, my 'waywardness' with fees pending, my 'flagrant shortcomings' in discipline. As if it were a court martial. He made me stand the whole time, despite my encumbrance.'

Encumbrance – he pondered on these words.

'He said I was unfit, morally unfit to teach. Stamp that on her papers, he said.'

'So they have let you go?'

Bella nodded miserably.

'Didn't I tell you,' Ma said, 'that you'd sup sorrow the day you took up with that Beaver?'

He was sent to help Bella fetch her things on her last day at the school. He knew his way around; he'd spent two years in this room looking up to her. Now he felt quite the big boy marching down the backstairs and into the basement hallway outside the schoolroom door. But there was no one to lord it over – Bella's infants had been released for the last time and she was dolefully moving around the room righting the slates and gathering the chalk.

'Oh,' she said looking up finally after he'd been standing there for several minutes. He liked to watch her and her unknowing; it was the only way these days he could steal a march on the bloody Bugler. 'It's you.'

She hazarded a weak smile. For the first time in his life he felt pity for her, though he didn't know why. Pity sits uneasily in a child and he railed against it.

'What do you want me to do?' he asked.

'Gather those books on my desk and I'll fetch a box for you to stow them in,' she said.

She went to the teacher's press, fishing out the key from her school ma'am's skirts and lodging it in the cupboard's scrolled escutcheon. Suddenly there was a commotion upstairs.

'Did you leave the street door open?' she demanded.

She made for the stairs but she had to fall back. Two men in caps were on their way down, manoeuvring a harmonium. The reverend was hovering behind them issuing directions.

'Keep it straight, now, men. Easy now, easy. Be gentle with her.'

Bella had to press herself against the wall to let them pass as they man-handled the instrument through the doorway of the schoolroom.

'Gift of Miss Eliza Griffin and the ladies of Zion Road,' the reverend said to Bella. 'Our Miss Blennerhassett has come with a dowry!'

'Miss Blennerhassett?' Bella asked.

'Our new teacher, Mrs Beaver!' he said. 'Your replacement.'

Bella stared after him. Once the men were inside, the reverend shut the schoolroom door with a resounding thud.

'You see how it is for me, Jack,' she said. 'Banished from the garden.'

The first he knew about the baby was when Doctor Sloper was called. When the birth pangs started. There was an awful flurry to summon him a full three weeks early.

'So much for the teacher's calculations,' his Ma said.

'That's Nature for you,' the doctor replied. 'The apple decides when it will fall from the tree.'

Still he didn't understand. He thought Bella just plain sick. He sneaked into his mother's room and lodged himself under the bed. This was where he retreated when there was too much female commotion. It was darkly soothing under there, away from the glare of light and the blare of rows. But within moments, that was where Bella was led, doctor on one side, his mother on the other, and he found himself trapped, unseen witness to Bella's undoing. He lay on the floor, transfixed, watching the mattress ticking bulge and writhe over his head. The springs protested. The bed frame seemed to cringe. He tried to gag himself when Bella hollered and groaned. Over and over she cried out, pleading, beseeching, one name on her lips. *Nick, Nick, Nick.* It was as if murder were afoot, as if she was at the wrong end of a terrible beating. His mother was in and out, flustered and full of grievance.

'The cheek of that medic charging a fee,' she complained when there was a break in hostilities, 'when I'm doing most of the work, running here and yon boiling India rubber gloves not once but twice over, as if the place was a sty!'

'It's the modern way, Mother,' he heard Bella say wearily but with a hint of admonition. 'Better than depending on a nosey old handywoman with a so-called lucky hand.'

He was relieved. That sounded more like the old Bella. But then the assault resumed. He clapped his hands over his ears as Bella wept and railed. Later, much later, he would wonder if Bella had spent the rage of a lifetime in that one long afternoon.

'Come on, Mrs Beaver, push,' Dr Sloper urged. 'It's crowning.'

As if a coronation were in progress. From under the bed, he couldn't work out what side the doctor was on. Was he with the assailants or agin them? And what was his mother doing, standing idly by? He would show them! But just as he was about to make himself known, a new cry joined the fray. Thin, feline, maligned. The doctor rushed from the room bearing the cry away – was he a ventriloquist? – with his mother following hot on his heels. He could see the pattern of their feet beneath the satin hem of the blankets. Gingerly he edged out from his cave, then knelt, peering up over the parapet of the high-built bed. Bella lay there, head averted, eyes closed, her hair a matted nest. Her nightie had been rent above. Her breast showed, cupped in lace trim. The shift's nether end was swaddled round her thighs; the sheets were bloodied. What had they done to her? He backed away from the bed. Oh Bella! Was she dead? He felt the weight of every mean thought he had held against her, as if his thoughts had had the power to kill. At the threshold he reversed into his mother, bustling her way in.

'Where have you been?' she demanded, thinking he had come in from the street. 'Run along now, there's nothing here a boy should see.'

'Is Bella alright?' he asked, heart in his mouth.

'Bella,' she said, 'has made her bed.'

'Is she dead?'

'Don't talk nonsense, child, of course she's not dead. She's just had a baby, is all.'

The first he knew.

Baby Susan was a full three months old before the Bugler got his furlough. Bella was determined to meet him off the HMS *Violet* due at the North Wall.

'His first sight of home should be his wife and child,' she declared.

'Can I come?' he asked.

'Well, I don't know,' Bella said, 'not if you're going to behave the way you did in Bray, all sullen and sulky when Nick was only being nice to you.'

He coloured at the injustice of the accusation. Wasn't it Bella who had behaved badly, carrying on with 'her Nick'? But he wanted to see the spectacle of a big ship coming in to dock and the drama of someone he knew disembarking, even if it was only the Bugler Beaver.

'Well?' Bella demanded.

'I'll keep an eye on the babby for you,' he said but he would make no pledges as regards the Bugler.

It was like her wedding day again, with all the preparations she went in for. Would she wear her white calico blouse with the lace trim, or her brown dimity skirt? Her best linen petticoat, certainly, and her good paisley shawl and her wedding hat, with the feather. For luck, she said. The hat was like a remnant crown, for the rest of Bella was strange to him now. Once he had come upon her and was aghast to see the baby's greedy mouth grazing against his sister's teat, red-raw and flayed looking. How had she become this farmyard creature, more animal than woman? He blamed the Bugler; this was *his* doing.

It was a humid July day and the streets seemed clamorous and full of threat.

'Will Nick recognise me, do you think?' Bella asked as the *Violet* came into view, belching a black cloud. It was a curious question. Why wouldn't the Bugler recognise her?

'Absence can wither what was once fair,' she said, answering her own question.

A crowd had gathered on the cobbled quay. A bustling crew of hectoring painted women.

'Gladnecks all,' Bella muttered, 'on the lookout for an officer.'

There was a couple of rough-looking men, brawny sailor types with bulging arms who lumbered about officiously pushing the women back and clipping the ears of urchins who looked intent on picking pockets. Bella clutched Susan tighter to her bosom, all of a jitter. Echoing her fright, little Susan woke and set up an awful racket, waving her fists in the air, her face screwed up in rancorous distaste, bawling all the while. The ship's claxon wailed and the avaricious throng of women surged forward, as the gangplank was laid down. Bella was so taken up trying to hush Susan that the Bugler came upon them unawares, Bella in preoccupied disarray and the baby overwrought.

'What's all this commotion, little girlie?' the Bugler asked, parting Bella's shawl and peering in at the child. The baby, on hearing a man's voice, stalled in her protests.

'What do you think, Nick?' Bella asked, full of trepidation. Since when had Bella become so timid?

'She has her mother's eyes and colouring, I see, and not much from the Beavers,' the Bugler said.

'Oh, but Nick, she has your nature,' Bella said.

'Loud and likes her grub, is it?' the Bugler said then pulled her to him. 'Take off that ould hat, would you, Bella for I can't get at you with the white feather in the way.'

He looked away as the Bugler enveloped her in scarlet.

They sat in the parlour, all formal as if the Bugler and Bella were official visitors, while his mother clattered about in the kitchen making the dinner.

'There's a deal of pot-walloping going on,' the Bugler said as the ill-tempered symphony continued. Bella rose and went into the kitchen, but Ma batted away her offers of help.

'No,' she insisted, 'you must be with your husband.'

They ate their dinner off the stiff white cloth brought out for the occasion. The house had been cleaned from stem to stern. His mother had surrendered her bed to the Bugler and Bella and dressed it with new linens but she was huffy with him all the same.

'And tell me, Nicholas,' she went on as they sat over the remains of the dinner – oh, she had put on a right show – a hock of meat, potatoes and a dish of curly kale – 'what are your intentions? For Bella here has a child to rear.'

'Well, Mrs C, I'm signed up till '93,' the Bugler said with a laugh in his voice for even when he was being serious there was a jocund air about him. 'And if I stay the course, I'll be honourably discharged and then I'll be back to look after my two girls.'

He winked broadly at Bella. As if some secret joke had passed between them.

*

The Bugler's military regalia was all laid out in his mother's room. His scarlet coat with the crescent epaulettes, his trousers with the red piping, his cocky Glengarry.

'Try it on there, Sonny,' the Bugler said, planting the hat on his head. He marched around the house, making battle sounds – the cannon's roar – and miming the beat of a drum. He slung the dress coat around his shoulders – it bore the Bugler's smell, the sweet tang of drink, the musty whiff of tobacco – and he inhaled and puffed out his chest. Was this how the Bugler felt when he strutted about? The gold trim and the brass buttons – is that what had dazzled Bella?

'I'm going to be a soldier,' he declared one evening to his mother, after showing his friend, Georgie Ecret his new props, a far cry from the usual run of play – sticks and stones.

'Not while I have breath in me,' Ma said. 'Haven't I already lost two sons to the forces?'

'Isn't it a right and sacred thing to serve?' Bella said.

'Is that so, now?' Ma said.

'Without the army, we'd all be flooded out with Fenians,' Bella went on.

'It isn't Fenians that Mick and Tom are fighting beyond in England.'

'My Nick says that it doesn't matter where you serve, so long as you're faithful to the Queen and honour the flag.'

'Isn't that a grand speech, altogether,' Ma said with her hands on her hips. He looked from one to the other, perplexed by all the aggravation. What was it all about?

The Bugler's leaves followed the same pattern as the first, he and Bella playing husband and wifey in the parlour while his mother retreated to the kitchen. Ma's chorus of resentments echoed his own. Yon Beaver had no manners, she would start, uses the saucer to drink his tea; treats the place like a barracks, sprawling around, expecting to be waited upon hand and foot; spends more time in the company of bowsies in wine lodges than with his lawful wife and child.

Bella would counter with her own litany. Her Nick was petrified of breaking the good china cups with the rose pattern, that was all. He was happy to pull his weight, but every time her Nick offered to set the fire, or bring the coal in from the yard, he would be batted off and told to sit, sit, wasn't he the visitor? And was it any wonder he preferred the rough company of the tavern? He wasn't treated like an interloper there.

It would have taken the wisdom of Solomon to fathom the truth between the warring women and he was an eleven-year-old boy. All he knew was that when the Bugler packed his kit bag to return to Aldershot, the only one to shed salt tears was Bella.

In the wake of his departure, Bella would sit at the pianola and play. If he closed his eyes, he could imagine them back in a time when there had been harmony, and not the stormy brew that now pervaded. The Aeolian had been left behind by the last tenant. It had once been cherished, but the ivories were yellowing and when you opened the door where the scrolls should have been, it was empty.

Bella would try her hand at a Beethoven sonata or a Boccherini minuet. He'd thought the music might soothe, but Bella's playing seemed to fuel his mother's ire.

'You won't have much leisure for the piano after you've borne the Bugler five or six more,' Ma would say.

Bella would stop playing and close the lid quietly as if she wanted to trap his mother's future for her in the darkness.

'Aren't you awful quick,' Bella lamented, 'to write me off completely?'

He was attending St Barnabas' now, a far cry from the order and calm of Bella's realm. The boys were a rowdy lot; there was a constant undertow of shuffling and spitting and the classroom was closer to the barred cages of the Zoological Gardens. Master Hogan was the ringmaster of the circus, more interested in wielding the leather and making entries in the Punishment Book than in educating.

'Casey,' he would bark — no first names here. 'Take up where Ecret left off.'

He hated reading aloud. He had to strain to keep the lines from running into one another. The Master took his poor sight for stupidity.

'Next,' Master Hogan would bark before he could stumble through two consecutive sentences. 'And you, Casey – out on the line!'

He came home daily with burning palms. He'd learn whole passages by heart from the anthology so that he might be prepared when next he was asked, but Master Hogan skipped about the book, so he could never be sure what chapter the Master might land on. He often feigned illness so that his mother would keep him back from school, pretending that his eyes were worse than they were.

'He shouldn't be kept from his books,' Bella complained. 'You're only encouraging him in rebellion.'

'Is that so?' Ma said.

'St Barnabas may not be a grand seat of learning but a school of a mediocre tenor is better than no school at all.'

'The Master singles him out and makes no allowances for his ailments,' Ma would say.

'I promised Pappie I would see to it he got his schooling.'

'Oh yes, my lady, we know all about your promises. If your poor father could see ...'

And then the old argument would be stirred up and he would be forgotten.

'If you're so worried about his education,' Ma said, 'fetch down your books and teach him yourself.'

*

Bella gave him lists to spell and tested him in the evenings as she wielded a hissing iron. She made him rattle off the capitals of the world while she folded the laundry. She would mark off poems for him to read aloud and parse and analyze.

'You must improve on your comprehension,' she would warn, 'you can't rely on memory alone.'

But it was a constant battle. If she wasn't quarrelling with his mother, it was baby Susan – her cough, how late she was to walk, her sacrosanct naps. In the schoolroom, where she had three dozen infants in her care, Bella had always been in charge and the pattern of patience. But at home her attention was fractured by just one. And it was never him. It rankled still, the childish hurt of it, his first expulsion.

One afternoon she set him a reading exercise from the *Poetry Treasury*. He loved that book, large as the bible with its gold-leafed pages and red leather covers. He was to read Tennyson's 'The Brook'.

'Quietly now, to yourself,' Bella instructed, 'and make sure you recognise and understand every word. Then later, when I've put Susan down, I'll examine you on it.'

Susan was on her lap, fractious, something to do with her teeth. He sat at the kitchen table, while Bella cradled Susan in her arms, crooning her into slumber. He worked for several minutes in silence. But he couldn't concentrate with all those lovey-dovey sounds Bella was making.

I come from haunts of coot and hern ... he started to declaim.

'Pipe down, now, Jack,' Bella said putting her fingers to her lips, 'for I've only just got Susan off.'

And sparkle out among the fern ... The music of the words made him want to sing them aloud.

'Didn't you hear me, Jack?' she hissed, 'You can do your recitation out loud in a little while.'

He shot her a glare. Wasn't it her idea to bring the school-room home? And wasn't he only doing as he was bid?

I wind about, and in and out, with here a blossom sailing ... he started again but this time at full tilt.

'Make him stop, Mother, would you?'

For men may come and men may go, but I go on forever ...

He was shouting now and Susan had started grizzling. Bella laid her carefully in the bassinet. Then she straightened and came at him. For a minute he thought she was going to strike him. In one swift movement she stretched across the table, whipped the book from under his nose. She waved it in the air showily, then placed it on the chair and sat on it.

'Give it back to me,' he yelled.

Susan added her own aggrieved cry to the clamour.

'I'll give it back when you're ready to behave yourself!'

'Ah Ma!'

'Oh for pity's sake, give the child his book, Bella.'

'I will not,' she said, her eyes fiery. 'Not until he shows me a bit of respect.'

Respect, was it? He'd show her. He leapt up and ran around to Bella's side of the table. He ducked behind her and locked his arms around her chest. With all his might, he tipped her back, chair and all, so that only two of the legs were on the floor. She made to tamp down her skirts to stop them riding up at this precarious angle.

'Hand it over,' he hissed in her ear.

'Let me go!'

'Hand over the book first,' he said.

'Mother,' she appealed. 'Make him let me go.'

'Jack,' Ma said warningly.

'I'll let you go,' he said, 'I'll let you go alright and see how you'll like it.'

He released his grip and stepped back. The chair teetered for a moment before Bella went toppling backwards. She reached out her arm to catch the edge of the table, but the cloth puckered at her flailing grasp and with a clinking jostle, it brought milk jug and sugar bowl to the floor with her. The jug broke in a temper. Bella was still caught in the upended chair, her legs in the air, her skirts all up around her. This time he saw everything, the gap of flesh between her stays and her bloomers, her dimpled thigh. He felt a hot rush of victory.

'If your Bugler could see you now,' he said with some satisfaction.

'Jack!' she cried as she tried to right herself, but one of her feet was caught in the rungs of the chair and she was hampered by her skirts.

'Mother, he attacked me!'

'Give over you two,' Ma said. 'Look what you've done!'

She surveyed the broken jug, the spilt milk.

'Help me up, Mother,' Bella pleaded and held out her hand.

'Help yourself up,' Ma said and went back to her mopping up.

He leaned over Bella, still seated in the upturned chair but with her head on the floor and her feet in the air. He scrabbled for the book beneath her skirts and pulled it free. He went back to his place at the table and putting his head down he stared blindly at the book, trying to quiet his thumping heart. He watched surreptitiously as Bella tried to right herself, crouching on all fours first, then hauling herself to standing. Her hair had come loose from her combs. Her skirts were stained with milk, her blouse was in disarray. A button had popped in the struggle, leaving a gape at her breast.

'Look at me,' she said to him. 'You have me ruined.'

And then the tears came. A great dam-burst, racking sobs that seemed to come from the pit of her stomach. Her face, when he dared to look, a mottled mess. He stared down at the *Treasury*. The back cover had come away from the spine in the tussle and was hanging on by the merest thread. Bella's *Treasury* torn in two ...

He stoops to retrieve the ball of scrunched-up paper from

the carpet at his feet. He tries to smoothe the pages out, to undo the damage, but the delicate carbon between the sheets has been irretrievably torn. A day's work destroyed, by a fit of bad temper. No great loss, in truth. What use were all these memories to him when he could make no sense of them? Bella had been right. It wasn't his memory that was at fault, it was his understanding. He would have to start again.

CADBY

CHANCE ENCOUNTERS

W hen Bella shut the street door of the new house on Rutland Place on May 1st, 1893, she felt a rush of victory. This was the fresh start she had longed for – Nick, discharged from the army and home permanently, her little family together. He'd secured a position as a porter with the Great Northern Railways, thanks to a letter from his commanding officer which described him as honest, steady and sober. She surveyed her belongings safely housed inside. The two-leafed mahogany table from her teacher's quarters, her framed prints, an iron bedstead with a green sateen eiderdown, a rocking chair she'd purchased from Rafters' Auction Rooms on the never-never, a horse-hair sofa with wine trim, her china wedding bowl with scalloped edges the colour of clotted cream. But her proudest possession was a vertical Cadby, on which she'd made a down-payment at Butler's Instruments. It would not have been a proper home without a piano, and though it was in the plain mission style, it was finished in a mottled burr walnut and had a most pleasing timbre.

Nick came in from the scullery. He had to bend for the lintel was exceedingly low. Dressed in his civvies, he seemed lesser, somehow, and she worried he might feel reduced by their little kingdom. There was a spacious yard, big enough for two washing lines, but after the broad expanses of the parade ground, would he feel hemmed in here?

'Well?' she demanded.

'It's a new billet, Bel, is all,' he said.

'For you, maybe,' she told him, 'but this is your home now, Nick, *our* home.'

To celebrate she'd bought Eccles cake in the Miss Edwards' shop on Cavendish Row. She sat Susan on a butter-box which she had covered with a piece of red velvet to pretty it up.

'Well, look at this fancy grub, Susie,' Nick said when she brought in the tray. 'Bought cake, no less.'

He whisked her on to his lap; Nick's gestures with the children would always be broad. He'd catch them from behind and swing them in the air until they were dizzy, or tickle them unmercifully.

'Look, Susie, look,' Nick said as Bella cut up a piece of the cake. 'Mama's going to make you eat crushed flies.'

'Oh Nick,' she chastised.

'What?' Nick said. 'What?'

'We'll have none of your barrack-room humour here, thank you very much,' she said.

There was a muffled cry from upstairs. The new baby waking. Christened Bella, but called Babsie. That was Nick's pet name for her.

'So as not to confuse her with you, Bel,' he had decreed. 'There's only one Isabella in this household and that, my sweet, is you.'

But things had not always been so sweet regarding Babsie. When Bella had found herself pregnant again, she had thought *this* baby would be the lucky one. There would be none of the dread associated with Susan, no whiff of illegitimacy to haunt her, no ugly ultimatums to be delivered. She had been dying to break the good news to Nick, waiting anxiously for his next leave, deliciously rehearsing in her mind how she would tell him. But once he arrived, she found herself holding back. Even after three years of marriage, she was still not quite sure of Nick. She blamed it on his soldiering. His intermittent leaves home meant they were more separated sweethearts than man and wife. They might have known continuity but there was no ease in it. Every time he came home, Nick was like a stranger, someone she had to reacquaint herself with, as if they were constantly replaying their courtship but never reaching engagement. She found herself discovering traits in him as if she were a new bride. He did all his own sewing for one. It was a skill he'd picked up in the ranks. He could stitch a hem and darn a rip quicker than any girl. The first time she saw him bent over a brass button whipping the needle back and forth she almost laughed for it seemed an oddly feminine occupation, but she was grateful for these unexpected gifts. They reassured her; a man adept at needlework must surely have refinement lodged somewhere in his soul. But other discoveries were less welcome. Nick might have looked neat as a bandbox but when he undressed he left his clothes where they fell, like scarlet rubble on the floor. His presence in the bed was a surprise to her, he sprawled so. He was a restless sleeper, bucking like an unbroken horse when he turned, snorting into wakefulness; in the mornings he hawked up phlegm. His smell, of smoke and ale houses, all had to be learned again and accommodated. And then he would be gone and she would be left with Mother – always more peevish after Nick's visits – a widow in all but name.

It was the evening before Nick's return to Aldershot and she still hadn't announced the new baby. She decided she would make an occasion of it, to make a distinction between this annunciation and the last. Nick was out playing bagatelle with his pals, so in the late afternoon she left Susan with Mother and made her way to Byrne's on Buckingham Street. She would cook calf's liver for his tea for Nick was partial to it and then she would tell him. She was in a merry mood and flushed with the bloom of anticipation. Even Mr Byrne, the butcher, noticed, and when she told him who the liver and lights was for, he patted her hand and said, 'He's the lucky man, then, Missus.'

Emboldened by the sensation of well-being, she stepped on to the street and straight into the person of Leeper. She felt her stomach turn. What was he doing here, completely outside his quotidian territory? It had been three years since she had seen him, not since that last day at the schoolroom, but all the old oppressions – the menace of his presence, her own puniness in the face of it – rose up in her.

'Miss Casey,' he said and doffed his bowler for he was in street clothes.

'It's Mrs Beaver, Reverend Leeper,' she said.

'Of course, of course,' he said, 'please forgive me, Mrs Beaver. It's just that you will always be Miss Casey to me. '

She was carrying a soaking bag of offal. It seemed an offence, somehow, some indiscretion in plain view.

'I trust you are keeping well?'

'Very well,' she said emphatically, then remembering her manners added a thank you.

'Well,' he said expansively fingering the rim of his hat, 'I must say the married state appears to be suiting you.'

He glanced at her appraisingly and she was forced to thank him again though she knew the treachery of his compliments. But she was glad of her burnished hair and her high colour – she had the luck never to look plain in pregnancy – even if her errand was mundane. She found herself perusing his features now in the same way as she had guiltily examined Susan's, for any trace of him in her. Thanks be to God she didn't have Susan with her.

He, of all people, must never set eyes on the child for fear that his greedy gaze might recognise the kinship.

'And your baby?' he asked, 'we hear you had a little girl.'

He used the royal plural as if putting himself up there at the right hand of the Lord.

'Our Susan is a baby no longer,' she replied. 'She's coming up for three.' *As you well know.*

'Is she indeed?' he said with an air of rumination as if he were doing the arithmetic in his head.

'And we,' Bella said with a declarative tone for two could play at that game, 'are expecting our second.'

The moment it was out, she felt a pang of betrayal. That Leeper should know the news before Nick, made her feel utterly abject. How was it that he had the power to turn every joyous thing in her life sour? Suddenly she wanted to be away, for fear of what other unforced admissions she might let slip.

'Well,' he said, 'that's very good news, altogether, Mrs Beaver. My congratulations.'

'I must be hurrying along now, Reverend Leeper, for my husband will be wondering where I've got to. I just stepped out to get some victuals for him. He's home on leave from Aldershot . . .'

'Still soldiering then, your husband? ' He leaned in close to her. 'But then, hasn't he the joy of a furlough baby to look forward to?'

The way he said it – a furlough baby – it made the new child sound like the fruit of some squalid encounter, the product of some hurried lust. Then he changed tack, pinning her with his conversation.

'You'll be glad to hear,' he went on, 'that your successor Miss Blennerhassett is doing very nicely. A charming girl and willing, too.'

Willing — every word out of his mouth reeked of perfidy. Once, Bella thought, he had probably described me so.

'The children are devoted to her and she's most effective in whipping in those fees.'

Bella felt a tremor of regret for Miss Blennerhassett. She had met her only once when the new teacher had arrived to inspect the teacher's quarters. Inspect was the word for it, for the young woman eyed up everything unashamedly, including Bella's encumbrance. Bella, in reply, had flourished her hand with the gold band. Miss Blennerhassett was a pert young thing with a high colour, dark tresses and a slender figure. Bella had wondered if she should warn her, but how would she have put it? There wasn't civilised language for what she had to say. Perhaps, she reasoned, Leeper had learned his lesson. Anyway, Miss Blennerhassett, being of a different nature, might not ignite his ugly passion and then any prophecies of hers would have been for naught. But in truth, even at that late stage, she was still afraid of Leeper and what he might be able to do to her.

'. . . and,' Leeper continued, 'she has qualified for two increments already and is studying for her promotion examinations. Oh yes, we shall have our Miss Blennerhassett with us for a long time. She intends to make a vocation of her teaching . . .' He smiled at Bella then, pityingly. 'But then, some of us have other callings, isn't that so, Mrs Beaver?'

And with that he doffed his hat and with a clipped good day he left. Bella felt the street spin around her and had to sit, choosing the steps of a house to sink on, though it was an indecorous pose. But her heart was thumping loudly and she thought that she might faint. She had never before been prone to the vapours, but it took her a full ten minutes to compose herself. When she did, she scurried home as if fleeing from the scene of a crime.

'Bella, is that you?'

The voice that greeted her was Nick's. She walked down the hallway with a tiny clutch of fear in her breast. She turned in at the parlour door and met a clouded brow. She had never seen such a thundery aspect on Nick's face and he had a dishevelled air, his jacket hanging open with his vest showing and flecks of tobacco on his trousers. He stood swaying by the mantel.

'And where have you been?' he demanded pointing to the clock which showed ten minutes after six.

'I've been off to buy your tea is all,' she said and raised the package as proof.

'And how long does that take, pray tell?'

'I got held up.'

'You did and all,' he said, 'your mother says you've been gone an age.'

Wasn't that an unexpected alliance, Bella thought, her Nick and Mother ranged on one side against her. 'And aren't you all kitted out for a woman just out doing the messages?'

She'd worn her good maroon skirt and a blouse of duck-egg blue, so that she would look her best when she delivered her news.

'Are you sure you didn't have something else on your mind?'

'I don't know what you mean.'

'Don't you, indeed!'

He moved uncertainly towards her and she realised the reason for his surliness. His breath oozed porter. She was ashamed for him. To be footless at this hour! She tried to calculate where Mother might be for she mustn't see him in such a state.

'You've been carrying on behind my back,' he said, 'and that's the reason you're tricked up like this.'

'No, Nick, no,' she said. She was bewildered by the turn of the conversation, the strange reversal in their disputation. Wasn't he the errant husband returning home in a drunken state?

'I spotted you,' he said and lurched forward jabbing his finger in the air. 'As I was coming out of Bergin's. I seen you with yer man in broad daylight chatting away like there was no tomorrow, dawdling and making eyes at him.'

'That was the Reverend Leeper that you saw, you know, from the school at St Mary's. There's nothing sinister afoot . . . '

She coloured when she said that and Nick pounced on her discomfiture for it seemed the porter hadn't dimmed his senses entirely.

'So why the pretty blush on your cheeks, my dear?' This soft voice of his frightened her much more than the barking that had preceded it. 'Like a woman with something to hide.'

He'd hit upon the truth even in his ignorance.

'It isn't that at all, Nick.' She tried a soothing tone, the kind she used when Susan was throwing one of her tantrums. 'Sure, isn't he a man of the cloth, and married with it?'

'Did you let him have you in some doorway? Is that what kept you?'

'Nick!'

'You hear me, Bella Beaver, and hear me good,' he bellowed, grabbing her by the forearms and shaking her, his face twisted in rage. 'Don't you think you can play me for a jackass!'

He unmanacled her arms and took a step backwards. She smoothed her sleeves and the creased collar of her blouse.

'All tarted up and swanning about as soon as my back is turned like some pattern wife . . .'

'Oh Nick, it's for you I'm all dressed up.'

He snorted. She decided to tell him about the baby there and then; that would surely sweeten his temper.

'I'm expecting, Nick,' she said. Once again, it was not how she'd planned it. Would the circumstances between them ever be just right?

'She's expecting,' he repeated stonily. 'And how can I be sure it's mine?'

The past seemed to rear up between them as if Nick were only catching up to it. It was as if for a moment the world had tipped, like a capsizing ship, and the familiar had become contrary. The next thing, out of nowhere, he struck her, landing a blow on her cheekbone so sudden and so hard that she didn't quite know what had hit her. Down she went. Then quite calmly, Nick stepped over her and stormed off, nearly taking the hinges of the street door with him.

He did not return until close to midnight. Bella had taken Susan into bed with her for she had taken an age to settle after the earlier commotion. She was glad of the child's distress if only to give her a chance to escape into the silent darkness of the back room and be alone rather than having to suffer Mother's withering looks. Had the neighbours heard their dispute, she wondered. How could they not have with Nick bellowing at the top of his lungs and their business being aired to all and sundry? Susan settled eventually but Bella lay where she was, fully clothed for fear of disturbing her. She hadn't the energy to disrobe. She was numb, but it was with a surfeit of feeling, not a want of it. Her biggest fear was that Nick would not return at all. How would she manage then with a baby on the way and no money coming in? To what new depths would she have to sink? An hour passed, then another, then three. She was still involved in her petrified calculations when the door of the room opened and Nick's silent figure entered. She felt his weight sink down on the bed beside her. Susan whimpered and stirred. He sat bowed in the dark with his back to her. She wanted to stretch out her hand and touch him but she was afraid of what fresh fury it might excite so she lay there utterly still, curled around Susan and played dead. A few moments earlier, the prospect of his return seemed inconceivable; now he was here, she didn't know how to act. Is this how it would be from now on, an icy calm between them? Would that be so bad? Wouldn't it be superior to raised fists? Better surely than disgrace and destitution. It had never occurred to her that the married state would be so full of negotiation.

'Bel,' he whispered coarsely, 'are you awake?'

She knew then that his rage was all spent. She reached out to him. Her fingers met the crested wing of his shoulder blade and suddenly he seemed to crumple. The broad expanse of his back shuddered and he collapsed into weeping, choking sobs and loud snuffles when he couldn't find a handkerchief to stem the flow.

'Don't know what came over me.' He spoke into the darkness, still with his back turned. 'Must be those damn jabs the medic's been giving me. I'm all out of sorts.'

There were always fevers running through the barrack rooms with all those men at close quarters. But she didn't ask what he meant for fear any interrogation might be taken as quarrelsome and the truce would be destroyed. She let it pass, trading knowledge for the sake of peace.

She had a rainbow face for days. She did her best to cover her coloured eye with powder, but even if others couldn't see it, she knew it was there. Normally she would not have ventured out looking like that, but Susan wanted to wave her daddy off at Custom House Quay, and with all the commotion that the child had witnessed, Bella wanted to appease her. It was a stiff kind of farewell. The events of the night before had chastened them. There had been no making up, just a chilly estrangement tinged with shame. For once, Bella was relieved to see him go. When he had embarked, she turned away where once she would have waited to see the ship disappear into the clouded distance. But all she wanted was the safe harbour of home. She hurried away, Susan in tow, with her eyes cast downward so as not to draw attention to herself. So intent was she on invisibility, that at the corner of D'Olier Street, she crashed into a woman with a plumed hat. In the collision, Susan lost her footing and fell. She shrieked, her face creased in protest at the fall.

'Oh dear, is the little girl alright?' the woman in the hat asked.

Bella was stooped over Susan, trying to find out where it hurt. But the voice made her look up. It was Lily Clesham.

'Bella Casey!' Lily cried.

She moved into action, sweeping Susan up in her arms, the feather of her hat grazing Bella's bruised face. She pressed her lips against the child's scraped knee.

'And what's your name, little girl?' she cooed at Susan who was so surprised by this lavish show of affection that she stopped whimpering. 'Is she yours, Bella?'

Bella nodded, surveying Lily's finery, her dapper velvet jacket, her peacock hat.

'Oh look how bad I've been about keeping in touch!' she lamented. 'You are married and with child!'

Susan began to fret and make strange so Lily reluctantly handed her back.

'Oh, have I upset the poor mite?' she said. 'Forgive me. And I'm forgetting my manners. Let me introduce my fiancé.'

The man who had stood quietly by her side stepped forward.

'This,' she said, 'is Mr McNeice. And this, Fred, is my dear friend, Bella . . . '

'Beaver,' Bella supplied. 'Mrs Bella Beaver.'

'Pleased, I'm sure,' he said. 'Lily often mentions you.'

An indulgent look passed between him and Lily. They might have been stepping out for several years, but their fondness seemed newly-minted. He wore a three-piece suit, with a paisley waistcoat, and he had a most elegant bearing. Not as manly as her Nick, Bella thought, but manliness had its drawbacks as she had discovered.

'We're going to have our photograph taken at Lauder Brothers, which is why we're all dolled up. I hope you don't think this is how I generally go about,' Lily said. 'I'm teaching in Galway as I had planned and John is hoping to enroll in Trinity College. He will have to have a degree before the church will take him. In the meantime, he's teaching school in Dr Benson's in Rathmines.'

She stopped to draw breath. Lily has got both a teacher and a clergyman, Bella thought sourly.

'And your husband, Bella?'

'My Nicholas is in the army. He's stationed in Aldershot at present.'

'That must be hard on you,' she said and she looked squarely at Bella. Despite her disguise, Bella felt Lily could see the blossoming bruise on her cheek and beyond it to the shame in her heart.

'Fred and I must make do with one weekend in four but he does not have to cross the sea to visit,' she went on. 'And for the little one, without a father.'

She has a father, Bella wanted to shout, but she checked herself. This was Lily, dear Lily, who meant only well.

'Dear Bella,' she sighed, and it was as if her name stood in for all that was unspoken between them. 'We absolutely must correspond.'

She took a little notebook from her purse and insisted on taking Bella's address. They exchanged a few more pleasantries, but it was awkward, and Bella was glad when Susan set up a whimpering and she could use it as an excuse to move on. As she made for home, she could not help compare their circumstances. Lily with her schoolmaster beau soon to be a minister of the church, while all she had to show, she thought savagely, was the shameful badge of a conjugal furlough.

A fortnight later a large brown box was delivered to Hawthorn

Terrace. When Bella opened it, it was a gift from Lily, a pair of candlesticks – real silver, not plate – with an ivy branch embossed on their columns. They must have cost a small fortune. There was a card inside. 'To dearest Bella,' Lily had written, 'let us not be strangers.' But Bella realised they already were.

WORTHY OF INSPECTION

In time Bella's ambitions would turn to rising above Rutland Place. It was not the house, but the neighbours she objected to. Many of them were Romanists and she was anxious to emphasise the distinction between them. She never left the front door open, as was *their* habit, for through such an aperture the malevolence of tittle-tattle would march in and travel out. She would not halt on the pavement trading small talk though sometimes it was unavoidable.

'A fine-looking man, your husband,' Mrs Gildea said to her one day having ambushed her on the street. She lived three doors up and was given to being more familiar with Bella than their association warranted.

'Aren't you afraid to let him out of your sight? I seen him at the station and honest to God, Mrs Beaver, he's the smartest-looking porter I ever clapped eyes on.'

'He's a parcels clerk, actually,' Bella said for Nick had worked his way up.

'And no surprise,' she replied. 'Tricked out like that, he could be taken for the stationmaster himself. Turned heads, I can tell you.'

Bella often wondered how other women might look on Nick. She knew he was not above a flirtatious glance if a well-turned heel passed him on the street, but was that not true of all men? But then, what did she know of *all* men?

Joan Gildea knew what kind of man Nicholas Beaver was. She'd seen him in the North Star Hotel, a glimpse, mind you, through the brown portal of the snug, his arm thrown around a girl half his age in a purple costume with a fur stole thrown over it, its tails dripping and the two eyes of the fox looking straight at her.

'All the same,' Mrs Gildea went on, coming over all womanly. 'Sure it doesn't matter where they gets their appetites once they ate at home.'

It was just such coarseness Bella wanted to shut out.

But Nick made no such distinctions. Pretty soon every man on the street had tramped through their parlour and scullery and out into the back yard – as much of it as was free – to view his birds. He had built a pigeon coop and populated it fully. The pigeons were ugly creatures with their dull grey coats and scaly claws. No better than vermin, Bella thought, and they were distinctly unclean. Even their brightly-coloured fantails couldn't save them from being common, like street judies wearing powder to hide evidence of the French Disease.

'Ah Bel, you don't understand,' Nick would say as he stood in the yard with one of them clutched on his wrist, another perched on his head. The rest clustered about him making a cooing racket while he fed them from his palm.

'Here,' he would say, wanting her to pet one.

But she hated the feel of those feathers and the throbbing pulse of their crops. She did not want them lodged in her back yard, housed in their rotten barracks one on top of another, breeding fiercely and carrying infection. But there was no gainsaying Nick's affection for them. He was quite motherly with them. She would peer out the scullery window when he was feeding them. He knew each of them by sight and spoke to them in endearments more suited to the bed-chamber. If Tommy Owens or Needle Nugent was out there with him, their talk was so hushed and admiring, it was as if a string of chorus girls were out in the yard, not a coven of slate-coloured birds.

'Clean as a barracks on inspection day,' Nick would say about the lofts. He was fastidious in his care of the birds' quarters. But she saw only evidence of their dirty ways, leaving their calling cards on her newly-cleaned windows and her sheets hanging out to dry. When Nick had first taken to racing homers, Bella was delighted to see him disappear off out of the house with a basket of the creatures, all fidgety and fretting at their sudden transport. Hours later he would return home with the empty wicker and stand out in the yard anxiously eyeing the skies. Sometimes she prayed that they might get lost or become so intoxicated with their freedom that they might fail to return; if she were a pigeon, it is what she would have chosen. But by dusk the sky would be sooty with wings as they made their jubilant homecoming.

Nick would often ramble down to the Bird Market on Bride Street to buy another of what he called his feathered friends. Once, Bella remembered, he came home from the market with a goldfinch in a tiny lantern cage.

'Come the good weather,' he said 'we'll hang it outside the front door and won't it brighten up the street?'

We will in our eye, Bella thought to herself. She did not hold with any class of boastful decoration on the house, but she said nothing for she had learned that sometimes it was wiser to yield in small *contretemps*. She was just relieved that it was not another beller or a bard, a red mealie or a white-tip, or a fresh pair of tumblers for they were already over-run with those. She knew the names of all the blessed pigeons. It was impossible for her not to pick up knowledge, even if it was knowledge she didn't care to have. Mostly, though, she pretended ignorance for she did not want to be drawn into the care of the detestable creatures.

'Look, Bel,' Nick breathed, 'look at her plumage, the wing feathers tipped with gold.' He caressed the splash of crimson on the goldfinch's crown. 'Isn't she a pure beauty?'

She was always impressed by the elegance with which Nick spoke about the birds and how soft he was about them, like a woman in love.

'Isn't it a shame to keep her under lock and key?' she asked.

'Ah Bel, see, your finch becomes quite docile in captivity.'

Unlike the cursed pigeons with their throaty racket, she thought.

'Isn't that right, my little beauty?' Nick said and folded the bird to his chest, pressing his lips to its crown.

The next morning Nick went out to check on the bird. Bella heard the creak of the cage door, followed by an oath.

'A pox on him!'

When Nick was riled, he spoke plain soldier. Bella rushed out into the backyard where a dun-coloured impostor sat on the perch. Mixed in with the grain on the floor of the cage was a carpet of gold and crimson glinting cruelly in the morning light. That was all that remained of the magnificent uniform of the day before.

'That blackguard sold me a spadger and painted it up to look like a brassy hoor.' Nick paced up and down the yard. 'I've been done.'

In that moment, she saw how it would be if Nick knew how else he'd been deceived.

'If I ever clap eyes on the poltroon who did this, I'll wring his bloody neck for him.'

He reached into the cage and catching the trembling bird he throttled it to death with his bare hand. Bella watched, open-mouthed, as he flung the abject creature into the gutter. The memory of the day Nick had struck her in Mother's house came back to her. The same shock and disbelief, even though this time the sudden inflammation of his temper had been directed not at her, but at a helpless bird.

'What are you gaping at?' he barked at her.

The poor pretender finch, she wanted to say.

When she looked back on the early years of her marriage, Bella preferred to dwell on happier moments. The day Baby James said his first word. He heard Nick's footfall outside and when his father pushed open the door, the child raised his fist in mock salute – as if he still saw the soldier in Nick though he had never known him in uniform – and out it came, triumphantly, two syllables, clear as a bell. Dada! Nick was as proud as Bella had ever seen him. He whisked the child off to the dairy for a toffee apple. Or she would recall seeing her girls setting off to the Model School, as she had once done. Bella had insisted they should get the best of schooling, though Nick had baulked at the fees. Babsie being the more robust and adventurous of the pair, usually took charge of these expeditions. She was a feisty little thing whereas Susan was complicated and secretive. Bella was forever on the lookout where Susan was concerned, vigilant for any slyness or cruelty of tongue or any weakness for fabulation, anything that might lead back to Leeper. She had decided from the time Susan could walk that she would have to be protected more than the others. She would not be sending her eldest out to work, Bella decided; no, she would keep her at home until she was ready to be wed so that history would not be allowed to repeat itself.

Sundays in those early years were spent *en famille*. The entire Casey clan would descend for dinner. Mick and Tom, back on civvy street, were delighted to be in cahoots with their old pal, the Beaver, and even Mother deigned to visit. They were merry occasions over which Nick presided with a proprietary pride. He was in charge of portions and always saved the crackling for Mother or held back the white of the chicken for Bella. If Mick or Tom's conversation got too boisterous, he would raise the carving knife and admonish them.

'Ladies present, boys, ladies present.'

After dinner there would invariably be a sing-song. Gathered around the Cadby, they would take turns at their party pieces. Bella would sing 'I Dreamt I Dwelt in Marble Halls', followed by Jack piping up with Foster's 'Hard Times'. Nick favoured 'The Star of the County Down', which always brought Bella back to that night in the kitchen in Innisfallen Parade when they had first met. Come seven, the men would disappear off to the pub and Bella would sit with the children and Mother and Jack around the fire, sinking into the sated torpor of the Sabbath and the easeful harmony of the hearth.

Jack would always have his head in a book even though he was no longer in school. Mother had decreed he should be out earning and had called a halt to his schooling at fourteen, despite Bella's protestations.

'Pappie would have wanted him to finish his education. It will give him chances . . .'

'You had your chances,' Mother said, 'And look what you did with them.'

The only way she could help Jack was to school him for an interview at Hampton Leedom's as an office boy and write him a letter of reference. She used the school address on Dominick Street, a deception but one in a good cause.

'The Bearer,' she wrote, 'has been a pupil in the above school, during which time he has proved to be a truthful, honest and obedient boy. He has applied himself to his books and I am confident that in the matter of employment he would give perfect satisfaction.' She signed it Isabella Beaver, School Teacher, using her married name so as to give no clue to their relation.

It was a queer sensation to see herself as a teacher once more and it gave her authority, even though it was a false one. The imposture provoked a twinge of regret; it gave the lie momentarily to her housewifely achievements in the neat house with the indoor plumbing, the three children and a steady-earning husband. Not that Bella could imagine trading her place with this mythical 'I. Beaver' with her Marlborough College script and her smooth words of praise. Which in the end weren't needed. Jack got the job because he was a Protestant, no questions asked.

But when she tried to guide the boy in his reading, he'd argue against her.

'Walter Scott,' he'd snort, 'he's old hat.'

As if she'd lost the right to influence him. It seemed the only distinction she had in her brother's eyes was what she once had been, a school teacher who would never teach again. She could have told him that a mother was always teaching – right from wrong, left foot from right, the stars in the sky and the portion of love in her heart. But there was little room for literature when she had to rise in pitch darkness to get the fire going and have the kettle steaming on the hob. When there were the flags to scrub, pots and pans to scour, rugs to be beaten, windows to be cleaned, laundry to be done and clothes to be got dry under a louring sky. It was hard even for Bella to believe in the midst of blacking the stove or turning the mattresses that once her Monday mornings had been given over to the argument of the Second Book of *Paradise Lost* or sketching Milton's delineation of Adam and Eve before their fall. But drudgery apart, she could at least say that her daily life was once again worthy of the Lord's inspection. And to Bella that was worth a great deal.

THE RELIEF OF LADYSMITH

What was it only a date? One minute before midnight the big hand inching towards the twelve, the next, a paroxysm of time, a century turning. The thought of it was too big for Bella to contemplate, it made her feel her own smallness and it was not a sensation she liked, even though it was a Christian reminder that we are all only grains of sand in comparison to the Almighty. But Bella preferred to stick to the notion that it was another year waning, that was all. Only a date, she said, even as she kept the children up way past their bedtime so that they could see the fireworks peppering the night sky and bathing the city in a silvery munificence. The only chiming she felt with the dawning of 1 January 1900, with its two round globes at the end, was, that like her own new beginning seven years before, this was a fresh start for *all*. What she hadn't bargained for was that the door flung open on a new century, also allowed the world, *out there* as she had always thought it, to infect her little household.

Time and event seemed to twin and quicken. The Boer War was the beginning of it. Her brothers were called out of army reserves. Mick was sent to England, but Tom was shipped out to South Africa to fight in the Relief of Ladysmith. It sounded to Bella like they were engaged in defending the honour of a high-born woman rather than a place of battle. She remembered the day Tom left because she was still counting Valentine's age in weeks. Jack accompanied his brother to the boat, carrying Tom's rifle on his shoulder. Tom certainly looked the part with his plumed busby and dress uniform though there were bands of ruffians waving flags of the Transvaal along the route and sporting badges and pin buttons bearing the names of Kruger and Joubert, who booed at every passing red-coat. Or so Jack said. He came by Rutland Place on his way back all fired up from the hectic farewell. It reminded Bella of the day when he'd accompanied her to greet Nick coming home on his first leave. He had only been a child then. Now he was nineteen and a bit of a beanpole. But for a boy whom Mother feared would not outpace his childhood, his spurt of growth into manhood, his speckled jaw and lanky frame was a triumph. There was not much else to be triumphant about. He had been through two jobs, losing both through insubordination. That was the official version, though Bella suspected that he had been pilfering on the job. While he was working for Hampdon's, tiny cargoes of matches, boxes of candles, borax, and night-lights found their way into Mother's hands. Once he had come around to Bella, offering Goddard's Plate Powder for Nick to polish his buttons.

'Where did this come from?' she demanded.

'Ah Bella, don't look a gift horse in the mouth.'

'This is a respectable household and we won't be taking things that are not rightly our due, thank you very much. So you can put that right back into those long pockets of yours.'

Duly admonished, he had slunk away with his ill-gotten gains.

On the foggy February night of Tom's embarkation, it was well past ten when she opened the door to him. If Mick had made a social call at this hour Bella could be sure that he would be well-oiled, but Jack did not have his brothers' weakness for the drop. He stood on the threshold in cloth cap and open collar, like a common labourer when, paradoxically, he was idle as a lord.

'Will you have tea?' she asked as he sat beside the fire and drew in close.

She settled Valentine in the crook of the sofa and put the kettle on in the scullery, calling on Nick who was out the back with his birds. Lately, he had acquired a parrot, the only species she would tolerate inside the house once it was safely caged. There it sat, beady-eyed and beak agape.

'There was a mighty crowd, alright,' said Jack, 'it was all the world like a magnificent procession. Die with joy, one woman shouted as the boys marched by.'

'As it should be, Jack me boyo,' said Nick coming in from the back yard, his jacket speckled with the fine mist that was falling.

For Queen and Country, screeched the parrot for Nick had been grooming him.

Nick bent down to the cage hanging off the mantel and made kissing sounds with his lips at the bird.

'That's all fine and well,' Jack retorted. 'But what is it our boys might be dying for out there beyond in the veldt?'

'For Queen and country, what else?' Nick said mildly and settled himself into the rocker.

'For the diamond mines of Johannesburg, more like,' Jack said, quick as gunfire, and there was a surly aspect to his face. 'Sure it's all just a grab for gold.'

Who's the pretty lady? the parrot cried.

It pained Bella to see Nick and Jack at loggerheads like this, for they were the two closest to her heart. She lifted Valentine and moved him upstairs for fear of fireworks. In the few short minutes it took to put the child down, the temperature in the parlour had risen. When she reached the last step of the stairs, Nick was standing with his back to the hearth and drawn to his full height.

'I'll not have such seditious talk in my house,' he was saying.

'Ask me arse,' Jack said.

'You watch your tongue, do you hear, I'll remind you there's a lady present.'

'England'll put the sign of death on Kruger and his gang,' Nick said.

'But it isn't rightly our battle,' Jack shot back, 'to be siding against the Boer.'

'And whose battle is it, then?' Nick demanded. 'Would you spit on the service of your brothers?' For a moment they all fell into reflection for those recently departed.

'They're inoffensive peoples, the Boer, and closer to our plight than any Crown of England.'

'Our?' Nick exploded. 'Our, who's this our?'

Who's the pretty lady? the parrot repeated, sensing the rising tempers and mimicking the indignation. Like a third person in the argument and making as much sense as the other two, Bella thought.

'Ireland,' Jack said emphatically, 'the Irish.'

'And what about General Roberts and French and Kitchener – Irishmen all and fighting for Empire.' Nick's voice had risen to such a pitch that Bella feared he'd lose his temper.

'Now, now,' she tried to intercede.

'This war divides our world against itself,' Jack said warningly.

'There's no division in this house,' Nick said, 'is there, Bella?'

There was no right answer to this question, but both of them looked to her.

Bella, Bella, Bella, the parrot mocked.

The mantel clock ticked.

'All I want is for Mick and Tom to come home, alive and well,'

Bella said. But her words sounded plaintive, if not plain mealy-mouthed.

Jack stood up and marched towards the door where he halted.

'When England's in a quandary, it's our boys who do her bidding,' he said. 'That's all we're good for. Doing their dirty work for them.'

'Would you have Mick or Tom die to prove your point?' Bella asked him.

'Divide and conquer, Bella, that's how they do it,' he said.

Queen and Country, the parrot rejoiced as Jack exited, leaving a chilly backwash in his wake.

'Do you know who that fella reminds me of, Bel,' Nick said finally. 'A certain Jimmy Connolly, a Liverpools' man like myself. We did the death watch on Myles Joyce the night they hanged him.'

'What did he do?' Bella asked.

'Slaughtered his entire family over a piece of land. Like some savage in a lair, he was, gabbling away in that Gaelic patois of his, no better than a wild Hottentot. He deserved to swing.'

Nick got up and poked at the fire.

'But this Connolly chap, he was all shook up about it. Turned out to be a right hothead, full of old claptrap about the history of injustice to the native Irish. Native is right, and he a Scotsman into the bargain and all too ready to whip up bad feeling against the English. And this when he himself was in regimentals!'

Bella wondered how this pertained to Jack.

'I should have reported him, rightly. A fellow could be drummed out for the things Connolly said that night.'

'But you didn't.'

'Different rules apply the night before a man swings. But I ask your pardon, Bel, what was a chap like that doing in the army in the first place – biting the hand that fed him?'

'Whatever happened to this Connolly?' she asked.

'Deserted, so I heard,' Nick said and laughed. 'Not much surprise in that. That's who that boy of yours reminds of – a yellow-bellied soldier.'

Years later, Bella would hear the name James Connolly again when a bunch of firebrands made to take over on Easter Day 1916, turning Dublin to ruins and she would wonder if it was the same man, but by then it was too late to ask.

Nick stood magisterially with his back to the dying grate.

'I can tell you one thing for nothing, Bel. Jack Casey's no longer one of us and he's not welcome in this house. Not while I draw breath.'

Bella railed inwardly against this injunction. True, she and Jack had had their rifts and rows, but she would have argued, the love between a brother and sister was dictated by blood, unlike the union of a man and wife that could be moulded to fit any shape. And blood cannot be denied, she could have told Nick. But she said nothing. Instead she worked covertly to come to an arrangement that would allow her to see her brother without openly defying her husband.

An opportunity came along with the birth of the new baby Nicholas. With two small babies like steps of stairs, she found herself falling behind with the laundry. She hit upon a scheme to pay Mother – sixpence and a glass of porter for each load – to do the surfeit for her. The plan had the charm of killing two birds with the one stone. Mother's circumstances had faltered with Mick and Tom again in colours and Jack idle so it was half-charity, though Mother never divined that intention in it.

She had been forced to quit Hawthorn Terrace for a shabby house on Abercorn Road where they were reduced to two rooms upstairs and a privy in the yard. The worst of it was that Mother could not call the place her own. There was a family downstairs of the Other persuasion, all eight of them the progeny of a Mr Seamus Shields, a man who swept the streets.

But when Bella would make her weekly visitations, Jack remained installed in the front room, as intent on boycotting Bella, as Nick was in barring him. When she enquired of Mother what kept him sequestered, she said haughtily:

'He says he's educating himself.'

As if he'd never known a day's schooling, Bella thought, and conveniently forgetting the many hours she had spent teaching him. Though now he was not trawling through Bunyan's *Pilgrim's Progress* or Plutrarch's *Lives* but O'Growney's *Simple Lessons in Irish*. He had taken to learning the Gaelic, the argot of peasants and rowdies. Not only that but he was insisting on calling himself

Seán, the Irish pidgin for his own proper name. Not that Bella would acquiesce to this. To her he would always be Jack Casey and she saw no earthly reason why she should call him anything else. Her dirty washing might have gained her proximity to him, but she felt she had never been further removed from his heart.

Once started, the sickness for change seemed to spread. After several months of courtship, Isaac announced he was to wed Miss Johanna Fairtlough, a young Catholic lady. To add insult to injury, Isaac declared that along with his forthcoming nuptials he himself was being instructed in the Other Faith. He took the name of Joseph as if, like Jack, mere nomenclature could change his nature. Not enough that he had married out, but that he had converted too. Bella wondered what Pappie would have made of all of this since his life's work had been devoted to conversion in the other direction. Mother was incandescent.

'How could he do this?' she asked. 'To spite me, is it?'

'He's marrying into money, at least,' Bella pointed out, thinking that such an argument might appeal. Johanna's father was a merchant with a string of grocery shops to his name.

It was a strange reversal that she should be the one speaking up for a despised suitor. At least her Nick had been of the right faith; he who had been once considered the worst that had been imposed on the Caseys.

'Sure, Isaac never troubled himself with religious observance,' Bella went on when Mother refused to be placated. 'He'll probably take to not attending chapel with the same indifference as he has done with church.'

But neither reason nor disparagement would move Mother. She would never speak to Isaac again.

In time, the family got invitations to afternoon tea at Isaac's new abode on Gloucester Street. Mother, of course, would have none of it. She wouldn't darken the door of a son who'd turned. But Bella conquered her qualms and brought Susan with her. She thought it would do Susan good to see refined company even if it was Johanna Fairtlough's striving brand of it. Johanna was a glossy, well-upholstered girl with the placid air of one who had seldom been disappointed and though she looked as though butter wouldn't melt in her mouth, she was firm-willed with it. She insisted that stiff collars and Sunday best be worn to her soireés, as she called them, though the French in her mouth came out much garbled. Swarries, Mick would call them behind Johanna's back, though he suffered the dress code and the silver service in silence for when Johanna was done with her fingers of fruit cake and iced fancies, Isaac would produce the bottle and, thanks to his father-in-law, could afford a generous pour. Despite her new sister-in-law's comical pretentions (a Catholic trying to ape her betters) Bella found herself sneakily admiring Johanna. She might have notions above her station, but she held her empty head high and everyone kow-towed to her.

*

Bella might have disapproved of Isaac's choice but she could at least see that he had gained in prosperity what he had lost in faith. When Tom, newly returned from the war, followed in Isaac's footsteps by becoming engaged to a certain Mary Kelly, Bella was mystified. Was it the absence of Pappie's guiding hand, she wondered, or some ungovernable spirit that impelled the boys towards such unsuitable women?

'Are *all* my sons intent on breaking my heart?' Mother wailed when Tom's news was broken.

Poor Mary Kelly had neither looks nor wealth to recommend her; she was plain and thin with a sallow hue to her skin and a strange affliction where one eyelid drooped as if the leftover of a childhood palsy. Her dress was dowdy, bordering on the care-less, and she had clearly never had the wit to get beyond First Standard. She worked as a char, which, more than anything else, marked her out as several notches below the Caseys.

'We've a real scrubber in the family now,' Mick said.

Why Tom should fasten on to such a specimen, Bella had no idea. If Mary had had a slender heel or a fiery spirit, she might have understood.

'Is there not a nice Protestant girl out there you could marry?' she asked Tom for she happened to be in Abercorn Road when he brought his prospective bride around to meet Mother.

'Ah Bella, don't be like that,' he hissed at her. 'I thought you, at least, would not be so quick to judge.'

They sat all together in the front room. Mary in her caved-in hat and egg stains on her bodice, her paw clasped around a glass of beer, for Tom had brought drink in the hope of lubricating the occasion. But even so, it was hard to get a word out of her, bar yes and no, though Bella tried.

'And where is it you'll live after wedding?' she asked Mary.

Mary stared glumly at Bella with her one good eye. Her expression – a mixture of timidity and obstinacy – Bella remembered from backward children in the schoolroom.

'Don't mind her, Mary,' Tom reassured her, 'Bella's not the sergeant-major she appears.'

The girl smiled tightly with downcast eyes, fingering her mouse-brown hair.

'Now Bella, don't be giving her the third degree.'

'I was only making conversation.'

But it appeared that this was another social grace Mary Kelly lacked.

'We'll be moving to Richmond Terrace, a grand place, isn't it, Mary?' Tom said airily.

Mary nodded dully.

Poor Mother, Bella thought. Richmond Terrace was a stone's throw from Mother's old place on Hawthorn Terrace. The houses there had the same brown stone, large bay windows and pretty little gardens. If anything, they were bigger and airier. Bella knew what her mother would be thinking. As they moved down, the likes of Mary Kelly was moving up.

A LOST BOY

Bella arrived at Mother's one Monday morning with a basket of washing and little Nicholas in her arms. She hallooed a greeting as she climbed the stairs as much to warn off the Shieldses downstairs as to alert Mother of her arrival. Jack was in the front room, as usual, the door left ajar. For months now he had been studiously ignoring her on her visits, keeping to himself and his books. She halted on the landing and set the washing down. She sent Nicholas tottering towards the kitchen. Enough, she thought, I have been punished long enough and for a crime not of my doing. This fight had not been with her, but with Nick and she was tired of tip-toeing round it. She would have it out with Jack once and for all. She peered through the crack in the door to see where he was in the room. There was the sound of lapping water and she saw that the hip-bath had been set down before the hearth. He must be at his ablutions. She made to step away but just at that moment, Jack rose out of the water. For the first time since he was a child, Bella saw him naked. She lingered, gazing at him through the aperture. These very limbs she'd washed, this chest she'd swathed in soap, this hair doused, these eyes bathed, and yet she could not take her eyes off him. Her face was afire – not because she was unused to nakedness for when you are a married woman there is not much novelty in that – but because she was viewing her brother as a man, as if in that moment he had sprung full-grown into manhood. She could not stop from looking. What was wrong with her, roused by the sight of her naked brother? She, who had once been so high and mighty in her purity, awash now with a strange glow that made her more mistress than mother, more slattern than sister. This body is but the physical self, Bella, she admonished herself, only the shell we inhabit like the creatures scuttling on the sea bed. She had gazed too long and it had alerted him. Jack hurriedly cloaked himself in a towel.

'Who's there?' he called out.

'It's me, Bella,' she called out as she rapped on the door. 'Are you decent?'

To hide her own shame.

Dia dhuit, he chanted when she entered. There he was again spouting his new Gaelic lingo. *Conas atá tú?*

He wore the towel around him like some savage in a grass skirt.

Tabhair póg dom, he said with a cheesy smile and when that elicited no response he reverted to the vernacular.

'Is it yourself?'

She bristled, but at least, she thought, they were talking.

'And who were you expecting? The King of England?'

'I'd sooner have Cathleen Ní Houlihan,' he replied, fishing up his shirt and shrugging it on.

'And who's she when she's at home?' Bella said. She was piqued by his cryptic talk, half-English and half this other peasant patois but they seemed to have fallen into conversation as if there had never been any trouble between them.

'Heard a bit of news that might interest you,' he said, pulling on his trousers. She averted her eyes, as much a show of modesty for herself as for the sake of decorum. 'Remember that Reverend of yours?'

She blushed to the roots of her hair. The possessive haunted her. Not mine, she wanted to say, not mine.

'What's his name, now?' Jack was musing as he buttoned up his shirt.

Superstition would not allow her to supply the name.

'Ah, you know him, the curate in St Mary's.'

Still, Bella would not utter it.

'Leeper,' he said saving her, 'that's it!'

'What of him?' she asked, his name producing the old leaden feeling of dread.

'Poor devil,' Jack said.

A surge of relief ran through her.

'Dead?' she prompted. Let him be dead, she wished, then I would be free, my sins washed away. She wanted the sentence to be pronounced not once, but twice.

'No, no,' Jack said, tapping his temple, 'something gone in the upper storey.'

'What happened?'

'He lost the run of himself completely – started pressing himself upon some young teacher at the school. She reported him to the Board.'

'You don't say,' Bella replied, for despite the blood thrumming through her veins, she wanted to maintain the appearance of disinterest. But in her heart she was exultant. 'He's been removed,' Jack was saying but she paid no more attention. The Devil mend him, she thought savagely. Not dead, then, but the next best thing. She was jubilant. She showed no mercy even in her private thoughts. She thought only this – now, at last, I can be free of him.

It was shortly after this that little Nicholas began to fail. He had been a very starling of a child with a mop of black birth hair. He was small and a little jaundiced on delivery but he had come without a doctor, suckled well and appeared to thrive. The illness started with his being out of sorts and not interested in eating but Bella did not pay that much mind. Then all he wanted to do was sleep. She would rouse him with the others in the morning but he crawled on to the sofa after breakfast and was deep in slumber by the time she had packed the older ones off to school. For several days he stayed drowsy like this, but his trouble seemed so vague she did not worry. It was a bit of a blessing, for he was at that age when he was stuck in everything, burrowing under her feet, or gathering her pot lids and clattering them together as if he were in a recruiting band. Some small fever, she thought, for he was a little hot and bothered. If it had been croup or scarlatina, she would have known the signs, but there was nothing to report bar this listlessness and a cloudy look to his eye. There were little spots of copper-coloured rash too, but she paid no heed to it. Hadn't she taught whole classrooms of infants, their faces blossoming with roseola? When he started refusing his food she determined to take him to the dispensary, but Nick put her off.

'He probably got into the bird feed and made a pig of himself.'

She decided to take him into their bed, nonetheless. Nick did not approve.

'What if you overlay him in your sleep?' he asked for such a thing had happened to his mother who suffocated a new-born in that manner.

'Our Nicholas is too big for that,' she told him, 'it would take a whale to snuff the life out of him.'

'That's all very well, Bel, but the marriage bed is no place for a child.'

And by that he made his meaning clear.

There were times when Bella had to submit to Nick's demands when she had not much mind for them. Having borne five children, her desires ran to the simpler pleasures of unmolested rest and dreamless sleep. But a man's appetite remains youthful for longer and Nick would have his way. She would never refuse him, if only for the memory of her youthful surrender and how it had saved her. She had never been one of those women who stared up at the ceiling finding maps of Corsica and Spain in the stains there, while their husbands satisfied their marital entitlements. There was a tender place in the nape of her neck – she often thought it the last seat of her innocence, a location untouched, unseen by others – that if Nick were to press his lips to, she would find herself melting . . . Was that what made her go against her better judgement that night? If only she rightly knew. What made her lift Nicholas from the hollow of their bed and place him back between his brothers when it came time to sleep? What sweet word or inflamed need of Nick's persuaded her to abandon her baby in favour of the marriage contract? The pity of it was that afterwards, Bella could not remember how it came about; she could only remember the consequences.

She rose in the graveyard hours to check on Nicholas and found blood streaming from his nose. It took an age to staunch the flow. When she had, she bundled him tightly in a shawl and went straight to the doctor's house on Rutland Square, by-passing the dispensary which would not be open at this hour. And even if it were, she would only be given a red ticket and made to wait. It was gone the time to be quibbling over a doctor's fee. It was an ungodly hour to be knocking on a door with a shiny plate outside but she did not care a jot anymore. The fierceness of mother love overtook her and turned her docile nature suddenly, if belatedly, pugnacious.

She had visited Dr Phineas Wood once before with Babsie when she'd come down with the croup, remembering how quickly a child could succumb to that dread disease from her two dead brothers long ago, and he had not let her down. This time a maid opened the door after she had rapped fiercely several times.

'Is the doctor at home, Miss?' she asked but she didn't wait for an answer for Bella knew by the cut of her she was ripe for refusal. She marched past her into the dim hallway.

'This child needs attention,' she said, 'go and get the doctor directly, if you please.'

Nicholas stirred in her arms. The maid scurried off. If God would only spare her son, she prayed, she would never . . . The doctor appeared from the back of the house, crumbs on his vest, his cravat crooked from being hurriedly put on.

'What's all of this, now?' he said, lifting his fob watch from his vest pocket and consulting it like a railway inspector. He was put out by being called from his breakfast.

'It's Mrs Beaver, Sir,' she said. 'This here is my Nicholas, he's been poorly for days, sleeping all the time, and now this . . .' She gestured to the blood on her breast, the child's laboured breathing.

The doctor peered darkly at Nicholas's face.

'Why was this child left so long?' he asked sharply, narrowing his eyes suspiciously. And what could Bella say? Because I would not stand up to my husband? That was no excuse.

'Well?' he demanded, no longer the kindly gent, but the judge and executioner.

'I thought,' she began, 'I thought he was just off his food, maybe his teeth. I thought it might pass . . . He's always been so strong, never sick a day in his life.'

She could hear the feeble pleading in her voice as if Dr Wood stood in for God and she was begging for his absolution.

'This rash here, how long has the child had it?'

Before she could reply, Nicholas came alive in her arms, his eyes wide with astonishment. His face turned puce, his little body went rigid. He flailed in her grasp like a slippery fish. If the early part of his illness was marked by acquiescence, this part was swift, noisy agony. He wailed and thrashed and screamed as if possessed by an evil spirit and then as suddenly as it had started, his animation ceased and he lay quiet again. The convulsion over, the doctor tried to prize him from Bella's arms.

'Hand him over, Mrs Beaver,' Dr Wood said. 'He's gone.'

'Gone?' she repeated dully. She tried to waken Nicholas, shaking his damp head, crushing her lips to his mouth.

'You're a doctor, do something,' she screamed.

'Mrs Beaver,' the doctor insisted. 'God has come for him . . .'

'No!' she cried as the two of them tussled over the child. 'No!

Is it that I did not come in time, is that it?'

'Mrs Beaver, it would not have mattered when you came, this child was doomed from the start.'

She relinquished her hold then, remembering before the blackness took hold that not so long ago she had wished Leeper dead. Now she had been sent the cup of her deserving.

He couldn't be sure since he'd never had the chance to examine the Beaver child. And then the mother fainting clean away like that. The maid examined her person but she carried no identification, so Dr Wood had to consult his files to find an address for her. Didn't the woman say she had brought another child to him? But that child only had the croup; he'd known how to treat that. The maid had to be sent to summon the husband while he lay the dead child on the ottoman in the hall. He saw to Mrs Beaver with some smelling salts. But when she came to, she made strange with him, beating at him with her fists and mistaking him for someone called Leeper. He had the damnedest job trying to control her. The husband came then – a healthy looking brute, despite it all – and he had to be told. The maid, on instruction, had only said there was an emergency. So there was a distraught wife and a dead son for Mr Beaver to deal with, and between the jigs and the reels, Phineas Wood couldn't bring himself to ask medical questions in the midst of all that grief. So he wrote convulsions on the death cert. It wasn't a lie. That's what had killed the boy, regardless of what had led up to it.

THE BALLSBRIDGE EXHIBITION

The girls were abject at the loss of Nicholas. Susan and Babsie had doted on him, vying with one another to have him sit on their laps and bringing him out on the street to show him off in his best petticoats. James did not make much remark about the passing of the baby; Nicholas had been too small to play taws or climb trees or skim stones on the canal. But Valentine, being closest in age, was baffled by his absence. He searched the house for days convinced that his little brother had gone to play the hidey game and was still undetected in a musty, overlooked corner. But after several weeks, even he gave up the ghost. There was no such surrender for Bella and Nick. The dead child weighed, heavy as an anchor. It was as if Nicholas still lay there on the sheets, in the hollow of their bed, his cries lingering in the night as if in protest at the selfish embraces that had dislodged him, while they had attended to their own desires. Each time Nick reached out to touch Bella's arm in the night or throw a lazy arm across her, she would remove it, even if it happened in the unknowingness of sleep. They suffered in silence though in her heart, Bella knew that between them – Nick by stubborn will and she by weak submission – they had let their lovely son die.

There was one punishing consequence that ensured they could never forget. Another child was on the way. John was born with the navel cord twice around the neck and once around the shoulder, which caused Bella hours of hard labour. Afterwards she had to go to the Adelaide. The afterbirth had grown to her side and when that was taken away she had to be syringed to stop the mortification. The doctor had to tear the afterbirth away with his fingers. When it was done, he warned Bella that it would be dangerous to bear any more. She did not think this would be any sacrifice. Since John had been conceived, Nick had not troubled her. But directly after his birth he began to insist once more upon his conjugal due, except this time he did it not with a tempting word but with a maddened eye. Five babies – no, six, for Nicholas had still to be counted – had been reared in their house, and though, by times, they had all bawled their heads off, it had never knocked a feather out of Nick. He had, indeed, slept soundly through night feeds and added to the racket by his own not inconsiderable trumpeting. But, for some reason, Nick could not bear *this* new-born's cries. They seemed to magnify in his head and he made such a fuss about the noise that Bella had to wean John early. She thought that Nick wanted only for tranquility. When baby John woke in the night she supposed that Nick, like her, heard Nicholas' cries – the ones that had gone unanswered – and the guilt was too much to bear. But as soon as she moved the baby out of the bed, she realised how mistaken she was. It was his own voluptuous wishes Nick wanted satisfied and he was in no mood for tepid refusals.

'The doctor says I cannot be with child again, Nick,' she said to him the first night he came in from the alehouse, bloated with beer and insistent with it.

'And is the medicine man to decree what goes on between a man and his wife?' he snarled back at her under the covers. He made a grab at her chemise. 'I'll have no witch-doctor tell me what my rights are.'

He pulled her roughly towards him. 'I'm only asking for my due, Bel.'

'Please Nick,' she begged.

'Please Nick,' he mimicked in a high-pitched whine. 'Don't give me that old guff, Bel. Pull down your bloomers and give your husband his satisfaction.'

He bunched a fist at her face while grappling at her nether regions to gain entry.

'Or I'll make you.'

She could feel the hard rod of his appetite.

'How so?' she asked in the hope her talking might distract or exhaust him.

'Is this an effing debating society or will I have to give you a belt to get my way?'

'You wouldn't,' she said.

The memory of the first time he had struck her assailed her all in a rush and though many peaceful years had intervened, she saw in the demented set of his face, the capacity for another blow.

'Wouldn't I?' he asked between gritted teeth and then with no more ceremony he straddled her and made his way into her ruined interior.

His appetite could not be sated. It knew no bounds nor could it be safely corralled within the privacy of the bed-chamber. This new ravaging lust could manifest itself at any time of the day or night. Bella could only hope that if James or Valentine woke in the night they would mistake the sounds Nick made – for he was noisy in his demands – as coming from the street, or the plumbing. He became like another child who had to be given in to or there would be a tantrum. Once or twice, when Bella demurred, he would take her in his arms by force, there in front of the little ones. There were scenes of degradation that Baby John witnessed that haunted her for years. She prayed that what the baby saw before he had words, would be lost in the murky depths and stay beyond the reach of the memory. Nick would have his way regardless of the location – by the lofts amidst the gurgle of the birds, in the scullery even when Bella was awash with Reckitt's Blue. He came upon her one morning cleaning out the grate, a bundle of kindling in her arms, which was scattered on the rug in the parlour as he launched himself at her. What a sight she must have been, her brow smudged with coal dust, her bodice flecked with ash and twigs nestling in her hair. But Nick did not seem to see any of that, Bella realised. He saw instead some darkness that he desperately wanted to possess and she was merely the portal.

Her greatest fear was for the girls. Susan had just finished Final Standard at the Model School but had not proved bright enough to get the call to training. Bella was not altogether surprised; the girl's spelling was atrocious and her mathematics a disgrace regardless of the time Bella devoted to her. They had fought bitterly over long division and square measure, matters Susan thought were open to disputation. She refused to believe there was only one method to achieve the right result. They were often at loggerheads like this; their natures seemed to grate against one another. In some of Susan's strange refusals, Bella detected the whiff of Leeper, the father she would never know, but she pushed the thought away. He was finally out of her orbit and she was determined that was where he would stay.

'The girl's as giddy as a foal,' Nick would complain.

Susan was his favourite, which in the past had been a comfort to Bella, the crowning glory of her deception. But in this new dispensation, it became a thorn. Susan had always had a way of insinuating herself into Nick's good books, no matter how ill-favoured his temper was. With him she played the coquette,

Adele to his Mr Rochester. If she wanted something of him, she would follow him out to the yard when he was feeding the birds, though she hated them as much as Bella did. Bella would watch as Susan billed and cooed, pretending to adore them, then giving a shrill frightened cry when they flapped about her. Nick would put his arm about her and draw her in, which was what she wanted all along. Then she would pounce with her request – a pair of button boots, a trim for her petticoat. That was all well and good before, but with Nick's new recklessness, Bella did not know what he might make of such overtures.

All of her attempts to protect Susan from the arbitrary lusts of men had been rendered futile. Wasn't it *she* who wanted Susan to pass from home to marriage without the slightest blemish on her character? Wasn't it by *her* decree that Susan was idle at home to spare her from the precise danger that had now lodged itself at the heart of their home in the person of Nick?

She would make excuses to get Susan out of the house in the morning when Nick was at his most insistent. Bring the children to school, she would say, which the boys regarded as a great mortification – to be accompanied by their big sister to the school gates. Or she would send Susan off to pay some credit off at the dairy, or to O'Neill's on Marlborough Street to buy blood pudding – best to get there early, she would tell her, practically pushing her out the door and into who knew what dangers on the street. Susan was perplexed by Bella's queer requests to go here and there, but she complied with her mother's wishes.

Guiltily, Bella worried less about Babsie. She had started work at the box factory. The very moment she turned fourteen she wanted out of the traps of school. Bella had tried to talk her out of it but she was determined to follow her friend Cissie Bayliss to Harrison's Box and Card, where she had already got a start and was earning seven bob a week. Babsie was plucky and being next to two brothers she was better able to fight her corner. She had a bit of a temper – from the Beaver side – but that was no harm for Bella couldn't see any man take advantage of her without getting a clout for his trouble. But Bella was not sure how any girl, even one with Babsie's mettle, might deal with the improprieties of a wayward father, dressed in the mental uniform of a man half his age.

One Sunday afternoon she was at the Cadby in a rare moment of peace. Baby John was asleep, the boys were over with their Granny Casey and Susan and Babsie had gone to the Exhibition in Ballsbridge. She was tinkering with Handel's *Largo*, reading from the sheet music published by Mr Boosey with engravings of trumpets, viols and vine leaves on the title page. She was playing *pianissimo*, using the under-damper pedal which made the music seem remote as if it were being played in another room. It suited her purpose entirely. She wanted merely to lull herself without rousing Nick who was taking a nap upstairs. But her touch wasn't soft enough for after a while she heard the creak of a floorboard overhead and the tramp of his boot on the stair.

Her music faltered, her ear tuned now to his tread as she tried to decipher the language of his footfalls. Without turning, she sensed him right behind her and held her hands quite still above the keys. She acted as if she were a statue in the hope that Nick would take her for a piece of the furniture. Lately, his eyesight was failing him so that he frequently mistook people if the light was low. Bella prayed he might take her for some figment of his imagination and walk on past.

The ruse did not work for suddenly he had her neck in an arm-hold almost choking the life out of her as he lifted her off her feet and sent her sprawling with a loud discord over the Cadby. Without the slightest ceremony he hoiked up her skirts at the back – his own encumbrances he had already unbuttoned – and parting her legs roughly with his hands he took possession of her – she could barely say it to herself – in the rear of the premises. Her face crushed against the edge of the Cadby raised a weal but that was as nothing to his depraved assault, all of it conducted without a word. The silence seemed to amplify the bestial act. Then just as casually, Nick withdrew, righted himself and set down a tanner on top of the piano like a liveried young fellow swaggering about a bawdy house. Lifting his coat nonchalantly off a hook by the door, he disappeared out into the street closing the door quietly behind him. Bella stared at the dully glinting coin. She wasn't even worthy of silver.

When the girls returned, Bella told them she had missed a step on the stair to account for the mark on her face. They were so full of reports from the Exhibition – there was a replica of a Swahili village with natives dressed up in grass skirts and chiefs with war paint and head-dresses – that her explanation raised no queries. She was lying to everyone now, as if she'd been born to it. But the time came when she could dissemble no longer.

One evening, thankfully after the boys had gone to bed, Nick came home a bit the worse for wear. Bella made no remark about his state. Sometimes the drink invalidated his performance and it spared her. He would not eat, although she had kept dinner for him. But she did not labour the point. He sat by the fire and fell into a fitful doze. Susan was at the other side of the hearth at her embroidery; Babsie, at the table, was helping Bella darn socks. After a brief spell, Nick awoke suddenly, snorting and startled-looking. Babsie cast Bella a baleful look.

'The dead arose,' she said sourly. 'And appeared to many.'

'Hush now,' Bella said, 'see to your work.'

Babsie probably thought her craven, but she knew that Nick, hearing the tiniest wisp of conversation, would be convinced that he was the subject of it and that it must be derogatory. Too late.

'What's that, what's that?' Nick bellowed and rose from the chair, using his arms to lever himself up to full standing.

'Nothing, Nick, nothing at all,' Bella said, also rising and dropping the sock she was working on. 'Babsie was just saying . . . '

He pushed her roughly out of his way and fixed on Babsie. She stared back at him in a way Bella knew he would take as defiant. It had become her habit to try to guess what Nick was thinking one step before he knew himself. Despite his lack of book learning, he had always been quick-witted, but lately it was as if his mind was slowing up like the inner movements of a clock that had not been wound.

'The cheek of you, Sir,' he said to Babsie. 'What the hell are you doing in my house?'

Babsie looked at Bella, bewildered.

'Are you making improper advances to this lady? This lady is my wife, I'll have you know!'

His eyes narrowed but his expression was clouded as if even he wasn't sure what he was seeing.

'On your feet,' he shouted at Babsie, 'when an officer addresses you!'

In a kind of daze Babsie complied, for madness has its own authority.

'Have you no respect for your superiors? You have no right to wear the uniform of the Liverpools, Sir!'

Bella could see Susan rising slowly behind him, open-mouthed. She moved to intervene, silently grateful that whatever phantasm had taken hold of Nick, he had mistaken Babsie for a soldier and not some glad-neck from the street. She interposed herself in front of Babsie just as Nick raised his fist so she caught the full force of the blow. It all but felled her and she staggered back, almost falling over. Susan was whimpering with the fright of it all, but Babsie was just plain aggravated.

'Look what you've done now,' she cried at Nick.

He stood there swaying gently, his brow more perplexed than stormy, then suddenly he retreated back to his chair and slumped into it.

'Are you alright, Mam?' Babsie asked, only now beginning to sound panicky.

'There, there,' she said. Useless words of comfort. 'Your father was just moithered, that's all. Woke up from a bad dream and thought himself still in it.'

They spoke in whispers as Nick had resumed his torpor. But he was wide-eyed and present – bodily, that is. Bella knew then she must quell the girls' suspicions. With great trepidation, for she did not know what reception she would get, she went over to where Nick was sitting and put her arm around his shoulders, kissing the crown of his head. He closed his eyes and moaned softly.

'How's my brave soldier boy?' Bella crooned as if he were a baby.

'All serene, Ma'am,' he replied, 'all serene.'

THE SILVER CANDLESTICK

From then on, Nick became a full-time inhabitant of his past. He took to donning his old regimentals to go to work and had to be cajoled out of it. He looked a sight for it was his dress uniform he chose, the crimson coat with the full skirt. Since the trews of this outfit had long since gone the way of all evil, he teamed the jacket with a pair of knickerbockers laced at the knee that used to be worn for musketry. He'd gained some weight since the last time he'd worn the coat, so the gilded buttons didn't meet and the torn scarlet lining was visible for all to see. Bella would have to strip him like a child and force him into his postal serge, all the while convincing him that he was not Lance Corporal Beaver of the King's Liverpools presenting himself for duty. He had to be chastised firmly out of the notion that he was stationed in Aldershot and set to go off to India.

Then one morning, he failed to rise at all. Bella did not insist on rousing him for it saved her the usual dismal morning routine. She kept James back from school and bade him to run over to Amiens Street instead and tell the Station Master that his father was sick and would not be turning up for duty. It was a filthy March morning, dimpled pools on the street, the sky leaden with mournful cloud as if the very world were disconsolate with itself. James was back within the half hour and he was not alone. The Station Master was with him, all rigged out in a tailed coat but with a cape thrown over it to protect it, rather than him, from the weather. Rain dripped from the peak of his cap like a guttering eave as he stood on the threshold and poor James was soaked through for he'd gone out without his coat. Courtesy demanded that Bella invite Mr Devereux in, though she shuddered to think what Nick would make of his boss standing in the parlour, discussing him behind his back. She prayed that, like a fractious child, he might sleep through the entire encounter.

She put the kettle on and told Mr Devereux to unburden himself of his wet Ulster. When she'd made the tea and fished out the good cups to serve, she told James to go out and feed his father's birds.

'I'm sorry to hear, Mrs Beaver, that your husband is indisposed,' Mr Devereux began as soon as James was out of hearing. He spoke in a confidentially loud manner. 'But it comes as no surprise.'

Bella dreaded what he was about to say next – that the railways did not encourage malingering and that Nick would have to go.

'The reason I've called today – and I hope you will forgive the intrusion – but I thought when the boy came, I should, in a manner of speaking, strike while the iron was hot.'

He slurped noisily at his tea. Bella noticed his large hands, wet and red from the cold, and worried that the china might slip from his ham-fisted grasp. He carried the cup tremulously to his nervous lips but lost all finesse on the return journey, so that it collided noisily with the slope of the saucer.

'But it has been brought to our attention – when I say our, I mean, actually, Mrs Beaver, mine – that your husband has become, how shall I put this, a trifle distracted of late, which has impaired the efficient pursuit of his duties. We were, at first, inclined to put his forgetfulness down to over-indulgence at the wine lodge and were prepared to make allowances. What one of us . . .'

Here Mr Devereux halted and laughed nervously.

'Well, be that as it may, Ma'am . . .' He hesitated and made another attempt at the tea. Cup to mouth, then back again without a sip being taken.

'Your husband, Mrs Beaver,' he began, 'your husband has taken to wandering.'

If only that was all, Bella thought.

'And that's not the end of it, I'm sorry to have to say. He seems to get agitated for no reason and has been witnessed raising his voice at members of the public in what I can only describe as a highly undignified fashion.'

He raised the cup again and then thought better of it. Another tiny crash ensued.

'He became most irate with a woman on the platform the other day when she asked him for directions.'

Mr Devereux leaned forward, casting an eye over one shoulder and then the other before whispering dramatically. 'He seemed to mistake her for a lady of the night, Ma'am.'

Relieved that he had got this unpleasantness over with, Mr Devereux reverted momentarily to his own vernacular.

'We're at our wits' end, Mrs Beaver.'

Bella felt the urge to confide in this kindly man since his heartfelt despair chimed so closely with her own. But she stifled it. She knew she must, yet again, feign innocence. If she admitted she knew there was something amiss with Nick, she would only be handing Mr Devereux a club to beat her with. In her mind's eye, she could already envisage the eviction notice, her children ragged and barefoot, their belongings heaped on a cart on the side of the street for all the neighbours to see . . . but no, she shook herself, she must not court disaster like this.

'So we feel it's no longer appropriate for him to hold a position of authority.'

There, at last, it was said. There was a certain relief in it. At least it was an end to pretence – though the pretence had been comforting – that there was nothing wrong with Nick. She waited then for the final hammer blow.

'So we've decided, given how impeccable his record has been, and the fact that he has served his country, that he should be given a less demanding occupation . . .'

He must have seen her face fall and mistook her relief for disappointment.

'Until, that is,' he hurriedly added, 'he recovers his full health.'

Nick was put to work on half-pay sweeping the floors. He was forbidden to go near the Parcels Hall for fear he would be mocked by his former underlings, and being an army man, he followed these orders without objection. It was still a terrible comedown for him, even if he was too far gone to realise the full import of his demotion. Bella found excuses to pass by the station. There she would see him leaning on his broom, the dust-pan idle at his feet as he stared off into the mid-distance as if stalled in some deep entrancement, the warning drums of an approaching army that only he could hear. Sometimes he would point, hand raised aloft, his eyes shaded by his fingers as he peered through some red mist that seemed to have obscured his eyesight. He had always been fastidious, but in his new position this trait became enlarged. He would fix on one patch of the chequered tiles in the station forecourt and sweep it over and over again, chasing ribbons of dust only he could see. But as long as the Great Northern Railways would pay Nick, no matter how measly the remuneration, it was imperative that he turn up and clock in. For that reason, Bella sent James to accompany Nick to the station in the mornings and Susan to escort him back in the evening so that he wouldn't stray *en route*. Then one Thursday when Susan went to collect him, Nick was nowhere to be found.

One of the counter clerks, Reggie Elliott, helped her to scour the station for Nick. Something of her distress must have bound them together for shortly afterwards they began stepping out, but on that night their mission was fruitless. It transpired that Rocliffe, one of the men in the Parcels Hall, had collared Nick on the steps of the station and had lured him off to Bergin's. They'd stayed drinking until ten when the landlord refused to put any more up on the slate. The upshot of the escapade was that when Nick finally arrived home, he was quite evil with spirits, staggering and wild-eyed. He'd always been able to hold his drink, but now even a single measure seemed to inflame him. He demanded food, of which there was little in the house, it being the night before pay-day. Bella and the children had eaten earlier. Not much of a repast – a head of cabbage and some bread and scrape. There was one large potato left in the larder which she'd boiled and held back for Nick. When she set it down on a plate before him, it looked plain miserly.

She was busying herself in the scullery, hoping that by re-opening the door of the cold press several times, some exotic morsel might come to light that she had somehow overlooked, when Nick came to the doorway. He held the cold potato in his hand as if it were a cannon ball.

'What's this?' he roared.

'It's all there is, Nick,' she said. 'I'll put the kettle on.'

'Tea,' he bellowed, 'is that all you're offering to a man after a hard day's work?'

Behind him she could see the anxious faces of James and Valentine.

'It's Thursday, Nick,' she said, 'we're a bit low.'

'We're a bit low,' he repeated. He turned around to find his sons examining him intently. 'Hear that, boys? Her Ladyship is too high and mighty now to stock the cupboards.'

'Please, Nick,' she said, hoping he wouldn't embroil the young ones in his fury.

But her pleading seemed to enrage him. He raised his hand and flung the potato into the grate. She thought he was going to make a hash of the place, break plates or turn on the furniture, but instead he took one well-aimed swing at her. She reeled backwards, striking her head against the corner of the cold press door which was swinging agape. By the time she'd slithered down on to the floor, her temple was bleeding and her lip was cut. She tried to hoist herself up so that the boys would not see her sprawled so inelegantly thus. But Nick was standing over her so menacingly she thought that if she stood, it would be as if she were standing up to him. James ducked under his father's arm still guarding the doorway and tried to help her up but she was too much of a weight for him. His son standing there between them seemed to bring Nick to his senses and he retreated to the parlour and sat himself at the table, grumbling softly to himself.

'Come home to find not a decent bit of grub in the house, a cold spud, if you please, and a cup of tea with the leaves used twice over, no doubt. Not the whisper of a sausage even. A fine how do you do for General Beaver . . . '

In the midst of the mayhem, a wry thought struck her – Nick's madness was outranking him.

She staggered to standing and tried to comfort Valentine who was hiccoughing with the fright of the encounter. Though the sight she presented must have offered little solace. Her lip split, her front tooth cracked, her brow bleeding profusely.

'There, there,' Bella said, 'hush now.'

But she was speaking as much to herself as to the child.

Leaning heavily on the rim of the sink, she ran the water and bathed her face with the hem of her apron. She stole gingerly into the parlour, for fear even her footsteps might offend, but Nick was slumped in the armchair beside the dying embers of the fire. His eyes were closed, but she wasn't sure whether that indicated he was asleep or in one of his vivid trances. She sat on one of the hard chairs at the table, the one with the gammy rung, for most of the furniture in the house sported a wound of some kind from Nick's fits, and she waited. For what she did not know. She had ordered the boys back to bed. James, at first, refused to go.

'I won't leave you alone with him, Mam,' he declared.

Had it come to this, Bella wondered, that her thirteen-year-old

son had to shoulder the responsibility of protecting her from his
father?

'He's quiet now, James, he'll be no more trouble.'

'But what happens if he gets worked up again?'

'Go to bed, James,' she warned.

'But Mam . . .'

'Do as you're bid, James, that's how you can be a help to me.'

The kettle began to scream then and Bella answered its piercing call numbly making the unwanted tea. When she returned,
James was gone.

She watched Nick now, the sad downturn of his features in
repose, his closed lids and jutting lower lip, his fine jaw gone
slack and loose and felt an appalling fondness for him, despite
her throbbing lip and aching head. In this state, there was no
malice in him; he looked both innocent child and defeated man.

The house fell into a kind of shocked harmony, the aftermath
of the storm with only the mantel clock ticking, parsing out the
truce. Nick's tea curdled in the cup. If anyone were to look in
at the scene, lit only by the dying firelight – the tired husband
dozing in the chair, his wife sitting at the table seemingly lost
in a homely reverie, the children abed – how would he know
that anything was amiss? Bella got up quietly and tiptoed to
the dresser, fetching down one of the candlesticks. There was the
stump of a red candle in it, the wax falling down in frozen icicles.
She searched in the pockets of her apron for matches but found
none. Just as well, she thought, for even the tiny sulphurous seethe

of a match might unsettle the delicate calm. Better to sit in the tranquil shadows and leave the peace undisturbed.

Susan came home presently from a night out with her Reggie, a romance that had blossomed from the night that Nick had gone missing. Bella put her finger to her lips to forestall any questions about the ruin of her face. She motioned Susan to go to bed. Babsie came in shortly afterwards.

'I'm dying for a drop of tea,' she said, glancing over at her father then fixing on Bella's split lip. 'What's this?'

'Don't start now, Babsie,' Bella urged her, 'all is peaceful and we want to keep it that way.'

Nick stirred then and opened a beady eye.

'Go,' Bella urged, 'go on.'

But Babsie hovered. Spittle flecked Nick's tunic where he had drooled.

'Did you wake up?' Bella asked in as pleasant a voice as she could muster.

He rose unsteadily to his feet and Bella went to help him, to hold the crook of his arm and steer him upstairs to bed. But something about the way she touched him – was it too maternal or did he divine pity in it? – ignited the rage she had thought was spent.

'Get your hands off me, you Jezebel,' he muttered and pummelled her arm with his fist. Another blow hit her across the cheek.

'Please Nick, no more.'

'What have you done to Mam?' Babsie shouted at him. 'You're nothing but a bully!' Oh my fiery girl, Bella thought.

Nick halted in his tracks. Then he began to circle the table so that Bella was forced on the move. He prowled around once, then twice the perimeter of the table, stalking her. Then suddenly he stopped, his bleary gaze settling on the candlestick. He swiped it up and came at her again brandishing it over his head like a sabre.

'Please Nick, please, don't hit me again. Please . . .'

At which point the door to the street burst open and Jack stood there with James at his side. The boy must have gone for his uncle when all the time Bella had thought him safely in bed. She didn't know which shamed her more – that his father had frightened the boy so that he'd gone looking for help, or that Jack was standing there in the doorway witnessing her pleadings.

'I told you Uncle Jack, he's nearly murdering her . . .' James said.

On hearing the childish voice, Nick paused in his assault, frozen in an attitude of battle and Jack, seizing the opportunity, swung a frenzied fist at him and sent him sprawling.

'Take that, you bloody villain,' he said so quietly it came out conversational.

He wrenched the candlestick from Nick's grasp and brought it down on his head felling him completely. From nowhere a stray memory came to Bella of a small boy smashing a crab to pulp on the strand in Bray.

NEW SPECTACLES

The whole house was up by now – and half the street as well, probably. Bella had often heard marital disharmony in other houses late at night like this; now it seemed, despite her best efforts, the Beavers were at the one level with their neighbours. Susan, flitting about in her chemise was trying to quieten Valentine and Baby John, both wide-eyed at the bloody spectacle. Babsie hadn't even had a chance to take off her coat. Armed with a bottle of iodine, she was tending Bella's bleeding brow. Bella's fissured tooth throbbed, but there was nothing Babsie could do for that. James set to and rebuilt the fire in the grate. Jack, meanwhile, was out in the yard, dishing out some stern words to Nick who had come to and sat cowed in a corner like a schoolroom dunce.

'You'll have no more gyp from him tonight,' Jack said when he came back in. 'Leave him out there till he sobers up.'

What would the neighbours make of that? Nick corralled in the yard with his birds until morning.

'This is what he's reduced you to, Bella,' Jack said, and with those doubtful words of benediction, he left her to the disarray.

'Maybe he needs spectacles,' Susan said as she viewed her father through the window of the scullery. 'Remember when he mistook Babsie for a man that time?'

Even now, after seeing Nick carted out feet first into the yard and dumped there like a bag of meal, Susan was too sheltered to see what was before her eyes. And the worst of it was, Bella thought, it was she who had schooled her daughter in this foolish optimism.

'Didn't Uncle Jack see a surgeon about his eyes? Maybe he could help?' Susan persisted.

And to humour her, Bella agreed.

She let some days pass before she could face calling around to Abercorn Road. Jack was sitting huddled by the fire, poring over a journal which he clapped shut as soon as he saw her.

'Bella,' he declared a shade too brightly, 'what brings you here at this hour?'

She sat down beside him on the sorry sofa, and glimpsed the title of his pamphlet. *The Irish Peasant*.

'What's that you're hiding?'

'Not hiding,' he replied, 'it's something I wrote, my first

publication. About Augustine Birrell and the hames he's trying to make of our schools.'

'Show me so,' she said.

He handed it over. She began to read his piece about the Chief Secretary. 'And though our poor children – the Hope of the Nation – will have to herd together in dismal places which a short-sighted yet well-meaning Government calls schools – though their tender and quick-witted minds be de-Irished and stupefied by a system which a paternal Government calls education; though they are taught to admire and revere the things of Europe, Asia, Africa, America, Australia and especially England; while their own country is to them bare of all useful and inspiring memories – her history unknown, her language unspoken, her music unheard, her achievements despised and her character unloved . . .'

Bella halted there for she could read no more of this sedition, its ill-tempered tone and the division the author tried to sow between Ireland and the Crown.

'Can't you manage any more?' Jack asked with a curl to his lip. 'I suppose *Elizabeth The Exile of Siberia* is more your style now, or some other penny dreadful.'

'I haven't lost my mind, you know,' Bella snapped.

'Unlike the Bugler Beaver.'

'It's about him I've come. Susan thinks he needs eye glasses.'

'Oh Bella,' Jack said with feeling, 'it's not his eyes are the trouble.'

'No, no really . . . hear me out.'

'That man has brought you down,' he said. 'Ruined every fine thing in you.'

He talked of her as if she was already dead.

'No, Jack, you are mistaken. It wasn't Nick who brought me down.'

Hot with denial, she almost divulged the secret she swore she'd never tell a living soul. How sweet it would have been to set aside Jack's certainties and clear Nick's name once and for all. But she couldn't for then she would have to admit to a lifetime of deceit and subterfuge.

'So what I saw the other night, that was a thing of nothing, was it?'

'He's not a well man,' Bella said, trying to appeal to Jack's better nature.

'That may well be so,' he conceded, 'but a pair of spectacles won't cure him.'

'What am I to do?' she all but wailed and did not give a fig what he thought of her. He had seen her at her lowest, a whimpering wreck and her children goggle-eyed with terror, so it was only a little further to give into despair in front of him. Was that what he was waiting to hear – this final abject admission? Was that what unfroze his heart that day?

'I'll look after it,' Jack said, 'but we'll be taking him to no eye doctor.'

They led Nick, one on each arm to a certain Dr Leavitt's rooms on Merrion Square. Nick was docile enough. He'd got it into his head that he was being presented to some high muckety-muck to receive a medal so when Dr Leavitt showed them into his well-appointed rooms – the oak desk, framed certificates of his prowess on the wall and an air of gloomy learning about it – Nick stood squarely and saluted. The doctor cannily enough took in the situation immediately.

'At ease, soldier,' he commanded.

Nick sat between them as the doctor did his examination. He shone a light into his eyes and tapped his chest.

'What year is it?' the doctor demanded.

'1889, Sir,' Nick said. The year they were married, Bella thought.

'And where are we, good man?'

'South Camp, Aldershot, sir.'

'Very good,' Dr Leavitt said, 'and why are we here?'

'I am the best shot in the regiment and I'm about to receive my prize plus a good conduct badge.'

Dr Leavitt stroked his bushy grey beard, tinted here and there with the russet of his youth. He was completely bald on top and so the whiskers were like ebullient compensation.

'And this lady, my good man, who is she?'

Nick turned his head and looked quizzically at Bella. What he saw was a patchwork of his own handiwork – a yellowed eye, a cracked tooth.

'Some doxy, sir, if you'll pardon me. Camp is full of them.'

Bella flinched. This was more cruel a blow than any inflicted by his fists. It was as if he saw through her at that moment, saw through all her pretences, as if each swipe he'd taken at her had been a righteous retribution for her ancient deception of him.

'I shall have to conduct a further examination,' Dr Leavitt said. 'Of an intimate nature. Would you both kindly wait outside?'

Nick looked at her with childish panic.

'He's not good with strangers,' Bella said.

'It's quite alright, Mrs Beaver. I have the measure of him.'

Jack opened the door and she stepped out into the hallway with him.

'What's all that in aid of, do you think?' she asked Jack once the door was shut on them. She found herself looking to him to have the answers, in the same way he had once looked to her.

'He's checking out his privates, Bella,' Jack said.

Before she had time to reply to this lewd candour, Dr Leavitt opened the door and ushered them back into the room of scrolls.

'Do yourself up, soldier,' he said to Nick.

'Take him out, Mr Casey, would you?' he said to Jack.

'Beaver,' Jack said in a clipped manner to Nick, 'this way.'

He had to direct Nick out for he had trouble negotiating rooms with which he was unfamiliar. He found it hard to find the exit.

'You do know what's happening to your husband, Mrs Beaver,' Dr Leavitt said when the door had closed behind them.

Bella shook her head.

'He's going mad. I was going to say quietly, but by the looks of you, he's quiet no longer.'

She blushed as if some terrible secret had been revealed, but it was written on her face.

'He has the general paralysis of the insane, the GPI, we call it.'

'Insane?' she repeated dully.

'He was a soldiering man, your husband, was he not?'

'Yes, the King's First Liverpools,' she replied, feeling a debt to be as proud of Nick's position as he once had been.

'I see,' the doctor said.

'I thought it was just the drink and maybe some trouble with his eyes. If I could only wean him off the whiskey, he might be more quiescent. It makes him agitated, you see, more prone to . . .'

'I'm afraid, Mrs Beaver,' the doctor interrupted, 'we cannot blame the demon drink for his condition. It goes a long way back, to his youth, if you know what I mean.'

But still she did not know what he was driving at. For the first time in her life Bella felt stupid and knew what it must be like to be the dullard in the classroom.

'You have children, Mrs Beaver?'

'Yes, five living.'

'And dead?'

'Just the one, our Nicholas, he died of the convulsions."

'I see . . . convulsions, you say?'

The image of baby Nicholas came to her mind, his sudden, awful end.

'And you, Mrs Beaver, are you quite well? Enjoy good health, do you?'

It seemed a queer thing for him to be making small talk about her health.

'No sores. Rashes? Complaints?' he queried. 'I mean, besides the obvious . . .'

Her broken features kept on intruding.

'I don't understand, Dr Leavitt, what has my health got to do with Nick?'

'Quite a deal, my dear,' he said.

The endearment caught her off guard so out of place was it.

'Listen to me, Mrs Beaver,' he said, leaning low over the desk like a conspirator. 'There is only one thing to be done here. You must certify your husband, sign the papers and have him committed.'

'The asylum?'

'Exactly so, Mrs Beaver,' he said rising from behind the desk and leaning his hands on the green leather inset with the gold trim. It was a beautiful piece with scrolled legs and brass detail. 'The Richmond is the only place for him.'

'Oh, I couldn't do that. Couldn't you give him something to calm his nerves?'

'It's gone beyond that now,' the doctor said. 'He is a danger to himself and to others. Certify him, Mrs Beaver, there's nothing else for it.'

He opened the door for her and stood sentry by it as she passed out.

Nick and Jack were waiting in the hall. Bella walked ahead

with Nick, steering him towards the hall door. Blessedly, he'd forgotten about the medal he was expecting to receive; otherwise, there might have been an unholy row for he could not bear to be denied even in the smallest things. The only medal that was handed over was the silver for the doctor's fee. She heard Jack and the doctor talking in low tones together, man to man, as she made her way out with Nick on her arm.

'Is it a case of whores-de-combat?' she heard Jack ask.

She turned her head in time to see the doctor nod.

Then, only then did she understand. Like Alfie Baxter coming slowly to his alphabet. It was the pox Nick had. The French disease, the syph. Whatever you called it, the shame of it was just the same. The plague caught from street girls who sold their wares to all-comers, who didn't give a fig for keeping clean or changing their drawers. She'd known Nick was no saint when he was a young man. And being away from home for months on end, he might have given in to temptations but he'd been out of uniform nigh on fifteen years, so why was the affliction only showing itself now? Unless . . . unless. Previously unimagined scenes began playing in her head. Unless when she was sitting at home nursing his children, he had still been lording it about with floozies. Was that it? And then she thought of baby Nicholas. Was that why he had succumbed? Why else did Dr Leavitt enquire? Did his father bring home some germ, a maggot picked up from a judy, that made her little boy sicken and fail? Bella had never felt such fury. She wanted to tear Nick's eyes out; to beat him bloody with her bare hands. She caught him bruisingly by the arm, just as he had often done with her. But when she raised her fist, she met not the proud swank of the Bugler Beaver, but the trusting eye and shambling mien of a madman, a helpless creature who couldn't tell his daughter from a soldier, who thought the doctor an awarding general, who could no longer find his own way home unaided. She let her hand fall and turned to Jack.

'Can you arrange it?'

'The clutchers, is it?'

She did not want the children – or the neighbours, indeed – to witness their father's incarceration. Or to know the awful truth of what it was that ailed him. So some days later when she'd signed the necessaries she brought Nick around to Abercorn Road so that he could be taken from a place where no one knew him.

'We're going round to Mother's,' she said to Nick,' for a nice little visit. We haven't been in ages.'

'I'll have to wear my scarlets so,' Nick replied, 'for I'm sure she don't approve of me.'

He was lost somewhere in the folds of time, as if they were a courting couple and he was still waiting for Mother's blessing, a blessing that would never come. Nothing would do him, though, but to don his uniform with the encrusted breastplate and the barley-twisted bugle cord. He wore his railway twills below so that he seemed a centaur, half-man half-beast, ill-fittingly put together. Bella had held the younger ones back from school so they could bid him goodbye. She'd told them their father was bound for the Blind Asylum. The subterfuge – no, she thought, the lies in which she had become so adept – was primarily for Susan's sake, who still nursed fond feelings for Nick despite the evidence before her eyes. James and Valentine did not think to question Bella's story either. Only Babsie remained sceptical.

'Will it cure him of the drink where he's going?' she asked.

When the time came Susan marshalled the boys into a row and Nick walked jaggedly before them as if inspecting a miniature parade.

'Your father's going away for a little while, to get his eyes fixed up,' Bella announced.

Nick shook their hands gravely, the man as trusting as the children, and all recognising the solemnity of the occasion without properly understanding it.

'Come,' she said to Nick tugging on his embossed cuff for she was afraid she might be overcome and the children must not see her upset.

'Why is that young lady crying?' he asked noticing poor Susan's trembling lower lip and brimming eyes. 'Did I make her cry?'

Bella's temper tightened. Too late, she thought savagely, too late for contrition now.

'Never mind that now, Nick,' she said in her firmest schoolmistress tone. 'We must be on our way.'

*

The black cab was standing outside by the time they reached Abercorn Road. It was not a long distance, but they had travelled slowly for Nick often made blindly for turns that weren't there and he got places muddled in his mind. He mistook Great Britain Street for College Green and nothing would persuade him that the Custom House was not Trinity College. The pewter-coloured river gave off its porter whiff, the barges bearing barrels from the brewery cruised by, the business of the city carried on regardless as they strolled, to all intents and purposes, a respectable couple taking a constitutional. Albeit that the gentleman looked a trifle odd, attired in motley, and the lady a little down-at-heel. Bella had thrown a shawl over her shoulders and worn a hat borrowed from Susan, but otherwise she'd not paid much heed to her appearance. It is not what a woman thinks of when she's about to have her husband locked away.

Nick did not register the cab. Jack was standing at the open door and when he saw Bella approach he gave the nod to the two coated keepers who were leaning against the hansom, smoking. They stubbed their butts out in the gutter.

'That's him,' Jack said.

Bella handed them the papers.

'Is he likely to go quiet, Ma'am?' one of them asked. He was a pale-faced ginger fellow with a pocked face.

'Where's Mrs C?' Nick asked.

'Change of plan, squire,' the other keeper said, a big bald brute.

'These kind gentlemen are to take you on a trip first, Nick. To tour a new barracks where you may stay awhile. So, just as well you wore the garb.'

She kissed him then on the lips, a Judas embrace. But there would be no pieces of silver for this particular transaction.

'Has he got the old delusions?' the ginger keeper asked as she let go of Nick's arm.

'Not another Napoleon,' said the bald one loudly, 'we have three of them already. Not to speak of several duchesses in the female block.'

'No,' Bella said, 'he thinks only that he is himself.'

She stood back as the two of them bundled him into the cab. She thought their unceremonious manner might arouse Nick's suspicions, but he was meekness itself. There was part of her, a contrary part to be sure, that wanted him to fight them off, if only to prove that his old spirit was somewhere intact, but it was a perverse wish. For that old spirit was so distorted now, its only expression was in rages and blows. She and Jack did not exchange a word as Nick was settled in the back. It was a terrible contract they had drawn up between them. Was this, she wondered, the fate he'd wished on Nick all along?

'Onward chaps!' she heard Nick command.

The cab lurched off with Nick shouting out from within: '*Nil desperandum*, Bella, *nil desperandum!*'

THE ORIGINAL SIN

The impressive pair of wrought-iron gates were firmly pad-locked, the chains bound tightly around the lock. Her ungloved hands fell to her side like a sigh. She peered in through the bars but could see no factotum she could appeal to. She stepped back and looked up at the spears of iron pointing sky-wards and was about to turn away, thankful to be thwarted. Then she noticed the small wicket diminutively hammered out of the large gates. Was it only the florid mad who got to use the grand entrance, she wondered. She pushed it open and slipped through. In the distance she caught a glimpse of granite, tur-rets and buttresses. She was bare-headed and empty-handed. She toiled up the driveway. Crows cawed crankily. On the stubbled grass she could see inmates bent at work. Some were lugging hessian sacks; others, armed with garden forks, the docile ones surely, were spearing leaves. They took no notice of her; madness, as she knew, bred incurious solipsism. The sky showed the remnants of summer. Nature smiled even on the feeble-minded, she thought, though she had fully expected pewter-coloured weather inside the confines of the Richmond Asylum, in keeping with her own creeping dread. She climbed the steps leading to the imposing front hallway, a mosaic of black-and-white tile and empty of furniture bar a marble-topped reception desk close by the door. A wardress in a brown uniform and stiff bonnet stood behind it.

'Yes?' she demanded.

'I'm here to visit my husband,' she said. She would maintain the pretence of decorum, even if her interlocutor wouldn't.

'Name?'

'Nicholas Beaver.' His name was her only identification in this place.

'Date of admission?'

'July 5th.'

It had been three months, she realised, and this was the first time she could face the ordeal of a visit. She contemplated the word. Wouldn't view be more accurate? As you would animals in a zoological exhibit. The wardress flicked the pages back and ran her fingers down the columns like a blind woman feeling her way through history. When she located Nick's entry, she drew a bell from a hidden compartment in the counter and rang it loudly.

'A beadle will come,' she said shortly and turned away.

Bella had to pace up and down for there was nowhere to sit in the echoing vestibule. At the far end stood two opposing arched doorways with the words MALES and FEMALES emblazoned in red overhead. This is the way life should be arranged, she thought grimly, to keep us free from the perdition that our coupling brings.

Suddenly her name was called. A beadle had appeared at the door marked MEN.

'Mrs Beaver, Mrs Isabella Beaver,' he intoned as if she were being presented at a Castle ball.

She wanted to flee. But what would the wardress make of such behaviour – as mad as any inmate within these walls? She quailed at the thought of facing Nick. Numbly, she followed the beadle. He was a portly man with an oily black handlebar moustache, all the world like a ringmaster in the circus. He wore a navy suit, and not the brown coats of the keepers, and clearly was of a higher rank. He took the chit the wardress had given her and pushed open the heavy door.

They were engulfed at once in a wave of sound, an underground roar as if they had been released into the very heart of a volcano. Down the corridor they trod past doors flung open on grim wards. The iron bedsteads were set so close to one another that the inmates' knees touched each other when they sat. Their suits were made of rough-hewn stuff, the trousers shapeless things, having accommodated themselves to a hundred nameless haunches. Their mealy jackets hung slack from their defeated shoulders. Pale forms slunk along the corridors close to the oat-coloured walls, skulking like dogs that expected to be kicked. They tugged at their neckerchiefs, scraping and scrabbling at themselves like animals with fleas. One man – though he hardly qualified for the term for he was a scraggy bag of bones with weasel eyes and matted hair – stretched out his hand imploringly to touch her arm, but the beadle, quick as mercury, yanked the creature's cravat so it closed around his throat and produced a ghastly choking sound. But it was barely audible above the woeful lamentation that seemed to emanate from every mouth. From one a demented muttering, from another avid calculation – the nine times table – and yet another engaged in full-throated bellows. It was a veritable symphony of pain. The beadle halted at a door at the end of the corridor and ushered Bella in with a flourish of his hand.

There were long sash windows in this room, but the sills were sloped making it impossible to gain purchase and were sited too high for any man to reach, even climbing on the shoulders of another. The grimy glass looked down on those within like the eyes of a mournful Master gazing down on those he'd decreed should suffer. As flies to wanton boys are we to the Gods, she thought. The light that filtered into the ward bore no relation to the nosegay sky outside. It was wan and dolorous as if it had grown thin and sickly in such surrounds. In this room all the men were tethered to their beds. Some lay on the naked ticking resigned to their incarceration, but the majority made play of even the most limited territory awarded them. They paced as far as their tethers would allow though their footfalls made no sound. No boots were worn in this ward – a man could string himself up by his own laces – so they sported woollen pampootees, those who weren't barefoot. Some sat on their beds rocking back and forth and moaning softly their private catalogues of grief and complaint. Others strained like dogs, spittle flying, trying to carry their beds with them – though they were like anvils since the frames were bolted to the floor.

Nick was one of these, though it was difficult at first to distinguish him so alike did all these creatures seem, a twitching mass of humanity, ants in drab engaged in minute, meaningless toil. Though his manacles were bound in cloth, one of them had chafed his ankle, yet still he applied all his strength to shift the bed. He was like an aviator and the bed a craft he was attempting to get airborne. But instead of making for the tantalisingly open door, he was straining towards a dun-coloured press at the far end of the ward. Its door was resolutely shut though the key lodged in the escutcheon was clearly visible. Like a lone swimmer, or an oarsman rowing against the current, he stood arms bulging with the effort, the cords on his neck in rigour, as he yearned towards the door he thought would lead to freedom. Even though during her visit, an orderly turned the key of the press to reveal shelves of metal chamber pots, Nick kept on eyeing it, convinced that escape lay in that direction.

'There he is Ma'am,' the beadle said pointing his finger. 'Number 0214.'

They'd let his hair grow, his lovely glossy hair once oiled and slicked back from his face, now hung in drifts around his blue unshaven jowls. He seemed to have shrunk not in height but in breadth; his shoulders once so broad and straight had caved in. The jacket he'd been assigned was too tight across his chest and gaped, the trousers were for a smaller man so they hung at half-mast. When Bella looked down, his feet were bare. That was the worst part. Never part a soldier from his bluchers, Nick used to say, for he feels naked without them. An orderly patrolled the small passageway between the beds.

'His eyesight is disordered, Ma'am, he may not recognise you,' he said. 'If you explain to him who you are, it will pacify him.'

'Nick, Nick, Nick,' she called out for in this room the noise was less underground swell and more roaring sea.

'It's your wife, Nicholas,' the orderly said as Nick looked past her at the cupboard door.

'Here,' he said catching Nick's chin and turning his face back towards Bella. Even in this, the simple act of looking her in the eye, he had to be directed. But finally, his face broke into a wreath of smiles.

'Nora!' he said.

'No, it's Bella,' she said evenly.

'Nora?'

'No,' she repeated, 'Bella.'

'It's Jennie,' he said emphatically this time.

She shook her head.

'Juno?'

She did not even bother to demur .

'Ethel?'

Molly, Bessie, Mary, Rose – with each new name he would beam at her, sure that he had her now. And each time she shook her head, his gormless glee would give way to a crestfallen dejection until he dredged another jade from his pantheon. All her feeling for him evaporated. She rushed from the room, brushing against a fellow inmate, who stood in her path frozen in an attitude of paralytic stillness. She fled down the corridor with its sickly hue and gaping portals of protest. The beadle who had escorted her was in his habitual position on guard by the main door.

'There you are, Mrs Beaver,' he said heartily like a flunkey in a fun palace. 'Leaving us so soon?'

'Open the door, if you please,' she said.

He got the measure of her mood then. He fished one key from a jangling loop that dangled from his capacious waist and inserted it showily in the big black lock. He heaved the heavy door open. It shut behind her with a thud, quenching the agonising clamour within and she was back in the Italianate hall.

The wardress had seen it a hundred times, a visitor emerging looking like the wreck of the Hesperus, as dishevelled and discombobulated as one of the inmates. What these innocents expected, she did not know. It was a madhouse, wasn't it? And yet some of them arrived as if to an Alpine sanatorium. Some even brought gifts! Tessie Archbold often thought of warning them beforehand, but she didn't. Better to keep your distance, keep it official. They would find out soon enough, anyway. And no warning could prepare them. They had to put their finger in the wound.

Bella took two or three deep breaths before moving away from the men's door. She longed to sit down but there was nowhere to sit in the hallway. It was a place for passing through, with dread on your way in and relief on your way out. Fresh air then, that's what she needed. She stumbled towards the main doorway but, like the destination in a dream, it seemed to recede as she went towards it. She did not remember the hall being so long, or was she, too, going mad? Behind her she heard the iron hinges of the men's door open again. She turned to look behind her, half-expecting to see Nick in pursuit, dragging his anchor bed behind him and still calling out names that didn't belong to her. But it was only two keepers being let out, escorting a chaplain. She stepped back out of their path as they passed her. Even a man of God needed protection here, she thought. The chaplain had a haughty bearing and a stately walk even though his suit looked oddly shabby. The keepers kept close to him as they halted by the counter at the far end of the hallway.

'Transfer,' barked the ginger keeper at the wardress. 'Leeper. Archie.'

The name, even in this slangy locution, reached Bella as if from a deep, watery recess.

'Where to?' the wardress asked.

No, it could not be! She felt for an instant an eerie sensation as if time were doubling up on itself. She was returned to the cowed young teacher standing on the threshold of St Mary's Infant School to be interviewed for the position of Principal Infant Teacher. She brushed the memory away. It must be another man of the same name.

'Incurables wing,' one of the keepers said loudly.

Bella pulled her plain shawl around her, hoping that might grant her invisibility. But something in her furtive gesture must have caught *this* Leeper's eye for suddenly the chaplain wheeled around and called out to her down the long passageway of time.

'Miss Casey?'

She could not mistake that voice.

'Yes, you, down there,' he repeated. 'Come out of the shadows so that I may see you.'

There were no shadows here, only the vast emptiness of the hallway and the darkness of her own heart. But meekly, Bella obeyed.

'Miss Casey, isn't it?' It was so long since she'd been Miss Casey that she barely recognised herself in the old appellation.

The clergyman shuffled forward flanked still by the keepers and they faced one another like chess pieces on the chequered floor. Bishop and pawn. There could be no doubt now. There was that inward face, the hair more unkempt than she remembered, that goitred eye. He seemed bowed down in some way, not as tall as she remembered. Her first impression of him that day of her interview in the schoolroom was that he was kindly. She recalled that when Miss Kidd asked her to play 'Abide With Me' on the harmonium and she stumbled over the second bar because she was so nervous and the instrument was new to her, it was he who had come to her aid. Laying a calming hand on her shoulder, he had motioned her to stop and turned to the Guardians.

'May Miss Casey go back to the beginning and start again . . . ?'

She felt lost in time, claimed by unruly recall. Was it this place? Could it unnerve you, render you as unstable as the people it housed?

'It *is* you,' he said.

And she had the self-same thought. This was no ghostly double, but the man himself, or a shadow of him. Leeper. His ministry among the mad now.

'Isabella!' He moved forward boldly.

She stepped back, her hands fluttering to her mouth like a nervous girl.

'I . . .' she began.

'I knew you'd come. I told them.' He jerked his head towards the two keepers. The ball of his jawbone chafed against his collar. 'Isabella will not let me rot in this place, I said . . .'

'Now Reverend,' the second keeper said. He was a rotund, bespectacled man with several chins. 'Why don't you leave this good lady in peace?'

Bella recognised the tone; she had often used it herself, a teacherly chiding of an obdurate child. Something on the keeper's wrist glinted, catching a shaft of sun glitter. It dazzled her momentarily until she realised what it was. It was a silvery bracelet with which Leeper was tethered to the fat keeper. He was an inmate of this place, not a servant to it!

'I have never stopped loving you, Isabella dear . . .'

'Steady on now Padré, less of the purple prose, if you please,' the keeper admonished.

'Isabella, please,' Leeper implored.

'Do you know this gentleman, Missus?' the keeper enquired.

But Bella was incapable of answering. Did she *know* him? The entire course of her life had been dictated by him. For thirty years she had been trying to escape his morbid sway. A wave of defeat washed over her. But then she looked at this supplicant creature in front of her with his quavering pleas, a sob in his voice. Wasn't he the one in chains? She felt a surge of power.

'No,' she said firmly, 'he has mistaken me for someone else.'

Leeper's face collapsed. He buried his face in his hands jerking the keeper's manacle in the process.

'Hear that, Padré, you're wasting your sweetness on the desert air. Come along, now, let's get you moving.'

'No, no wait,' Leeper cried out as they ushered him towards the main door. He tried to twist his head backwards to appeal to her again. 'Don't let them take me away.' He was shrieking now. 'Save me, Isabella, save me, save me, save me . . .'

Save him? She put her fists to her ear to drown out his dwindling cries. Save *him*? She made towards the counter so that she could have something solid to hold on to.

May Miss Casey go back to the beginning and start again?

Oh, if only she could go back to the beginning . . . if only she could start again. But to what point would she return? To which fork in the road? Was there any way to trace the root of her error?

'You look a little shook, Missus,' the wardress said.

She produced a water jug and tumbler and poured noisily.

'You mustn't mind them,' she said candidly, 'when the syph takes hold they fix on even complete strangers with their fancies.'

'The syph,' Bella repeated dully.

'Oh yes,' the wardress said.

'But he's a man of the cloth,' Bella heard herself say.

'Oh believe me, Missus, sometimes they're the worst. The Reverend there has had it for years. It goes quiet, see, and nothing shows, and then . . .'

Bella heard no more for she had passed into some nether region where every known truth was reversed. *He had the syph; he had the syph.* The words rang out as if an accusing jury had set up inside her temples. She pounded her forehead with her fists to drive the voices out. They fell silent but were replaced with a judge's cold arithmetic, a judge who had her own voice. *It is you who committed the original sin.* Her mind raced. If Leeper had had the syph, then it was he who was the source and she the wanton carrier, a typhus Mary ferrying disease between them and feeding her child the poisonous milk of death. And Nick? He was the wronged party, not once but twice over. It was *she* who had brought him to this hell. Every righteous conviction she'd held about her life had been mistaken. She was the guilty one; by right, she should be here among the spit-flecked mad. She had manoeuvred poor Nick into marriage with a terrible lie and brought to the degraded union a dowry of pernicious disease that had fingered its way into the deepest chambers of Nick's mind. No punishment was equal to *these* sins. In a moment, she had joined the company of the knowing damned.

'. . . and there's no saving them.' The wardress was winding up a speech she hadn't heard.

Bella took the water the wardress proffered and drank it in one clean gulp. The taste was pure, as she could never be again. Purity was the fortress of the innocent. There could be no escape for her. Everything in the end led back to Leeper.

She stumbled into the daylight like a dreamer woken from a hectic nightmare. She made blindly for the gates of the asylum, which were now thrown open, letting the pernicious influence of this wretched place free to seep out into the world. She did not stop running until she gained outside. She halted on the cobble to catch her breath. The liver-brick of the houses was solid, the beat of a rope and the chant of little girls skipping, beautifully quotidian. The drifting swirl of leaves, a golden reassurance. And yet she felt herself in a daze out in the unfettered world. It was like being new-born, with calf-legs, but ancient too with the burden of what she had just learned. It was not just that the last remnant of her innocence – or was it ignorance? – had been wrenched from her; it was that now, even in reminiscence, it could never be regained. *That* view of the world, and of herself in it, was entirely beyond her. She was a fallen woman, not just in the world's estimation, but in her own too.

TOTNES, DEVON, 1943

In the midst of the whimpering, there she was, starkly stretched out on the family bed, the clothes still disordered, part of her breast showing over the edge of a coarse shift made out of a flour sack. The remnants of the old shawl were still wrapped round her head, forming a rowdy cowl from which his sister's waxy face stared like that of a nun of the higher order of destitution salvaged from it for ever at last. He recognised in the dead face his sister of the long ago, for a swift bloom of a dead youth had come back to mock at the whimpering, squalid things arrayed around it ... Here lay all that remained of her piano-playing, her reading in French of Iphiegnia *and of her first-class way in freehand drawing. All that had to be done was to get rid of her quick as he could . . .*

There. The deed is done. He feels like a monster. His eyelids are on fire, the skin there craggy and folded like an elephant's jowl, a sticky yellow ooze snagged between what's left of his lashes. The old trouble with his eyes. He wants to rub them, strip away the layers of burning skin. He unhooks the rickety arms of his spectacles and lays them down on the scratched desk. Without them, what he has written is reduced to hieroglyphic waves.

The light in the upstairs room is brassy, autumn desperate in her late charms. His divan beckons but to stretch on it now would chime too much with the death-bed. There is no getting away from it. The incriminating scene may be an incomprehensible blur on the page lolling in the typewriter roller, but the memory of the moment is as sharp as pain. Now, as then, he cannot bear Bella's life, or her living of it. It has made a coward of him. He has just hurried her towards her end. He has played the magisterial god and chopped a decade from her sentence. With one stroke of his gavel, he has rendered Bella dead – again. It is a damnable business, this scribbling. Sometimes he longs to be the man whose only writing duty is the paper dart for the milkman – *two pints please*. He stares down at his assassin hands. They are strange to him, as if they belong to someone else.

Poor Bella. He cannot break the habit of appending the impoverished title. She seemed to attract misfortune, courted it, you could say. As soon as he thinks this, he berates himself. Blaming the poor for their condition, Comrade Casey? A nice how-do-you do! For a brief spell she'd played the bright scholar with her parcel of books, then the strict school ma'am ruling by arched eyebrow, before falling for the soldier, full of strange oaths. Oh and fall was the word for it. Once she'd met Beaver, Bella's life had been all fall. Trouble was that his sister's romance with destitution had demanded witness. His. He'd felt the burden of that witness. Too often he'd found himself playing walk-on parts in her mortification. Even with Beaver out of the way, committed. Committed indeed – the treachery of language!

The eviction was the beginning of it. No sooner was Beaver incarcerated in the Richmond than the notice was posted. It was he who'd brought Bella's attention to it. It had been plastered overnight on the front door in Rutland Place and was there when he'd come to call. He was allowed to visit Bella now since Beaver wasn't master of his own wits, let alone lord of this household. He felt a vague twinge of guilt. What kind of puerile superstition was that? As if their damned falling-out over the Boers had hastened the Bugler's decline. As if words of his had the power to madden! No, Beaver was a fool, wrongheaded, a bully who reached for boycott when he was outdone in argument. A pox on him!

He had just lifted the knocker on Bella's door when he

saw the notice to quit. *This is to declare* ... the proclamation of money-grubbers. His heart sank. He left the knocker fall heavily. The sound echoed in the rinsed early morning. The dawn-bleached street had not yet properly awoken. Red-brick snoozed, curtains drawn on bleary windows. As he stood there waiting for an answer, he remembered the Sundays he'd spent here as a boy, he and his brothers gathered around the piano in full-throated song while Bella accompanied. Even Ma had joined in then, when all was sweet-seeming domesticity.

Bella, with tumbledown hair and still in her nightgown, came to the door. He pointed wordlessly to the notice. She scrabbled at it desperately while looking furtively up and down the street for fear of prying neighbours. But it was a futile task. Jamie, the landlord, had used horse-glue. Anyway, even if she had managed to remove that one, there were two more pasted to the window panes.

The eviction was inevitable, any fool could have seen that. Any fool but Bella. The bully Beaver had at least provided; the madman Beaver couldn't. Babsie's pittance from the box factory was all that stood between Bella and penury. He'd heard Jamie making his threats.

'Eleven weeks Mrs Beaver and it's marked down agin you in black and white,' the creeping money-grubber had said.

'My husband ..,' Bella began, but Jamie waved her off.

'Everyone has a hard luck story,' he said.

No such thing as an hour of need with those boyos. Fumbling in the greasy till.

He was there, too, the day the bailiffs came. Three gruff fellas did the dirty work, making a funeral pyre of Bella's possessions on the street. How unprepossessing they seemed when piled out on the kerb. The sofa, a ragged beast upended. The wash-stand was forlorn, the fender bled rust-red in the rain. The dresser, once the bulwark of the house, seemed defenceless, the butter-box with the velvet seat, an abdicated throne, the tapestry screen, agape. Bella's pots and pans, thrifty on the stove, seemed patched and poor on the pavement. The beloved piano, stricken. Her bedstead – wretched source of her downfall – was like a ruined ship run aground.

He had stayed on guard with James and Valentine, while Bella took Susan and the baby and went hunting for somewhere they could lay their heads. Why she brought Susan along, he couldn't fathom. On Bella's say-so, the girl had been treated like a veiled novice. Another of Bella's vanities, that took on the hue of delusion. He could have told her that Susan's well-tended air, her neat bonnet and smart coat would be an obstacle on the mean streets where they would be forced to look for lodgings. The girl would be taken for the District Nurse, or, worse, the lady from the Cruelty Society and be distrusted *instanter*. And should she open her mouth, she would add to the suspicion that she was on some 'official' mission, for the girl had been encouraged in an accent. But he said nothing. Bella would only get uppity and accuse him of trying to peddle his ruffian politics.

She found a two-pair front room in a tenement on Fitzgibbon Street. The gable of the house was propped up by two great shafts of timber set in a field of rubble where its neighbour had once stood before it had collapsed. Truly, they were living in the ruins of Empire.

'The place is full of RCs,' Bella said as they stepped over the threshold. 'Who else would live in such parlous disarray?'

His argument, if he'd voiced it, would have been why should *anyone* be forced to live like this. It made his bile rise, not just for Bella's sake, but for the whole damned human race.

The walls were peeling – in places near the double windows, the plaster had come right away showing the pitiful skeleton of the house. Laths like fragile bones, innards of crumbling shale. The only clue to the room's former grandeur was in the ceiling rose. Centre-stage in the high-browed room. The floorboards creaked, the windows shivered. The lock on the door was gammy from too many forced entrances.

He watched as Bella and the girls scoured the floor – the place was crawling – and threw down rugs and pushed the sofa into familiar territory before the stove. Bella set the wash-stand behind the door. Here they would have to wash themselves and all they owned. The drop-leaf mahogany table that had come from Dorset Street, well-scored and scorch-ringed now, stood in front of the dresser, in a vain attempt to recreate the vintage comforts of Rutland Place. She ordered the piano to be placed in the Alcove Right. It might have looked the worse for wear out on the street, but in *this* room it seemed positively grand, as did Bella, though to her detriment. A tenement was no place for remnant respectability. The stage was set.

The boys slept top to tail on the one mattress in the Alcove Left. Bella and the girls shared the bed of shame. She had strung up a curtain around the girls' bedding – to preserve modesty, she told him, though in this squalid crush, how could anyone hold on to a modicum of dignity? He said as much, couldn't stop himself.

'Dignity,' Bella said, 'comes from within.'

Her pious certitudes infuriated him.

'It's slums like this that lost me my faith in god and man,' he said.

'Don't go conjoining our situation with any of your new-fangled notions,' Bella said sharply, 'for I won't have you spouting Darwin at me, who would have us all on the one level as chimpanzees.'

But looking at this crowded room – with the howls of children off-stage, the bellowing of husbands, the clatter of boots in rooms bereft of furniture and draperies – he thought the monkey in the jungle had a better situation.

*

The commode, as Bella termed it for she refused to call it the slop bucket, was housed behind the tapestry screen, once a proud appurtenance of the parlour. Susan was aghast at the lack of a lavatory.

'Nothing lah-di-da like that here, young Miss,' said Mr Pilgrim, the landlord's agent – a vile breed. 'You brings your own slops to the yard and the dung dodgers come twice a week.'

'It'll only be for a short while, Susie,' Bella said trying to quell alarm with falsehood. Was it to comfort the girl, or herself? But Susan refused to go when anyone else was in the room. So it became the drill for them all to be banished to the hallway while she attended to her duties. Visitors included. The neighbours found their exile hilarious and who would blame them? At first, they put it down to some Protestant practice of the Beavers.

'Is it like our Rosary?' one of the neighbours asked him, a raddled woman with a drinker's face, built solid as a street post box. Mrs Madigan, she was, though he didn't know her by name then. 'Or is it the indulgences, with all the travelling in and out youse are doing?'

The denizens of Fitzgibbon Street didn't beat around the bush. When they were curious, they asked, when they had something to say, they told you. Living cheek-by-jowl removed the niceties.

'No,' he said trying to make light of it. 'Nothing like that. Just taking the air, don't you know!'

'Watch out, so, for the air out here'll kill you,' she said. They followed the pathway of her laughter as she lumbered up two flights of stairs.

The lobby of Fitzgibbon Street was the front stage of the house. A constant traffic of cargo and humanity passed through trailing fumes and odours in its wake. It was impossible to do anything and be unobserved, someone always hovering in the wings. It didn't take long for the entire house to be privy to Susan's lavatorial excursions. When any of the ragged children saw Bella's brood gathered in the hall, they would holler out to all and sundry. 'Susan Beaver's on the throne!'

He was their only visitor. His mother kept away. Wouldn't lower herself, she said. But it was Bella's lowering Ma couldn't stomach. Bella came to them instead, bringing her dirty laundry, another matter of principle.

'I will not hang Beaver smalls out on their communal lines,' she declared. 'Even the most ragged shirt or threadbare skirt is likely to end up in their baskets. As for the girls' dainties, who knows what greasy paws of theirs might defile them?'

Everything in Fitzgibbon Street was *theirs*.

He did what he could. He couldn't offer money even though he'd got himself work on the railways. Casual labour, they called it, though there was nothing casual about it. His bones ached;

his hands were nicked and scarred. He wielded hammer and axe from dawn till dusk. It brought in measly spoils but at least it spared him having to doff the cap to some well-heeled boss. The gang he slaved with were like dumb animals, workhorses, silent for the most part, who lived blindly from one pay day to the next and poured the proceeds down their gullets. But they didn't trouble him with small-talk.

It was a paradox, but the mindless work freed his mind for his real vocation – writing. Articles and pamphlets and the like, just now, but he nursed ambitions he didn't talk about, so delicate did they seem, not robust enough for scrutiny. Particularly not Bella's. She would not approve. In this alone, he was still the awed and craven boy. Once he'd shown her an article he'd written. 'Sound the Loud Trumpet', it was, a broadside against the education system. Proud as a new parent, he'd handed it over, but she'd baulked after a few paragraphs. Hardship had mildewed her mind, and made her touchy with it. She seemed to take all of his propositions to heart. As if it were prim and proper Bella Casey and not the damned Chief Secretary Augustine Birrell he was having a go at. Still, he tried to help.

When he called to Fitzgibbon Street, he would set young Valentine mathematical problems for which he'd offer a small reward. It was a nod to the hours Bella had spent with him when he was at the same age poring over Tennyson and Wordsworth, though he had done such exercises for love, not reward.

'Would you not consider going back to the teaching, Bella?' he asked her, while Valentine laboured over his sums. 'You could start again.'

'From a place like this?' she said.

'Wouldn't you have somewhere to live, like the grand quarters you had in Dominick Street? And a fine salary and your children at their books instead of out slaving for the Bosses?'

She flinched, as well she might. She had just taken her eldest, James, out of school to be apprenticed to Swan's, the printers on Dame Street. Boy came home flecked with silver shavings but was paid in lowly coppers. He remembered the schemozzle when his mother had sent him out to work at fourteen. How Bella had berated her loudly, calling up the memory of his dead Da as ammunition. But she had been Miss Casey in spirit then: bright, indignant, full of mettle. First, the hardening of the heart, then the dimming of the intellect.

'I'm too long out of the teaching,' she said, 'too much water under the bridge entirely.'

'But Bella,' he countered, 'with all your experience and your gift for teaching . . .'

'Those gifts, as you put it, are of no earthly good to me here.' She gestured to the crumbling casements. 'And anyway, I don't see you putting your book learning to much good, bar agitation and rebellion.'

'But Bella,' he persisted.

'Look, Jack, leave it be, would you?' she hissed, casting a furtive eye on Valentine. 'You know why I cannot return to teaching. Must I spell it out? The computations can't be beyond you. Or do you still have only a child's understanding of my situation?'

'It's only,' he began, 'all this could have been avoided if . . .'

'If I hadn't married Nick, is that what you mean?' She was nettled now.

Valentine, totting up on his fingers, halted at the mention of his father's name.

'If you only knew the half of it,' she said.

'Not in front of the child, Bella,' he said with an edge of warning. He heard a kind of reckless imminence in her talk.

'Well, you're the one that brought it up. There's no undoing the past, we just have to wear our burdens with the grace of God.'

'God,' he snapped back, 'helps those who help themselves.' He wouldn't stand for her tambourine theology.

'Rich of you to be lecturing me about God, when Mr James Larkin of the Transport and General Workers Union is your only Lord and Master.'

Someone rapped at the door. The neighbours on Fitzgibbon Street kept theirs open at all times, but Bella would not join with the throng, not even in that. Her spirit showed itself in these adamant refusals. He half-admired her for them.

'There is nothing as desolate as the noise of poor humanity,' she had said. 'I try to shut it out.'

She went to answer the knock.

'Yes?' she demanded.

A child stood in the portal. Or rather a walking skeleton with the pallor of a ghost, her tiny claw gripping a chipped cup. There were two hectic spots of red on her cheeks like the powder on a corpse.

'Me Ma's looking for a cup of sugar,' the child said.

'Tell your mother we have none,' Bella replied. 'Off with you, now.'

She closed the door and put her shoulder up against it, as if the weakling child might try to storm the citadel.

'What ails her?' he asked

'Consumption,' Bella said.

'More victims,' he said 'of the inequitable system.'

'The system, is it?' Bella cried. 'A neglectful mother, more like, who sends a tubercular child out to walk the halls bare-foot, spreading her contagion.'

'Where is your mercy, Bella?'

'I cannot afford mercy towards those who despise me. You don't know how they treat me.'

But he did. To his shame, he'd seen it for himself.

One summer's evening he'd stood on the street and watched from the long shadows as the congregation of slatternly-looking women gathered on the steps. No 21 Fitzgibbon Street was a kingdom of women; the menfolk out working, or skiving more likely. That evening a child had been sent for a jug of beer so the talk on the doorstep was lubricated and the laughter raucous. In time he came to know them all. Mrs Gogan, Bessie Burgess, Mrs Madigan. Even little Rosie Redmond.

Mrs Burgess, who sold fruit on the street, was leaning on the handle of her perambulator, a perennial pose. She was a handsome woman, chestnut thatch chopped to her ears, her face a pocketful of florid jowls. Inside the pram was a stash of produce, soft fruit on the turn.

'Oh, here she comes,' she cried as Bella came along. Seeing the welcoming party, Bella stiffened. Playing the part; playing into their hands.

'If it isn't our lady Protestant,' Mrs Gogan chimed in. She was thin and beady, a pinny swaddled around her scrawny waist, vigilant eyes set deep in a skull-like face.

'Good day to you, Mrs Gogan,' Bella replied. She meant it to be civil, he knew, but it came out superior.

'Is Madawm taking the air?' Mrs Burgess said. 'Been on a prominawde, have we?'

This a take-off of Bella's diction. The assembled company erupted in guffaws. Mrs Burgess did a twirl, her pinkies cocked for imaginary tea. She stood in the doorway, blocking Bella's progress.

'Let me pass, Mrs Burgess.'

'Pray, let me paws,' Mrs Burgess mimicked to more hoots of

derision. It was, he thought, pure theatre. By rights he should have intervened. A man approaching would have punctured the female ribaldry. He could have piloted Bella by them and saved her from the worst of it. But something stopped him. Selfishly, he wanted to see how the drama would enfold.

'Give us an old song, there, Mrs Beaver,' Mrs Burgess insisted. 'Aren't we having a bit of a shindig here and you'd be welcome to join in.'

Bella remained flinty.

'Give us a bar of "Rule Britannia", why not? Isn't that what your lot would be singing?' Mrs Gogan said.

Bella stood her ground. The tableau stalled. He could see that scene to this very day; he'd used it on the stage, after all, but no amount of artful scripting could remove the original from his memory. Or was the opposite true? Had he killed the real people off by turning them into characters? Eventually, Mrs Burgess gave way when her goading failed to raise a row. Bella furled her shawl with a flourish, and made her way into the house, braying laughter in her wake.

'Snotty Orange bitch,' he heard Mrs Gogan call after her when she was out of hearing.

For him, it was different. He was saluted cheerily.

'There you are, Mr Casey, and no mistake!' they would greet him.

'Ladies!' he would say and doff his cap.

(Ladies, he could hear Bella explode, ladies how are you!)

They liked him in equal measure to their distrust of her. He thought his friendliness might soften their hearts towards Bella, but she undid his work each time. If he lingered on the steps for even passing pleasantries, she would call him in ostentatiously.

'Jack? Is that you?'

As if she were a mother summoning a child away from unsuitable companions. He saw the women's rolling eyes, the smirks behind their hands and knew what they were thinking. A mammy's boy, at Lady Beaver's beck and call.

Bella had more in common with the Greek chorus on the doorstep than they knew. She, too, was gathering coppers one by one to feed her children and to keep want at bay. Like them, she ducked and weaved to avoid the rent-collector, down to the pawn on a Monday and redeeming on a Thursday, hiding in the back room when the insurance man came to call. She used all their devious tricks to thwart old Pilgrim's Progress. When the agent called, she would get John to answer the knock while she hid behind the door and watched him through the crack.

'My mother's out,' the child would say exactly as Bella had instructed him. Or she's at the dairy or she's visiting my granny. Or she's gone to church. If Mr Pilgrim believed that, he must have come down in the last shower, for by John's accounts, Bella spent half the week on her knees. There would be no

Geography Generalised for John; no *Superseded Spelling*. Bella was schooling him to tell bare-faced fibs and hoping to trade on his big bright eyes, his curly hair, his angelic looks to beguile and to deceive.

No, the only difference between Bella and the other denizens of Fitzgibbon Street was that they had grown up with perpetual scrimp and save and she had not. They whiffed that off her, his scruffy sibyls. They thought she'd been born with a silver spoon in her mouth. So it was sport to them to take the Duchess down a peg or two. That was their nickname for her. The Duchess of Fitzgibbon Street. It was a source of glee to see a woman of better birth brought down and they delighted in it. Tuppence looking down on tuppence-halfpenny. The law of the jungle.

If only Bella could have seen what he saw. That their humour was a comic pride, the light-hearted twin to her po-faced disdain. That if she could have unbent a little, she might have made something honourable of her life on Fitzgibbon Street, mean and all as it appeared. She could have suckled from the solidarity of the working poor. But Bella insisted on her singularity.

'We may be equal in our hardship,' she would say, 'but not in our bearing of it. They're off down to that Society of theirs or calling round to the back door of the convent with their hand out. If that makes me Lady Beaver, too uppity to beg, then so be it.'

'You could take the Outdoor Relief,' he ventured. It wasn't much – two loaves, a few grains of tea, a pound of sugar weekly – but it would have kept the wolf from the door.

'I won't become a charity case,' Bella said. And that was the end of the discussion.

The world, both big and small, had changed around her, but she would not budge. She'd set her mind against it. *He'd* changed and she'd never forgiven him for it. He was a worker, a trades union man, an Irishman. He spoke a different language. When he had first started learning Gaelic, the words had sounded strange in his mouth, like clods of fresh-turned earth. But as his tongue found its way around them he grew to love their loamy texture. He'd even changed his name. Not plain, unadorned Jack Casey now, but Seán Ó Cathasaigh, a bardic handle drawn out long and slow by its ennobled vowels. Citizen now, not subject. But Bella remained constant despite her altered circumstances. The paradox of it was that she was more *herself* in mean Fitzgibbon Street, more the strict and proper schoolmarm than she had ever been when she'd stood before the infant class. The tenements had found the untested girl in her, except that on Fitzgibbon Street, that girl had been turned into a figure of fun.

Although he abhorred its very existence, he revelled guiltily in Bella's new world. Her degradation became the mother of his invention. Fitzgibbon Street was the large world writ small.

The plays that he would one day write were performed for him daily there. They came to him personified. What a cast these women made – his women, he came to think of them as – with all their fickle prurience, their rowdy ebullience, their self-serving pride! They were characters already, born and ready-made, roaming their foetid rooms in search of a writer. He'd changed their names, of course, but now when he remembers them they seem to have inherited his monikers and forgotten their own. Mrs Gogan, with her thin laughter and sly mimicry, or Mrs Burgess, brave with porter, letting fly with acid wit, were already on the stage before he ever came along, declaiming to the world from the steps of Fitzgibbon Street. Even the little street-walker, Rosie Redmond, all painted up and glam, who lived on the second floor and came home at all hours of the night found a way into his heart. He'd seen her often, trailing in, but he dared not to talk to her. Bella had outlawed all contact with her.

'An offence to decent people,' she said.

Her girls, she'd ruled, must not even greet the likes of Rosie, in case they'd be corrupted. Out of deference to Bella, he steered clear of Rosie in the house. But there was nothing to stop him seeking her out elsewhere.

He buttonholed her on Burgh Quay one night. Slip of a thing she was. Cap of limp hair, teeth too big for her crowded mouth, flashing her garter to all-comers and eyeing him up winsomely. She didn't recognise him at first. He was just another Mr Gentleman.

'Care for a squint at a trim little leg?'

He gloried in his incognito.

'Let us go in out of the cold,' he said.

It was a windswept place that quay, a gale blowing in off the river and she out in next to nothing. He led her to the snug of the White Horse and ordered for them both. A shandy for himself, a snifter for her. Her hands when cupped around the glass were red-raw.

'Oh,' she said, 'it's only you, Mister Casey.'

Then she brightened.

'Sure afterwards,' she said, stroking him on the arm, 'you and me'll go someplace quiet, isn't that so?'

'Let's just sit and talk,' he said. 'I'll pay you just the same.'

'Are you only for the talking, Mister Casey, is it? Sure who'd pay for that when he can gets it for free?'

'So tell me,' he began and then he stopped. Pen poised in his head. What was it he wanted to know? The squalid details, the sordid mechanics? No, nothing like that, only to hear her talk.

'Them's that have it, use it, them's that don't grows old and dry.'

As he was in in danger of doing. His comrades on the railways would go to Monto, take a twirl with a doxy there, but he was too busy in the world of men, arranging meetings, organising, preparing for the revolution that would sweep all before it. He smiled for the young man he had been. Too earnest by half, too lofty for his own good, but how else was the work to be done? He went with Rosie Redmond that night, all the same. She lifted off his glasses in a doorway on Mountjoy Street and took him expertly in hand.

The news of Bugler Beaver's death came to Abercorn Road since it was from there he had been carted off. He'd been the one to steer his brother-in-law into chains, now he had to pronounce his final punishment. It was evening, winter-dark. He walked under the clear delineation of the plough, his breath came in globes.

'Passed on this AM,' the telegram had said, as if Beaver had died a glorious death in battle. Out on a foreign field. Which, he supposed, the Richmond was, in a manner of speaking. He'd never been, but Bella had gone to visit. For what, he did not know. Beaver had retreated to infancy, become no more than a babbling baby, a talking shell. Yet, even though his brother-in-law had been counted already as good as dead, his children training to be orphans, and Bella girding herself for the widow's weeds, he still dreaded the delivery of the final verdict. Must he always be the bearer of bad news? This news, in particular. Because he'd wished for it, a lifetime ago, on the beach at Bray, with a stone in his hand.

The front door in Fitzgibbon Street was thrown open, despite the lateness of the hour. He knocked, then let himself in to Bella's room, bringing a gasp of the cold night in with him.

'Bella,' he said simply.

She was sitting in the rocker by the dimly glowing grate, the boys abed, the girls still abroad somewhere. She was reading, and for a moment some old admiring flame leapt in his heart, as if time had doubled back on itself and these past twenty years had been a nightmare from which he had just been roused. He saw the scholar Bella with her books spread about her, glow of the oil lamp on her bowed head. But he shook off the consoling fantasy. It wouldn't be Racine she'd be reading, or *Love's Labours Lost*; no, more likely some cheap novelette and when she looked up, it was not as Isabella Casey but as Bella Beaver. Her blouse warning of its end, a soiled apron, a pair of shattered boots.

'It's Beaver,' he said simply.

This was their new language with one another, a terminal shorthand.

'Nick?' she asked, rising slowly, the rocking chair nodding in her wake at lullaby pace. She moved to embrace him. Standing in the poor light, his coat and muffler making a soft embrace against her threadbare blouse, he felt like the ghostly embodiment of the man he'd come to bury. Bella's shoulder blades were like two crushed wings in his arms. He thought he felt something give inside her. A tiny knuckled cracking as if she had reached her breaking point. He expected tears but she merely clung to him, dry-eyed. Had she, too, mistaken him for the Bugler, the husband of old, the soldier returned? But whatever phantasm it was, it couldn't hold. The icy draught from the open door fingered its way into the room. Death entered the household.

'It's all over, so,' she said.

Amen, he breathed, amen.

By the time the funeral was paid for, it was bread and scrape for every meal. Bella's precious items - her candlesticks, the wedding bowl, her engagement ring – had been in and out of hock a dozen times, just to cover the necessities. A pair of boots for James, a bottle of quinine for the baby, Valentine's school fees. Meanwhile, Susan sat at home and embroidered squares, a proper little Lady Muck. That girl was like a statue behind glass, an object of veneration, the virgin child.

'Put Susan to work,' he told Bella. 'My god, woman you're in dire straits.'

'No, Jack, I can't, I promised ...'

'And who did you promise?' he persisted, thinking this was some youthful pledge she'd made to Beaver. Part of her loyalty to old things.

'I promised myself,' she said, 'that I would spare her that.'

'Spare her what?'

'She wasn't brought up to work.'

'And why not?'

'Because . . .' Bella seemed lost for words. 'She needs protecting.'

'From what, in god's name?'

'The slings and arrows . . .'

It was his rule never to lose his temper until it would be detrimental to keep it, but this was no time for Shakespeare. He raised his voice.

'It isn't natural, Bella. How can you keep her from life?'

'Susan is an innocent.'

'Only because you've *made* her so.'

She smiled at him. Not wanly, but as if this were some great victory.

Like all their arguments, it ended in uneasy truce. But, something in what he said must have struck home and spurred Bella into action. This time he entered in mid-scene. Bella standing by the stove, stirring a thin concoction.

'I've just been telling Susan that I've made arrangements for her to go out to work.' She said it in a tone that begged endorsement. Pitifully bright.

Susan glared at her mother with such hostility, it was as if Bella had just struck her. She was loitering by the window. Thin hands, thin face, a thin demanding nature, he'd always thought.

'Yes,' Bella replied.

'But you said . . .'

'I know what I said, Susan, but . . .'

'You said you would never allow me to roughen my hands, to mix with a bad crowd, to demean myself with common labour . . .' There followed a litany of all the foolish principles Bella must have declared when she could afford to have them. Before Susan could exhaust her list, Bella interrupted her.

'Look here, my lady. You eat, don't you?'

Susan nodded dumbly.

'Well, there's not enough food for you here.'

'You would deny me food?' Susan asked, incredulous.

For once, he was at one with Susan, aghast at his sister's shrewish ultimatum. Oh Bella . . . so against her nature was it that she had to reach for cruelty to go through with it.

'Yes,' Bella said, buoyed up by her imposture. 'From now on you have to earn what you eat.'

'If Dada were here, he wouldn't stand for this,' Susan said. The ghost of Beaver hovered, done honour by the only one who maintained tenderness for him.

'Well, he's not. So it's me you have to deal with now,' Bella said. 'And isn't he the reason we're in this pickle?'

'Is he to be blamed for being sick, and then to die?' Tears threatened.

Tell her, he willed Bella, tell her.

But Bella hadn't the bottle for the undiluted truth. She would not tell the girl that her precious father had brought the pox into the house and with it ruin on them all. If it were up to him, he would have ripped the scales from Susan's eyes.

He would have told her all and rid her of this useless, much-prized innocence of hers. Susan wiped her face. Hot tears gave way to sullen resignation.

'What class of work?' she asked.

'At the Misses Carolan on Sackville Street. Oh Susan, you should see it, those hats are only gorgeous, with feathers and plumes and my friend, Clarrie, is in charge there, and she'll look out for you.'

He imagined Bella going cap-in-hand to the plush milliner's, begging for a job. From Clarrie Hamilton, of all people! She who had never reached Final Standard! Whose forthright manner and lack of social graces Bella had once been so lightly mocking of. Now it was the likes of Clarrie Hamilton who had Bella's welfare in her gift. The new world, Bella, he wanted to say, welcome to the new world.

'And what will I be doing?' Susan asked.

'I told Clarrie how good you were with a needle and she said you'd be just the ticket for all those small finicky bits on the hats and the like.'

This, he thought, is what your mother has been saving you for. A life of miniature slavery.

Work was a rude awakening for Susan. For the first time he felt for the girl. She slaved in a dark, ill-lit room behind the Misses Carolan shop, where oil lamps burned all day and a cluster of girls slaved over trimmings for the gentry. Luckily for her, she didn't understand the mechanics of her exploitation, how every fancy she sewed propped up the class divide. She only knew that her fingers bled for weeks from where she had inadvertently stabbed herself, that Miss Carolan threw any piece that was not picture-perfect back on the cutting-room table to be ripped and done again. In her first week, she spent three days - three days! - attaching sequins, one by one, to a hat bound for the lady of the Vice-Regal Lodge.

'Her perspiration was woven into that wretched piece,' Bella complained, 'so often did she have to go back over it.'

'It's a sweat shop, Bella,' he told her, 'that's what oils the capitalist engine.'

'But this was *your* idea!' Bella cried.

'That girl's sweat is all that stands between you and the workhouse ward.'

Only in Bella's other girl, Babsie, could he see the change he hoped would come. How she and Susan had grown up in the same household, fruit of the same loins, he could never fathom. Like chalk and cheese, they were. Babsie, stalwart and sound and wearing the ribbon, where Susan was brittle and fey. He cheered inwardly when she led her box factory girls out into the street.

'A strike, is it?' Bella was beside herself.

'The union, Mam, the Trades Union. One out, all out,' Babsie said.

'The same union your Uncle Jack's always preaching about, is it?'

Bella spoke of him as if he weren't there.

'They sacked Jennie Claffey,' Babsie said. 'We're all going to walk out for her.'

'Since when were you mixed up in that class of thing?'

'Ah Mam, you don't be listening to me, that's the trouble.'

Babsie had a point. Her mother fretted night and day over Susan, but Babsie, being resolute, was overlooked. The noisy world hears least of strongest minds.

'How are we going to manage with you out on the street?'

'It was a clear case of victimisation, Mam!'

'Isn't one victim enough for you?' Bella demanded.

He could hear the panic in her voice.

'Uncle Jack,' Babsie appealed. 'You're with me, aren't you?'

'Don't be looking to him,' Bella said, 'Uncle Jack is not going to put food on our table for all his talk.'

'You won't persuade me out of it, Mam, it's all decided. A principle's a principle.'

'It's all just empty talk, Babsie.'

Then Bella turned the residue of her ferocity on him. 'This is all your fault. I curse every incendiary word she's heard from you. And do you know the worst of it? I opened the door to this corruption. I let you in.'

Was this how she saw him? An agent of contamination?

When he was the sole guardian of all that was fine in her, even when Bella herself seemed to have forgotten it. He had cherished the memory of the young woman in the cape and skirt with the satchel full of books, and the careless, blooming mind. He had burnished it, for God's sake, daily. Love can do that, smooth away the weary lines, unwrinkle the puckered pouches beneath the eyes where unshed tears are stored. Unpepper hair. Halt the downward drift of mouth and hopes.

But there was some contagion even Bella couldn't blame him for. The Lock-Out had them all outside. At last, he thought, it begins! The city roused itself from its supplicant torpor. The toffs arriving for the Horse Show in Ballsbridge found the trams lying idle and deserted. Let them ride their stallions home. The match girls, the poplin workers, the foundry-men all followed suit, and made a theatre on the streets, instead of playing docile at their benches. He remembered still the foment, the rush of exhilaration like thousands finding infatuation at the one time. Larkin on the balcony, hands raised not in surrender, but in exhortation. Arise! Who runs the city now? *His* crowd, at last. Shoulder to shoulder, the over-worked, the under-paid, the ants that toiled by day and night, turned into one solid mass. Until the constabulary charged them with batons raised. Enemies of the people, drink on their breaths. Club us, he thought, and we will rise again for there are more of us than you can imagine. Orators sprouted on every corner in megaphone semaphore. *More pay! A shorter week! Down with scabs!*

Even Bella reaped the benefits. Her slate at the Pioneer Stores was into double figures, but Mr Heneghan had a son on the railways and he went easy on any family with a striker in their midst. Surely now, he thought, she will see how her plight is as one with those on the street, not separate to it. But, damn and blast it, if that flibbertigibbet Susan didn't drive her back into the arms of singular respectability.

When all the world was losing theirs, Susan ditched her job at the Misses Carolan. Some young man had turned her head and popped the question. The promise of ring papers finally brought Bella's poverty home to roost. If the girl was to wed, Bella had decided, it would have to be from a decent address.

She did a runner from Fitzgibbon Street, owing all around her. Stole away in the dead of night, leaving half her meagre appurtenances behind her. He didn't mind that – that wretch Pilgrim deserved no better, two bob a week for that hole! Fight fire with fire, that was his motto. But Bella had run out of places to run to; there was nowhere left but home. He arrived back to Abercorn Road late one evening to the invasion. Bella and her brood were ensconced in the front room. *His* room. Now a rag-and-bone shop. The house, once a sanctuary, was like a barracks hall. Nowhere to sit, not even a corner of a table at which to write, not a vacant chair that was not decorated with a child, or evidence of one. To think was nigh on impossible with an audience dumbly eyeing him as if he were a forbidding master, his nose forever in a book. That was Bella's constant complaint. As if reading were an indulgence and her need, obscurely, made into his doing. At night when they all bedded down together, the humid crush of small bodies was suffocating. The boys snuffled in their sleep like little animals suckling at an empty tit, they tossed and turned. He could not shut out their vivid nightmare cries.

He had not bargained for the venom in his heart when he saw his mother trying to divide her widow's mite like the loaves and bloody fishes. The kitchen turned into a souper's queue. All those mouths to feed. Like birds with gaping beaks. Bella's youngest, John, could speak testaments with his hollow eyes. Had she trained the child to look like that? His eyes yawning at each morsel. If a crumb were to drop, he swore the boy might go scurrying after it on all fours.

Bella tried to appease by exiling Valentine and John to the street during the day. For play, she said, but what capacity did those poor children have for play? It was only show, anyway, like Bella doing mathematical conjuring so that he and his mother might not notice that where there once had been three, there were eight now. She had turned home into a tenement and made them all the poorer for it.

If her children were quiescent, Bella's own need turned

voracious. Like a near-drowned fly in a jar of water, she flapped against the bowl of her confinement. When she was in the tenements, she would stoop to neither charity nor mendicancy. But now she preyed on all of them, him, his mother, did the rounds of Mick and Tom. A penny for this, sixpence for that. She wheedled and cajoled. Like a madam in a brothel selling her children's urgencies as forfeits for small change. The boys' schooling, the youngest's snotty nose, a piece of baffety for a wedding dress, if you don't mind, for the Lady Susan. Suddenly, after years of stubborn resistance, Bella surrendered. She stuck her hand out, hardly even resorting to words. She seemed all want. Wanton want. Even her pride, foolish and all as he had thought it, deserted her. Whatever obstinacy had fuelled her on Fitzgibbon Street, seemed to gutter and go out once in the bosom of her family. As if the only flame that had animated her was opposition. Against her neighbours, against the world on account of Beaver, as if the lifetime she'd spent defending him had exhausted her. (Can a life be lived like that, galvanised by trying to prove the contrary true?) And with the Beaver gone, there was no fight left in her.

He took to staying out himself. He'd rather walk the streets, than witness this last of Bella's diminishments. He'd have traded the haughty Duchess of the tenements any day for this new abjection, the impoverishment of her spirit. Dammit, though, he missed Fitzgibbon Street, those rancid rooms, that rancorous wit. But there was another reason he was avoiding home. She was a certain fresh-faced girl by the name of Máire Keating whom he'd met at the Laurence O'Toole drama club. She was twenty-two, with chestnut hair and hazel eyes which she hid under a broad-brimmed hat. There was always a ruffle at her full white throat, a sprig on her pert lapel, a fragrance of lavender dabbed behind her ears. She was a school teacher and a Catholic, so he couldn't bring her back to Abercorn Road. It would have broken his Ma's heart; another Casey son gone bad. Máire was a lovely thing, well brought-up, respectable. What would she make of Bella's hungry horde? He did not want her to see them, this shameful secret of his. But that was the least of it. How could he bring Máire face-to-face with Bella? It would have been like holding up a mirror. Here is what you were; this is what you could have been . . .

That looking-glass gaze was what decided him to finish her off. The candour of reflection. It was no easy task. He'd had to resort to all the Lazarus tricks of fiction to craft that final scene, and all sorts of stagecraft to populate it. Bella had been alone when she died. Unlike her other mortifications, there were no witnesses on that infant dawn when she slipped away, so he'd *had* to invent. He'd cast his mind back to another day altogether, a day of beginnings. The day when Susan was born, when he'd crawled out from under Bella's birth-bed and saw her stretched out, the globe of her breast on show, the sheets in a bloody tangle and he'd thought she *was* dead. He remembered the minutes slowing to the dead march of his own heartbeat, the whole world seeming to stop. The loss of her had been his childhood's most haunted dread; now he enacted it on the page.

He ranged her children all around because he couldn't bear to think of Bella alone. He summoned them from the night he clobbered Beaver with the candlestick. He remembered young James coming to his door, tears drying to grime on his cheeks, so terrified he could barely get the words out. *He's going to kill her, he's going to kill her*. Valentine and John, still babies then, hiccoughing with fright when he arrived – he drafted them in too, then added the shivering girls as part of the general squalor around Bella's death-bed. What did it matter if it wasn't fact? It was true, wasn't it? She had died as she had lived, a condemned woman.

The light has changed. The sky has turned bronze after the sudden vehemence of a hail shower. The 4.45 train rumbles by on its way to the station; is that Eileen's Ford he hears, back from an outing with the children? They have three evacuees staying with them, bright cheeky kids from London, who will scamper up the stairs, hallooing, and disperse the mood of the silent house. He sets down his pages. If there's a heaven, and god knows he doesn't believe there to be, he wants it to exist if only for Bella's sake. Who deserved an after-life more than she did? He laughs at himself. A Paradise specially constructed for his sister – now *there* was an imaginative perversity. In the meantime, this will have to do, he thinks, an immortality of sorts. Bella as glorious failure – in life and on the page.

He rises and pads blindly downstairs and into the kitchen. He stoops over the Belfast sink, deep as a trough, and turns on the tap. Cupping his fingers under the cold flow he splashes his face; it brings no relief. His eyes protest; if they could speak, they would scream. When he straightens he is assailed by a lurid crimson bloom. A blood-shot vision and no wonder after what he's done. But no, it's only the roses waving stalkily, the garden's velvety roar. Steady, he tells himself. It's a mercy kill-ing. He has put Bella out of *his* misery. He retraces his steps, up the stairs and into his study. The return room. He puts his spectacles back on, extricates the page from the typewriter and begins to read.

BROADWOOD

THE GREAT SILENCE

The first night home in Abercorn Road, Bella lay wakeful well into the night, gazing at the moon. Clouds scudded across its face so that it seemed to frown as if the very heavens disapproved. But the rest of the household slumbered not noticing the recrimination of the elements. It was an odd sensation to lie so close to Mother that she could almost hear her heartbeat, though when she turned on her side it was her own pulse she could hear and it disturbed her. For it was just one more thing she had no dominion over. She watched Mother's stony profile hoping that she might, in sleep, steal from her some glimmer of forgiving softness. But even in slumber, her mother did not seem to yield. Bella felt the leaden weight of her years, and the downward spiral of her circumstances like a clock running down, that had brought her back to the beginning again, but in such a reduced state. As the moon turned its eyelid down, Bella thought this must be what it is like to be dead, to have already entered the Great Silence.

But if her spirit was restless, her body was like as a corpse on a slab. As if an unseen hand, dispassionate as a coroner, had stripped her, bared her breast, her Mount of Venus, her very liver and lights, in search of the root of her ruin. That God was ever-watchful, she had always believed. Now she felt another presence, this one with a voice. Perhaps it was the voice of her conscience, so long dimmed in service to a respectable life. Bella Casey – for this is how the voice spoke as if she were starting out again – this is your epitaph. That you ruined a life in return for your own ruined life. An eye for an eye.

Even now, months after his death, the thought of Nick made her wither. Regret was too polite a word for it, too lady-like a sentiment. She could dispense with such refined feelings now for she did not merit them. She might as well have laced his porter with arsenic. Had she done so, at least he would have had a quick, intoxicated death, as opposed to the tormented end he had, straining after phantoms. There was no chance, either, of expiating her sin. Who was there left to tell? She envied those Catholics their weekly jaunt to the confessional. If she could only whisper her crime into the velvet darkness . . . but of, course there was always a clergyman present. And Bella would not confide in any clergyman. The Romanists talked of a place called Purgatory where sinners gathered awaiting a final verdict and from which they might be rescued by indulgences paid by the living. Bella had always found the idea repugnant, worse even, idolatrous. For how can a soul be *bought* into the light? That is in the Lord's dispensation, and His alone. But now if she could only believe that there was such a place for her, she would have gladly embraced it. She would have settled for anywhere that was not the eternal fires of Hell. Unless, of course, she was in Hell already. For surely it was the devil's own revenge that not only had she destroyed Nick with her false heart, but she had engendered in her children the possibility of repeating his madness. And how many years of reprieve could she expect for herself, before the dread syph would show itself again? She was on borrowed time, living in her own epilogue. I can't go on, she thought. But she did.

When she went to rouse the boys in the morning, Jack opened a sticky eye and cast her a baleful glance. This had been his kingdom, now it was strewn with bodies more like a pauper's ward than a parlour. There was a smell of stale breath exhaled and foetid socks and damp overcoats used to supplement the bedding. Mother was already up with the kettle boiling and a bleary-eyed Mick soon joined her. There wasn't space for all of them to eat in the kitchen so Bella brought the boys their bread and scrape to them where they lay. James had his downed and was up and dressed and gone in the space of five minutes as if he couldn't wait to get away. She did not know if it was shame or pride that made him so keen to escape. Of all her boys, he was the one who kept himself and his thoughts private from her.

Babsie busied herself with the tea and light-hearted banter with Mick, or as much banter as he could stand with a pounding head. The two of them stepped out together, he already late for his nine o'clock start at the GPO, and she hurrying off to pick up her union relief. Only Susan slept on, blissfully it seemed, as if their contingency was no longer a concern of hers.

Before she sent him off to school, she took Baby John into the yard and splashed water on his face from the tap. It was only a lick and a promise given the upheaval of the night before. They met Mrs Shields from downstairs dragging her own son to the tap on the same mission.

'Bella,' she said and nodded warily.

Mother did not fraternise with Mrs Shields on account of the Sacred Heart lamp she had installed in the hall with the ever-present light afore it. Mick used to joke he wouldn't have a word said against the said lamp for it had lit his staggers home many's the night. For her part, Mrs Shields objected to the Union flag Mother had hung out to mark the king's coronation. But Bella was grateful for Mrs Shields' measured salute, comparing it to the reception in Fitzgibbon Street where there would have been some smart remark to the tune of wasn't it a marvel how Protestants had to wash just like the rest of us. But Bella determined not to dwell on such thoughts. She was away from the tenements now.

*

She shook Susan from her slumber for she would not have her act the sleeping princess while she was under Mother's roof. Time enough for that when she was married to her Mr Elliott. She dispatched her off to escort Valentine and Baby John to school, admonishing them not to reveal to anyone where they'd moved in case they might be tempted to boast, as boys will, of the high excitement of being on the run. She could certainly trust Susan in this, for as she'd proved, dissembling about her circumstances had become second nature to her in their courtship. She had never once brought Reggie Elliott back to Fitzgibbon Street. She had pretended she was still living in Rutland Place and so when they stepped out, it was back to there that he would walk her and she had to linger by their old door until he went.

'No good will come of such deception,' Bella had warned her. But Susan had long since stopped heeding her advice, or taking any responsibility for their plight.

That was clear from the day she had arrived home from the Misses Carolan, announcing that she had thrown aside the job. The very job Bella had had to go begging for. She remembered the humiliation of having to don her best, which wasn't up to much these days, and throwing herself on the mercy of Clarrie Hamilton. Bella had let her friendship with Clarrie lapse; in Bella's mind she was too closely associated with the snaring of Nick.

'As I live and breathe, if it isn't Bella Beaver,' Clarrie had cried as soon as Bella had pushed open the weighted door of the shop which gave off a merry tinkle.

She came out from behind the counter and eyed Bella up and down, hands on hips. Then she embraced her warmly. Bella's hat got squashed in the encounter and she fished it from her head. She had thought it would be bad form to go hatless to a milliner's, regardless of her mission.

'I swear, Bella Beaver, if that isn't the self-same hat you bought off me in Mrs Falix's,' Clarrie had said unabashedly. 'How's that dashing husband of yours?'

'My Nick is dead,' Bella declared in a forthright fashion.

'Oh Bella,' she said, 'I'm frightful sorry to hear that and him still in his prime. What was it took him?'

'Tuberculosis,' Bella said. How quickly the falsehoods sprang to her lips. Followed hot on the heels by a sneaking admiration for the perverted audacity of it. Wasn't it a strange state of affairs when she considered consumption the lesser of two evils?

Clarrie put her hand up to her mouth.

'It's the reason that I'm here,' Bella began, dropping her voice though there was no one to hear bar the mirrors ranged about and the preening headgear – large brimmed hats with lacy falls and garlanded with florets of sateen, pearls and cameos, even plover feathers.

Clarrie took a step backwards and Bella could already see a creeping reservation, whether that was owing to the talk of tuberculosis or the fact that she knew something would be required of her. Before Clarrie could fend her off, Bella plunged into her story. 'You could say we've fallen on hard times with Nick gone and all. And our Susan, she's had her full schooling behind her. She's a bright girl, Clarrie, wait till you see her, very pretty and she has a beautiful hand. She'd be most presentable in the shop. She even has a little French . . .'

'Oh Bella,' Clarrie had said again, pityingly. 'The Misses Carolan do all the vetting for the floor staff. It's in their gift alone.'

She sighed as heavily as Bella did. Then Clarrie brightened.

'Is your Susan any good with a needle, by any chance?' she asked. 'We have a couple of girls who do the trimmings . . .'

Bella remembered the swell of charity she felt for Clarrie in that moment, though it was Clarrie who was dispensing the charity.

'It wouldn't be much, mind you,' she had said. 'And your Susan might find it a bit . . .'

'We're desperate, Clarrie,' Bella interjected for she didn't want Clarrie to talk herself out of the proposition. 'Anything, anything . . . she'd be glad of.'

That was when the threshold was crossed, when Bella had become poor. Not when all their belongings were piled high on the street, or even the move to Fitzgibbon Street, but there in the plush splendour of the Misses Carolan's. It was the weak supplication in her voice, her cloying gratitude and the first frank admission of their circumstances to an outsider. And now, all of that gone, for nothing, thrown over on a whim.

'After all this time, I'm still doing beads and fancies,' Susan wailed.

Bella's blood boiled. Was there ever a girl as fickle? Or so wilful. Or contrary. Though she knew from whom all these traits had come.

'You left because of that!' Bella couldn't hold the reprimand out of her voice while counting pennies in her head.

'It isn't fair,' she had said, '*your* Miss Hamilton gave me to believe that I might hope to serve in the shop one day, but look at me, there's not a budge and others have been put out front instead of me.'

Bella noticed how suddenly Clarrie had become her personal creature and was tarred with the same brush as herself – holding out the promise of better.

'Anyway,' Susan said with a toss of her head, 'I don't need that old job anymore. Hasn't Reggie asked me to marry him?'

Bella had felt a seize of dread. It was the queer way Susan announced it. Shouldn't the news of her engagement have been foremost?

'It's not a matter of necessity, is it?' She had had to ask. She would not be in the dark ever again through her own timidity.

'What do you mean?'

'Well, you know, Susan, sometimes a girl can . . .'

'Mother!' Susan had cried full of righteous indignation. 'What do you take me for?'

Susan had looked at her with such malice, it should have

wounded her. But she didn't care, so flooded was she with relief that there was no blot on Susan's character and that shortly, God forgive her, she would be off Bella's hands.

But they couldn't live off the promise of a marriage. Bella had scavenged through her things, trying to find pawn value in the most meagre of her belongings until her eye lit on the Cadby. Her neighbours on Fitzgibbon Street had thought the piano the personification of her pretensions and she wouldn't give them cannon balls to fire at her by playing nocturnes or gavottes in their hearing. She had not played it since that Sunday afternoon when Nick had done his worst to her. If she had struck the keys, she feared they would only release a piercing scream that would tell of what had been done there. Every time she looked at it, she saw not only that vile scene replayed over, but a repository of her own shaming guilt of what she had done to Nick.

'Think how much it'll fetch,' she had said to Babsie, hoping her new pragmatism would appeal to the most sensible of her children.

Babsie looked at her with frank dismay.

'But, Mam, it's your pride and joy.'

'Pride and joy will not keep us from the poorhouse,' she said firmly.

But the selling of the Cadby had only bought parole and Bella knew it was only a matter of time before she would have to throw herself once more on Mother's mercy. For where in the city could she have found a cheaper, meaner home than Fitzgibbon Street?

With all the children gone, the emptied house seemed to tick with grateful silence, aided by the mantel clock in the parlour. Then the general routine reasserted itself. His lordship, Jack Casey, stayed abed till mid-morning sometimes or at least until the parlour fire had warmed the place up. He would sit enthroned while Mother ferried in his tea and and toasted slices on the flames for him. Then she went about her chores in the kitchen. Bella came upon her washing up and suddenly saw how aged she had become, the evidence of those years apparent in her mother's craggy cheeks and the whorls of her elbows. It was as if this change had happened in the interval between Bella going into the parlour and stepping back into the kitchen. Mother rubbed a speck of soap from her eyelid with the back of her newly ancient hand – or was it a tear?

'Oh, Bella,' she sighed.

Bella wasn't even sure whether Mother knew she was standing there. But then she turned to face her and she said it again.

'Oh, Bella.'

All their battles had come to this. Bella had conquered her, not with her achievements as she'd imagined in her youth, but with her failure. She fled into the parlour and wept noisily. Jack came upon her in this state.

'So,' he intoned, pompous as a magistrate, 'this is how it ends, Bella.'

She felt a surge of revolt. He was the only one who could summon up rage in her with his pronouncements, and this one in particular, for he spoke as if she were already dead and buried.

'I'm not the first,' she replied, 'who with best meaning has incurred the worst.'

Everything was coloured by her crime and the secret of it. She was already judged and damned, so what matter now how low she stooped? What matter now those high-flown ideas of honour? Deceit might have been forced upon her all those years ago, but she had honed it over the years into a dubious art. She used it mercilessly now in the only way she knew how. She begged. Mick was the easiest touch. She'd place herself, as if by happenstance, near the GPO, and be sidling by the kerb at the hour she knew he came off shift. She'd hurry up to him, all breathless, as if some fresh crisis had overtaken her.

'Could you spare a shilling, Mick?' she'd say.

For John's coat is falling asunder; for Valentine must have a jotter for his sums; for the tab at Murphy's must be paid.

And he would hand it over.

'Better for you to get it than the publicans, I suppose,' he would grumble good-naturedly.

After a while it became such a regular performance that Bella would not have to furnish him with excuses. He would see her approach and be already digging in his pockets. Her aim was to gather up a little extra for a trousseau for Susan. But she did not pretend any of that to Mick, or anyone else she cadged off; instead, she used her children's growling stomachs, their coughs and sneezes as a blind.

She moved from one brother to the next. She propositioned Isaac at his place of work. He had left his father-in-law's employ and now held office in the Union. She made her way to the Northumberland Hotel, swishing past the throng queuing outside his door which had his name on a plaque outside.

'Whose yer wan?' she could hear them grumbling, as she strode purposefully up the stairs where these creatures clung to the rails, 'what gives her the right?'

'The claims secretary is my brother, if you must know,' Bella replied loudly when one of these doxies at the head of the queue laid a hand on her arm. 'My business is of a personal nature.'

She knocked firmly on the door but did not bother to wait for a reply. As she pushed it open, she could feel at her back the restless dissatisfaction of the crowd. She closed it quickly and stood face-to-face with her sister-in-law. Johanna Fairtlough was standing in the middle of the room, a vision amidst the sober brown wood, in a tight bodice dress of bright cerise with a matching high hat and a frothy parasol on which she leaned. She was never afraid of colour, was Johanna. She'd got stout since Bella had seen her last at one of her swarries. Which was a long time ago since a woman from the tenements was not a welcome guest at such affairs.

'Bella,' Johanna said and her eyes popped.

'Sis,' Isaac said rising from behind his desk, 'well, this is a surprise!'

The way he welcomed her, she couldn't help feeling that he welcomed the interruption more.

'Indeed,' Johanna said, looking her up and down as her colour rose and she drew herself up to her full height. The shelf of her bosom trembled under its shimmery fabric.

'I came to see my brother in his new high office,' Bella said.

'Joe's a very busy man,' Johanna said, giving off fumes of indignation.

How was it, wondered Bella, that her brothers were so keen to lose their given names? Jack first, then Isaac.

'Don't you worry about me, dear,' Isaac said, 'never too busy to see family, isn't that right, Sis?' He steered his portly wife towards the door and opened it for her. The mutinous clamour of the waiting crowd invaded the room for a moment. Isaac closed it quickly and stood with his back against it as if their need was contagious.

'I was awful sorry to hear about poor Beaver,' he said. 'I would have come to the funeral, but Johanna wouldn't have it, you know how it is.'

To be under the thumb of a domineering, overfed wife? No, Bella thought, she didn't know what that was like.

'Are you getting by?' he asked.

Isaac ambled back to his desk. He was smartly dressed in his high collar and cravat.

'Well, that's why I'm here.'

Bella did her well-practised spiel – her widow's lament, the fees owing at the Model School, Susan's upcoming nuptials.

'Isn't your Babsie on the relief already?' Isaac said.

'I'm asking you as a brother, Isaac, not as some factotum of the union,' she said to him.

He rattled the coins in his pocket as if to emphasise how few there were, but he opened the drawer nonetheless and drew out a union money order.

'I shouldn't be doing this at all, mind you,' he said.

He made it out to cash for twenty one and six and signed it with a flourish with his new name – Joe Casey. It was a fortune and she all but kissed him. I'll never see a poor day again, she thought. But wasn't that the treachery of money – even a gift horse like this. There was never enough of it.

She tried her luck with Jack, too, even though he wasn't earning. But she knew he had a metal box under his bed in which he guarded the petty cash (though not petty to her) for the Laurence O'Toole Pipe Band, an outlandish outfit he'd hooked up with. They were Irisheens, one and all, and ran a social club of sorts somewhere near the Five Lamps, where they put on theatricals and played music, if such the caterwauling Jack produced on his bagpipes could be called. He used to practise in the yard. It was a comical sight, the wheezy bag and sprawling legs of the pipes like an octopus around his shoulders and he huffing and puffing with all his might. What came out could not be classed as music, but a kind of screeching protest as if a bag of cats was being painfully strangled. But as he stood there, it put Bella in mind of Nick. Jack was a poor imitation for he had none of Nick's fine regalia, only a plain navy tunic over a pair of mended moleskins, but she wondered if the childish dream of being a soldier of the Crown was still lodged deep somewhere in his heart.

'Sure, who would miss a shilling from the band box?' she said to him.

'I won't dip into club funds,' he declared. 'On principle.'

'Would you see your own starve then?' Bella demanded. Her new situation had made her bold; timidity being the domain of the well-bred who have no need to importune. 'Even a tanner would do.'

'If I gave you a sixpence, I'd have to wait three more weeks for *La Débâcle*.'

He still had money for books, she noticed. Probably gleaned from the little bits of seditious scribbling he was doing.

'Will Zola feed my children?'

'Isn't it enough I have to eat my dinner with your brood bearing down on me?'

'They cannot help their situation,' she replied quick smart. 'They're only children, as you once were, when I provided for you. And now all you care about is damned books.'

'Damned books, is it, Bella, there's a fine contradiction! Wasn't it you who brought me to the books in the first place?'

'But not to worship them above all else. Not to put them higher than those in need.'

'I do my bit, and more.'

'But not for those close at hand. Oh no, you'd walk a mile for the pipe band or those fellows you hang about with drilling in the hills, but you wouldn't lend your sister a tanner to buy a schoolbook.'

'Lend?' He exploded then. 'And when exactly would I get it back? From now on, Bella, it's a borrower you'll forever be.'

The cheek of him, using the Bard to turn her down.

When she went to tap off her brother Tom, she was in for a shock. It was several years since they'd come face to face. Mother's boycott of his Catholic wife meant Tom was lost to Bella too.

'Bella, me old flower, what brings you to our neck of the woods?'

She was about to begin her litany of pleas – she always came right out it with it; no more beating about the bush for Bella Beaver – but she saw it was an effort for him to stand. She helped him from the open door. He held grimly to the wainscoting and paused on each step to draw in a lungful. They moved cautiously into the parlour where a cheery fire was set. His face was ashen and he was finding it hard to draw breath. She helped him into a chair close to the flames.

'What ails you, Tom?' she asked with sinking heart, selfishly feeling a downturn of disappointment for she could see he was in strife of a much graver hue than hers.

'I've been poorly this last while, Bella, haven't been to work in nigh on a month.' He smiled at her weakly. 'But once the spring sets in, I'm sure it'll all straighten itself out.'

Bella recognised the falseness of his optimism. There is a look that men get when the Lord is set to call them – a caving of the face and a bleak look to the eye – and Tom had that very look.

'Have you not been to the doctor?' she asked firmly for clearly, someone needed to take command here.

'My Mary's been looking after me and says there is no need,' he said.

'All the same . . .' Bella said, knowing the penalties of putting off a visit to the doctor.

The street door banged noisily and Mary Kelly appeared, looking much the same as she had ten years before, with her crooked eye and implacable manner.

'And who is this?' she demanded, looking at Bella crossly.

Bella wondered idly if her lazy eye affected what she saw, for she did not have the wit to play malicious.

'It's Bella, Mary, my sister Bella,' Tom said.

Bella rose and went to greet her, not sure if she should offer a hand or an embrace. One seemed too formal, the other too intimate.

'Bella?' Mary queried, gimlet-eyed and doubtful. She looked Bella up and down.

'My, my, Isabella,' she repeated, taking in Bella's mud-spattered skirt, her shawl threadbare from washing. It was a chastening experience for Mary Kelly to look aghast at her and make dim comparisons in her head that were evident on her face. And the name Isabella from this woman's lips seethed with a low sarcasm.

'Would it not be better,' Bella ventured, 'if Tom were to see the doctor?'

'I'll thank you, Isabella,' she said, 'to leave the nursing of my husband to me. I've managed to look after him all these years with no help from a cluster of ragged Caseys. Isn't that right, Tom?'

Tom looked at Bella, pleading with his eyes, not to draw cudgels with Mary, before he was smothered in a bout of coughing. Mary Kelly made a show of helping him, putting an arm around his shoulders as he buried his face in a handkerchief on which he left small pellets of blood. When the fit subsided, Bella rose to go, relieved she hadn't shown her hand.

It was a respectable ceremony. She had seen to it that Susan had a proper address from which to be married. Mick gave her away and paid for a portion of the celebration – although he had already contributed by Bella's sleight-of-hand to the plum gown Susan wore and the matching hat she'd bought from the Misses Carolan – the favourite item in her trousseau for she had swept into the shop where she had once slaved and ordered it to be custom-made.

Her new son-in-law, Bella discovered on the day, was a respectful young man who called her Ma'am. He was not what she would have called a looker, but perhaps Susan had learned more by observation than Bella had given her credit for. He was steady in his nature, was Reggie Elliott, and he treated Susan like an exquisite piece of china. Bella was secretly grateful for his pallid manner. He would not be one to make 'demands', she thought. When Susan walked down the aisle – steering a worse-for-wear Mick between the pews, instead of the other way round – she felt she had honoured her most solemn vow. Susan had arrived at the church door with all her female innocence intact. She did not, would not, think about the future. The children Susan might have, the sickness they might carry. There was no way of, or use in, warning Susan. She, like Bella, would have to trust to fate.

THE TREE OF HAPPENSTANCE

The Lock-Out was but a memory now and everyone worse off than before. The revolution Jack was forever talking about, the big change, the overturning of the old order had turned out to be a damp squib leaving him, and her Babsie, forlornly unemployed. Most of the girls who had worked beneath her at Harrison's had slunk back to their positions and glad to have them. But Babsie had been singled out as a ringleader and would be given no quarter. Her vouchers from the union exhausted, she spent weeks trawling through the city trying to find work. But everywhere she went she met the door. Bella watched her slip further each day into the slough of despond.

'I hate to be sponging off Granny Casey,' she would say.

Bella felt a pang of self-recrimination. Her stout-hearted daughter had not abdicated to charity as readily as she had. Her only answer to Babsie's situation was to stoop to counterfeit, the only tool at her disposal. She wrote a letter purporting to be from Babsie's supervisor at Harrison's declaring that she had been a good and loyal employee while in their employ, punctual and hard-working, who'd risen to the top of the assembly line when she'd had to give it up to tend to her sick mother.

Bella painted a portrait of herself as not alone an indigent widow, but a frail invalid troubled with the quinsy. It was an impudent assertion for her health had up to this time been robust. She wondered afterwards if she hadn't called down illness upon her head by indulging in such extravagant falsehood. Because Babsie's name might appear on some blacklist because of her association with the wretched union, Bella used Susan's instead, and dated her invented indisposition well before the strike so Babsie would not be tainted by any whiff of association.

It was a long time since Bella had had call to use her penmanship – or her imagination – in such a way. The last time was to secure Jack his first employ, and it felt strange to once again pick up a pen. How easily the lies came forth once she did; no, not lies, for all she said of Babsie was true, but once the ink began to flow she found herself carried away by the world she'd created on the page, in which she became Mr Frederick Leverett, general manager of a plant where she had never set foot. She made her hand bolder than it would be normally so no one might guess there was a female behind it.

'In all my years,' she wrote, 'I have never encountered a

brighter and more capable young woman, a bright star in a dark world, a jewel in the crown . . . .'

She had to do several drafts for Babsie said it was much too fancy.

'It's not a marriage proposal I'm after, Mam, just a job,' she said. 'And anyway, Mr Leverett would never talk like that.'

It was easier, though, to pretend herself this Mr Leverett Esquire than see herself as she was – a dejected woman with a polished hand, who had the instincts now of a charlatan, a conjurer trying to produce rabbits from a hat.

The ploy worked, no matter her misgivings, and Babsie landed herself a packing job in Jacobs Biscuit Factory. She had to endure a rigorous inquisition from the manager there, a certain Mr Dawson. Gone were the times when being a Protestant was enough to get a job. This Mr Dawson was a strict type and every girl before him had to submit to an inspection.

'Are you sure you're not one of Larkin's girls?' he barked at Babsie. 'Is this one of the Liberty Hall blouses I see?'

'I had to deny the Union, else I wouldn't have got in,' Babsie said miserably.

'Still and all,' Bella said, 'haven't you got a position and all that Union ever brought you was strife.'

'I'm no better than a scab,' Babsie said. 'That's what it means to be a Dawson girl.'

'I won't hear of such nonsense,' Bella replied, in case Babsie's conscience might get the better of her, for she was thinking, venally, only of the wage packet she would bring in. 'Just think, you're not doing this in your own name. According to your reference, aren't you Susan Beaver, so the crime is hers not yours.'

Once she would have died rather than impugn Susan's character in any way; now she was happily bartering her first-born's good name for profit. She knew that by her deception, Babsie was flourishing on the ill-luck of some other girl and at the expense of another hard-pressed family. But Bella would not surrender to such thoughts for they sounded too like the kind of opinion Jack would hold.

There was a time when she'd considered the houses on Brady's Lane as mean. They were no more than hovels, really, with their low-browed windows and sagging lintels but when a cottage came free there – she knew it by the dingy pyramid of shabby belongings piled up on the street outside – the prospect of having her own front door, no matter how humble, brought out the covetous in Bella. When they had been evicted from Rutland Place, there was already another family queuing to gain ingress; now she was the hawk circling on her prey, in this instance, an old woman, close to Mother's age, and with no living family to tend her, who was bound for the North Ward workhouse. But we are five, she told herself, and justified it by asking whose need was greater. Would her gain make any difference to that poor woman's plight? Bella stood guard in a doorway opposite the house until she saw the beadles come to take the old woman away. She had gone soft in the head, poor thing, for she mistook them for the constabulary and kept on crying out – 'I have done nothing wrong, Sir, please Sir, I have done nothing . . . .'

Bella hardened her heart against the woman's protests with strict words to herself. What had *she* done to deserve her fate? But there was no good in tracing the roots and branches of the tree of happenstance. Knowledge was a burden, not a cure.

No sooner had the beadles gone than several doors on the street opened and the occupants of Brady's Lane edged their way out as if they'd been waiting, hands on latches, for the commotion to die down. They set upon the rickety pile of goods like flies on dung, plucking a basin here or a chair there or hauling away the old woman's sunken mattress. Bella waited for the pilfering procession to peter out and only then did she make her way across and push open the beaten-looking door. She felt a great swell of possession as she stepped in, so much so that she camped out in the house so that it would not be left unattended for someone else to nab. She wanted to be well-established before the landlord made an appearance.

The landlord turned out to be a lady, a Mrs Irvine from Drumcondra, who owned several houses on the lane. She was a woman of the right persuasion and when she turned up to find a Protestant *in situ* – with three earners in the family, Bella was able to boast, with Babsie back in employ – she turned a blind eye to the fact that Bella had taken up residence by sharp practice. They were dingy quarters with only two small rooms and a scullery out the back in a lean-to. The old woman had let the place sadly go. It smelled something dreadful of unwashed skin and reeking odours of a personal nature, but it might as well have been the Lord Mayor's mansion, as far as Bella was concerned. They had so little left to transport that they were able to carry it in their embrace. A table, chairs, some crockery, the pickings from Mother's. Valentine and John took one end each of the bedstead and rolled it home. The candlesticks, the wedding bowl, her dainty gloves from the academy – this was the random flotsam that had washed to the shore. There was, she realised, no logic to the survival of things. No more than people. For it was on the day the Beavers moved into their new abode that Bella got the news of Tom's passing.

The last person she expected to see at the funeral was Johanna Fairtlough, particularly since Tom was buried according to the Anglican rite. But no sooner was Tom lowered into the ground than Johanna, disrespectfully late, stalked up the avenue of the graveyard beneath the tossing trees. She was all kitted out for mourning – a black suit with saucer buttons, a sombre high-necked blouse, a soft black hat, but her mood was far from solemn. Hardly waiting for the rector to say his piece she launched into a tirade.

'Is that you there, Bella Beaver?' she all but shouted. 'I hope you're satisfied now.'

'Whatever do you mean, Johanna,' Bella said, trying to steer Johanna out of Mother's hearing for she was pure distraught at having lost poor Tom. 'Please, Johanna, not here.'

She must have had drink on board. How else to explain such unseemly behaviour?

'Yes here, Mrs Beaver,' she said, 'right here in front of everyone who knows you.'

Bella wondered what she had done to excite Johanna's ire – bar breathing.

'Would any of you like to know where your precious Isaac Casey is? 'She must have been agitated for she didn't even call him Joe. 'And not able to be here to mourn his brother?'

None of them could supply an answer for they had all been perplexed by Isaac's absence.

'Beyond in England, he is, thanks to his sister here. Mrs Bloody Beaver!'

That was going too far, swearing in a churchyard!

Mick tried to intervene. 'Steady on, now Johanna, we're all upset this day of our Lord, so don't be adding to the anguish.'

But Johanna was not to be pacified.

'Had to set sail for Liverpool like some vagabond leaving me alone with three orphans, one of them in petticoats, and no money coming in.'

'She,' Johanna declared, pointing her umbrella in Bella's direction, '*she* has been the ruination of us.'

Bella blanched. The accusing finger never failed to terrify. She was always waiting for the terrible truths of her own life to be revealed. She felt all eyes on her, but she couldn't fathom what Johanna was talking about. What had she done? Was she forever to be guilty of crimes she didn't know about?

'Plants herself at the top of the queue for a hand-out from the union, even when her own daughter is on the Relief. And my Joe, out of the goodness of his heart, doles her out a bit on the QT, and what's the consequence? He's hauled over the coals for putting his hand in the till!'

She unleashed another noisy volley of tears.

'Sacked and disgraced. A blemish on his character for evermore – and on mine too and his poor orphaned children!'

'There, there, Johanna,' Mick said, trying to place a manly hand on her shoulder. 'I'm sure now there was more to it than the little bit he might have given Bella as a dig-out.'

'Get your paws off me, Mick Casey, and don't give me any of your old palaver.'

She brandished her umbrella like a sergeant major. 'I rue the day I got involved with a shower of black Protestants like yourselves. Mark my words, your lot are well and truly on the way out and you'll not be bringing the likes of me down with you!'

She marched off, having said her say. Bella felt all eyes turned on her, as if she were the one who had screamed like a fishwife.

'You didn't tell us, Bella,' said Mick ruefully, the only one to have an opinion on Johanna's outburst, 'that you'd been doing the rounds.'

She felt the scald of shame. With her devious conniving she'd even exhausted Mick's goodwill.

A few months later, Johanna and her children removed to Liverpool to join Isaac. He was never to set foot in Ireland again, an upheaval Bella felt uneasily responsible for, though she found it hard to credit that he had been driven from the country on account of the twenty one and six he'd given her. Surely not! But Johanna Fairtlough clearly believed that the puny extent of Bella's want had the power to topple those about her. If only it were true, she thought. Poverty, she could have told Johanna, has only one power – to mesmerise and weaken those within its grip.

THE EMPIRE'S HOUR

OF NEED

The slaughter of an archduke and his duchess by a madman on the streets of Sarajevo, seemed so unlikely to touch their small lives that Bella's only thought when it happened was that this young assassin must be a young man much like Jack, a hot-head bent on villainous upheaval. She issued a silent prayer that he might not end up like this Princip fellow – with bloodstained hands. Otherwise, the war in Europe made not much odds at the start, for everyone thought it a skirmish that would be over by Christmas. But when James made his announcement one Friday evening, it brought the Great War home.

'It's the Empire's hour of need,' he said plainly when Bella asked why.

She should not have been surprised. He'd finished his apprenticeship and with printer's ink on his hands he was churning out recruitment posters with Kitchener's pointed finger. Day in, day out he saw other young men going out on the troop ships and it must have seemed to him an exciting adventure to head off to a war. There were uniforms out and about the streets once again, but not the cocky regimentals of Nick's day, but workaday khaki.

James was a mystery to her. Young Valentine, her Baby John, she knew their hurts and prides as well as she knew her own. But James, being the eldest son and the pride of his father, had, in the end, to stand up to Nick on Bella's behalf. Ever since, he had held himself apart as if that dastardly business had demeaned him, not her.

'But we have need of you at home,' she replied.

'Ah Mam, I want to follow my father into colours,' he said, 'it's in the blood.'

What else, she wondered, was in the blood.

'But you're only a child.'

'Old men are being called – look at Uncle Mick called back to the Engineers. If he can serve, then I can. I won't be left out of it.'

There was no point in arguing that every soldier fighting meant a family at home going without for the Army paid a pittance for patriotism. There was no point in arguing at all. The boy's mind was made up.

When told of James's enlistment, Jack took up the contrary position.

'This war,' he said, 'is Ireland's opportunity.'

'Opportunity for what?' she asked, exasperated, for his cryptic words irritated her, laden with doom and foreknowledge.

'For Home Rule, for freedom, for revolution.'

It disturbed her, this kind of talk for it spoke of a cruel indifference to his own flesh and blood.

'How can you talk like that with two of your own heading for the fields of France?' she asked.

'Just like the business with the Boer,' he pronounced, 'it's not our war.'

There it was again, the old division. The us and them. What had started as an argument between her husband and her brother, two sides of the one coin she'd always thought, had spread out like a wasting disease, so that in the end not one of them was untouched. It had infected Tom and Isaac who'd thrown their lot in with the enemy and had been aggravated by her mother who'd used boycott as an antidote. Now the sickness was spreading. Wars and strife, assassination, revolution. She remembered a conversation she'd had with Valentine just days before James had enlisted.

'What would happen, do you think, Mam,' he had enquired, 'if all the coal that rested in the cellars of the gentry were to ignite like all hell broke loose and engulf all above ground in a consuming conflagration?'

He was apt to make such observations, was Valentine. He worked as a coal factor. Oh, it was a cruel job – out in all weathers and breathing in coal dust at every hand's turn. His skin was permanently sooted, his lungs clogged up. At night his coughing kept the entire house awake. It was a pain to Bella to see him age before her eyes for the work gave his face a pitted, haunted look. And he had been so bright at school, quick especially at the mathematics, but now all he calculated was the heft and haul of coal sacks on his back. His view was of gaping coal holes, which were, he said, like the very gates of Hades.

She did not have an answer for Valentine but she realised that her son's musings were taking on the hue of premonition. There were movements afoot too large to counter. What chance the puny turnings of a single heart when set against the angry baying of the crowd? Despite their kinship, she saw now that the division between her and Jack could never be undone. He would always side with the others – the Gaelic speakers, the Romanists, the haters of the Crown. There was no healing it, she realised. Truce couldn't do it, nor appeasement. Not even love. The big world would have its way and do them all down in the end. And then the Rising happened.

THE FAMILY SILVER

earing the strains of Beethoven's *Moonlight Sonata* emanating from the Beavers' front room, Sadie Kinch couldn't resist knocking. Was it a gramophone the Beavers were after getting? And where from? The music halted as soon as she rapped on the wood. Well, thought Sadie, her ladyship couldn't very well pretend she wasn't in – as she was wont to do – with that highfalutin' music going on inside. Mrs Beaver opened the door a fraction.

'Yes, Mrs Kinch?' she demanded in that way she did, as if she were a school warden or, worse, a police constable and you had been caught with your hand in the till.

'Oh, is it yourself playing that lovely music?' Sadie said, peering into the room through the restricted aperture and spying the decorated corner of the piano lid.

'Can I help you?' Mrs Beaver said, though she was not in the way of dispensing much in the way of largesse; the Beavers were as poor as church mice.

'I was just passing,' Sadie said, 'on my way into town . . . and then I heard that heavenly music.' A lie, for Sadie Kinch thought what she heard dreary as a funeral dirge. A good old come-all-ye, or something sentimental was more her style ('When You Said You Loved Me' was her own favourite; her husband had sung it at their wedding.) But Mrs Beaver would be too posh for that.

'It's Beethoven,' Mrs Beaver said, seeming to relent.

'Beethoven,' Sadie repeated sagely. Foreign, she thought.

'I didn't know you had a piano,' Sadie said, inching forward. 'Is it new?'

'A legacy,' Mrs Beaver said, opening the door a little wider. 'From a relation of ours.'

'Oh, I see,' Sadie said. 'Well, I always say no home is complete without a piano.'

'That's true,' Mrs Beaver replied, looking so moistly at the piano it could have been a sleeping child. Sadie felt the tide turning. This was the first time she and Mrs Beaver had agreed on anything.

'Would you play a little more?' she ventured. 'I'll just stand on the threshold here . . . and you carry on.' That way she could give the piano the once-over.

This suggestion seemed to discombobulate Mrs Beaver. She made no reply but shyly – yes, Sadie thought, who would have thought Mrs Beaver shy? – she sat on the kitchen chair pulled up in front of the piano and raised her hands above the keys. The legacy, Sadie noted, did not include a piano stool.

'Well, that's a very fine specimen, and no mistake,' Sadie said in the hope of forestalling the dreary music. 'What kind of wood is that?'

'Rosewood,' Mrs Beaver said, 'Indian rosewood.'

'An aunt did you say? That left it to you?' Sadie persisted. It was a month since the Rising and the flotsam of it was still bobbing up in houses across the city.

'I didn't say,' Mrs Beaver replied. She was a stickler for everything being present and correct – even when she was about to be unmasked as a looter. 'But yes, an aunt it was – from the Archer side of the family – my mother's people.'

'Isn't it a pity they didn't take more care of it?' Sadie said. 'There are a few scrapes here on the cabinet, I see, as if it had been mistreated.'

'The men who delivered it were none too gentle, Mrs Kinch, and so it got a bit damaged in transport.'

'Isn't that shocking altogether! Your beautiful legacy manhandled in that way! But I suppose the wonder of it is that they managed to deliver it at all with all the mayhem on the streets . . .'

Mrs Beaver gave Sadie her haughtiest look then, as if she'd detected a bad smell in the room. She looked her down and up, her eyes coming to rest on Sadie's hat, a black velvet confection with red and gold threaded through the band, on its first street outing.

'Isn't that a lovely hat you're wearing, Mrs Kinch?' she said. 'Did your husband get it for you?'

Damn her, Sadie thought, always getting the upper hand. She'd kept the hat under wraps for weeks.

'Well, I can't dawdle, Mrs Beaver. Thanks ever so for the recital.'

She hurried off – wait until Mrs Clarke heard this! Sure, an old hat was small beer when set against a piano.

The Broadwood was a worldly thing, a possession not rightly hers, a spoil of war. Everything about it was wrong. Bella knew the dangers of investing in the material, attaching to belongings emotions that more rightly sit with God. But the Broadwood made a fool of her. Made her bashful and blushing and all of a dither. For it was more than mere acquisition. It was as if she'd never owned a piano and this was her first. Which it was, in a roundabout way. She'd only had a lease on the Elysian. And the Cadby had been robbed from her long before it had been sold off. But the Broadwood, the Broadwood was all hers. Hadn't she come by it by her own efforts? Hadn't she risked life and limb for it? Her own and her son's. Not that she was proud of that. But she had it now with no harm done and possession made her defiant. She would not make the same mistake twice. This piano would not be taken to the pawn, or used to ward off want. No, she would never part with the Broadwood. It might have been ill-gotten but it stood in for every refinement she had nurtured in her breast through long years of privation. It seemed to open the door on her girlish self, so serious and high-minded and bent on improvement. When Bella considered *her*, she felt motherly towards her.

It was a queer sensation, like miraculously raising up a daughter who had been given up for dead. Thought lost but now found. For the first time in decades, Bella thought about her first vocation, and with it a string of propositions that she found herself in idle moments threading together like small beads. It was preposterous to believe that she could ever regain a schoolroom. Somewhere there were papers to the effect that she was an unfit person to be in charge of young minds, albeit stamped by a man deranged by his own corruption. But with a piano in residence, could not the schoolroom come to her? She saw herself again as a teacher, schooling the children of the gentry in scales and in notation and with it regaining some semblance of her former self. She imagined a brass shingle outside her door. She even sketched the wording. *Mrs Beaver, Music Teacher, Lessons Given in the Pianoforte. Rates Moderate.* That would put a stop to all those prophets of doom, her own flesh and blood included, who took her for some broken-down creature, who failed to see the flame of elevation that burned fiercely within. She was careful to say nothing of the run of her thoughts, lest she open herself up to ridicule. She could imagine her neighbours cackling at the very idea. Mrs Beaver – the teacher? To the hard-headed, to those done in by poverty of the mind, her ambitions might appear as fatuous or worse, a fabulation that a crazed mind might produce, as outlandish as Nick marching to Amiens Street Station in full regalia and thinking it to be Bombay.

Her present surroundings, she knew, could not support such fancies. What well-born child would venture down Brady's Lane to practise her Czerny five-finger exercises? What respectable gentlewoman from Rathgar or Malahide, would risk the slings and arrows of East Wall to perfect her polonaise? Polonaise – imagine Sadie Kinch trying to get her tongue around that? But if Bella were living at a *good* address, a little house in Portobello or Rathmines, maybe, where the neighbours kept their doors shut and passing strangers would not be subject to suspicious scrutiny or downright hostility, then . . . The phantasm only went this far but it sustained her, even though she could not see how she might make the journey from Brady's Lane to such Elysian fields.

It was her landlady, Mrs Irvine, who put the idea of charring work into her head for she asked outright when her regular woman let her down.

'Would you consider it, Mrs Beaver? You'd be doing me a great favour. A shilling a go,' she said, 'that's the going rate.'

Bella had never been so offended. What do you take me for, she was about to answer this woman's impertinence, I am a teacher, not a skivvy! (Her secretive ambition had got ahead of her.) But a shilling a go? Oh, the glinting silvery promise of it. *Here* was the means to effect her transformation. But in the same instant, she saw the parlous legacy of her own useless vanity. In their direst hour of need, she had never considered putting her own hand to work. She had relied on a kind of exalted innocence – but it was a treacherous innocence, she saw now. She had forced James and Valentine out of school and into manual labour; she'd even sacrificed her precious Susan to slavery, and never once had she thought to offer the sweat of her own brow to spare them. She had begged and borrowed, and now stolen; could scrubbing floors be lower than any of these? And wasn't it in service to a higher ideal – the little house in Rathmines, the teacher's shingle outside the door. She would open up a Post Office Savings Book and put a sum by weekly for this purpose alone so that it would not dwindle away in quotidian necessities. Two shillings a week, could she manage that. . .

'What do you say, Mrs Beaver?' Mrs Irvine asked.

'Yes,' Bella said, 'yes, I say yes.'

Her body revolted against the hard graft. Her skin erupted as if in some enraged passion. Great blisters sprouted on her hands and arms and travelled to her shoulders in angry suppuration as if her very being broke out against the work. The dispensary doctor diagnosed erysipales. The external signs could be easily explained away – too much lye and soap, she told the boys when her face took on a scaly aspect. A lifetime of deception had made her adept. But the internal symptoms were far more frightening for they seemed lodged in her mind and could not be put down to mere erysipales. Her temples would throb with piercing shafts of pain that altered the world of solid things, turning them into a miasma like sun glinting on water. It might have been a pleasant sensation – almost like a glimpse of Heaven itself so bright and shimmering was the light – but for the darting spasms of pain that accompanied it. But she didn't tell anyone of these blinding moments for they had the hue of another ailment whose signs she knew all too well. A disease whose name she would not utter.

No matter her affliction, though, she determined her work at Mrs Irvine's must go on. She douched the threshold, scoured the kitchen flags, polished the brasses and wiped the wainscots with an energy she had never applied in her own house for this work she saw now was both her punishment and her redemption.

Mrs Irvine had a fine red-brick in Drumcondra, two receptions and a garden. When she saw the comforts that Mrs Irvine enjoyed, Bella gave in momentarily to a mean misgiving. Our rent has kept her here in this high style, she thought. But it was a sentiment too close to Jack's line of sedition for her liking so she did not indulge it. She preferred to imagine progressing to such an establishment herself rather than waste her time on rancorous envy. Hadn't she escaped the tenements, after all? An establishment like this was not beyond her.

When she had proved herself a steady sort, Mrs Irvine promoted her to prestige tasks. She was even trusted with the silver.

A week before Christmas, when she arrived for duty, she was shown into the dining room and there it was, a splendid tea service arrayed on an inscribed tray.

'A wedding gift, Mrs Beaver,' she said, 'so treat it with kid gloves, if you please.'

The service looked as if it had never been used.

'Beautiful,' she mused, 'but dust collectors, I'm afraid, Mrs Beaver.'

If these were mine, Bella thought, I would have them out on show – the teapot with its swan's neck spout, the milk jug's puggish pour, the curlicued extravagance of the sugar bowl. She started with the teapot – something about its imperious spout. She poured the silver polish from the tin onto the rag, smearing it over the dulled contours of the pot. How quickly these beauties lost their sheen if left unattended. She worked the oozing fluid into the join of the spout and the hinges of the lid then let it be for a while so it could soak in. It was a strange thing, but when she applied the polish first, it muddied up the silver something dreadful. It made it cloudy and dull and left pinkish streaks behind, as if she were making more dirt, not getting rid of it. It was hard to credit that with several buffings the surface would come up so sparkling that it would give her back her own reflection, but enhanced.

The tray was the last to be done. She ran her fingers along the cursive lettering, feeling the tiny pieces of dirt lodged in the loops of the writing. This would be the very devil to clean. She smeared the polish on, working it into the pitted tracks the writing made. The silver drank the fluid greedily. She took off the rubber gloves that Mrs Irvine had given her, the better to work the cloth, cloaked around her thumb nail, into the etched inscription. She worked blindly. It was like trying to find the pearl in a shell of grit. She must have spent twenty minutes at it, edging her finger into each last indentation. When she was done, she brought the tray to the window to examine her handiwork. So intent had she been on perfection, of bringing the silver to a pitch of shine, she hadn't bothered to read what she'd been burnishing. She tilted the tray towards the blanched winter light. The inscription was perfectly legible now. Isabella Casey, it read, Mistress of her Circumstances.

NEW YEAR'S DAY, 1918

Babsie, coming in at noon, found her mother still abed. That in itself was strange for her mother was an early riser, but since Christmas she'd been poorly, laid low with a purulence of the lungs and a wild fever that had made her overheated one minute and perished the next. Babsie had put her husband's dinner on – oh, how she loved to say that, her husband; Babsie was a new bride – and leaving the door on Clarence Street on the latch she'd run around the corner to check on her mother. She was relieved to find a peaceful scene and not the wracking sounds of coughing that had been going on for days. There was some kind of infection going round. Some people blamed the soldiers for it; a Spanish flu, they called it. Others said it was some kind of swine fever. But that couldn't be what Mam had, Babsie thought, for when would her mother have been mixing with either of those? She had urged her mother to call in the doctor but Mam had set her face against it.

'It's just my old trouble,' she'd said to Babsie. 'It goes quiet, you see, for a long time and then . . . it emerges again.'

The erysipelas was her mother's old trouble. Soon after she'd taken up charring, her mother's skin had broken out in a rash. She'd had to wear gloves up to the elbow to hide her contagion. A dress pair with a pearl detail for these were the only gloves her mother owned. But the rash had spread anyway. It found its way to her face and washed up in a high tide close to her hairline. She had to wrap a turban of fabric round her head when going out to keep the condition a secret.

'People will think it a want of hygiene,' her mother had said. 'But it's a surfeit of cleanliness I'm suffering from, up to my oxters in suds all day.'

If you passed her on the street, you'd have given her a penny, Babsie thought, or be calling the clutchers what with the strange headgear and the dress gloves. The neighbours mistook it for another of her mother's eccentric affectations. My, my, the airs and graces, they would say, look at the Protestant wan, all tricked up as if going to a ball, and only off to do her charring.

Babsie's brother John was sitting at the scored table reading a book. Just like Uncle Jack he was, always stuck in a book. She poured tea from the cooling pot. The milk when she added it curdled.

'How's she been?' she asked him.

He shrugged, barely lifting his head from the pages.

'You've let the fire go out,' she said. She tried to raise a flame from the embers in the grate. The poker made a grinding sound as she hit the firebricks.

'Shh,' John said, 'you'll only wake her.'

'I wouldn't have to do it at all, if you kept the place warm for her. Is it too much to ask?'

Babsie was peppering for a fight so sick with worry was she about her mother. But she seemed to be the only one. She wanted only to be immersed in the newly-minted world of her marriage. Everything about this house, like every other house they'd lived in, spoke of struggle.

'Has she eaten anything?' Babsie persisted.

John shook his head. 'She hasn't moved since I got up.'

Only then did Babsie get up to investigate. She tiptoed into the back room and over to the bed. Drawing back the covers she placed a hand on her mother's forehead. She shook her gently by the shoulder.

'Mam,' she said gently, 'wake up.'

She shook again, this time more roughly.

'Mam,' she repeated, panicked.

She felt a tiny flicker of irritation. She was forever trying to shake Mam into action. She reached for her mother's scabbed wrist – peeled back one of the gloves; yes, she even wore them in bed for fear of scratching herself unbeknownst in her sleep – but

Babsie knew even before she tried for a pulse.

'John,' she said evenly, 'go and get Reverend Brabazon.'

'Ah Babs, I'm in the middle of me book,' he wailed.

Books, she thought, bloody books.

'Go,' she ordered, 'this very minute.'

When he was gone, Babsie drew the curtains and stopped the clock. There was no mirror to cloak, her mother having gone beyond gazing at her own reflection. She put the kettle to boil, for whom she did not know. It was just something to do so she would not have to approach the bed again and look on her mother's closed-in face. She could not take it in; that the end would come like this, so quietly, as if her mother had just suddenly upped and surrendered. Typical, Babsie thought, and inexplicably she felt her ire rising again. It was something she had never understood. It wasn't that her mother had lacked spirit – hadn't she raised up five of them as a widow? – but her striving seemed always directed at appearances, the look of things as opposed to how they were. Well, Babsie thought, looking around, something would have to be done here. The scene looked peaceful, though hardly dignified. Her mother's face had a par-boiled look where previous bouts of the erysipelas had left angry blotches. The gloves and the makeshift turban seemed foolish and pathetic, and Babsie set to, unwinding the scarf from her mother's head and peeling off the gloves, so that when the clergyman saw her, she would not look like something out of a harlequinade. She loosed her mother's hair from the matted mound the scarf had made of it. Babsie lifted her head then while she combed the tangles out of it. When she laid her mother's head back on the pillow, her hair settled like a tortoiseshell fan. Babsie laid her mottled arms by her side. Then she straightened the bed.

Something tinny fell off as she turned down the counterpane. She had to go down on all fours to retrieve it. It was her mother's little birdcage. It was a useless little thing, she thought, not even brass but brightly painted metal made up to look like silver. No pawn shop in town would look twice at it and so it had survived, a priceless treasure. She weighed it in her hand and then lifted her mother's and folded the stiffening fingers around it in a fist. Tears came then, but nothing operatic – that was not in Babsie's nature. She wiped her eyes and marched purposefully into the other room to fetch the two-pair candlesticks. There was a large dent in the stem of one, from what Babsie couldn't recall. A domestic skirmish with her father, no doubt. One of the many. She lit them with a taper from the reawakened fire and set one down on each side of the bed. She bent and kissed her mother on the brow. Then Babsie passed her fingers in swift benediction over her mother's eyelids and closed them, her lips moving to some silent prayer.

When John came back, she sent him off to fetch Susie. She left the Reverend to do his business behind closed doors. With a man of God in the house, her mother would not be alone; that was important. Now she would have to go to break the news to

Granny Casey. But when she got to Abercorn Road, she halted, not wanting to make the terrible announcement. The door was thrown open to the street – the Shieldses downstairs were not particular about it. Babsie felt a surge of fellow-feeling for them because Granny Casey had such a set against them, being Catholics and all. But Babsie had all but converted herself to marry her lovely Starry in St Laurence O'Toole church this November just gone by and she didn't care who knew it.

Granny Casey had been bitterly disappointed, Babsie could tell, though she had said nothing. But Granny Casey had a way of letting you know what she thought without ever opening her mouth. Both Uncle Tom and Uncle Isaac had married out and she'd never forgiven either of them; now the weakness was passing on to the next generation; that would be Granny Casey's view, Babsie knew.

The strange thing was that her own mother had barely turned a hair when Babsie broke the news. She had been expecting frosty silence, mute disapproval.

'He's a good man, isn't he?' her mother had asked, sounding vaguely quarrelsome.

'You know he is, Mam.'

'Well, that's the most important thing, so.'

'Then you'll come to the wedding?'

'I will, of course, and why wouldn't I?'

'Even though it'll be a Catholic ceremony?'

Babsie was incredulous. Her mother was always looking down

her nose at Catholics. When they lived in Fitzgibbon Street, sur-rounded by them, she could hardly bring herself to salute them. When I die, she used to say, the word Protestant will be found written on my heart as Queen Mary thought Calais would be on hers.

'It's just that Starry's people won't stand for him marrying me unless the children are brought up in his church,' Babsie said for she had all her arguments rallied and felt obliged to use them. 'Sure isn't it the one God we all go to in the end, that's what Starry says.'

'I don't hold with that at all,' her mother said and Babsie braced herself for a row, 'but I won't deny anyone's good nature.'

'But it's a lot to give up,' Babsie countered, playing devil's advocate despite herself. She had told Starry she would elope with him if her mother didn't give her consent, and the daring of such an escapade appealed to her. But her mother remained implacably in favour.

'A girl,' her mother had said, 'should give up a lot for love.' That was her final word.

AFTERWORD

Seán O'Casey (1880–1964) is one of Ireland's premier playwrights. He also wrote six volumes of autobiography, in which his only sister, Bella, featured. For reasons that have never been clear, O'Casey prematurely killed Bella off in his autobiographies – about ten years before her time. She actually died at the start of the Spanish flu epidemic of 1918.

The Rising of Bella Casey is a fictional reinterpretation of her life.